HIS SALVATION

THE ADA CHRONICLES: BOOK ONE

J.R. LOVELESS

GABRIEL

A FILE landed with a small slap on the desk in front of Gabriel Romero. He picked it up and flipped the cover open while his boss, Bryan Sorensen, gave him the lowdown on his newest assignment. "Twin brothers, Alexander and Jason Ryker. Nineteen years old and very powerful, telepathic and telekinetic. They were abducted forty-eight hours ago before we could get to them."

Gabriel stared down into the greenest eyes he'd ever seen. His chest tightened at the innocence shining up at him from the young man in the photograph.

"Gabe... Vincetti has them."

He whipped his head up at Bryan's words. "Vincetti? Are you sure?"

"Yes. Our inside intel tells us they were taken to a secret compound in Vermont. I need you to assemble your team and get them out of there." Bryan grimaced. Gabriel could tell Bryan felt guilty asking him, due to the events five years ago. "You're the only one I trust with this, Gabe."

Gabriel didn't say anything for several moments as he sifted through the file on the two teenagers. The boy who'd captivated him immediately was Alexander Ryker. The dossier stated that he stood at six foot even, with short dark-brown hair and green eyes. What it didn't state was how flawlessly smooth the man's face looked or how sexy the small dimple was that appeared in the corner of his mouth when he smiled. Gabriel forced himself to look at the next photograph of Jason Ryker. Jason had the same green eyes as his brother, but with a more worldly depth to them. His dark-brown hair hung to his shoulders, and a small silver hoop pierced the lower right corner of his mouth. The agency had been aware of them for a little over a year, and had been tracking them up until two days ago, when they'd been forced into a nondescript white van outside a convenience store.

"Level five?" Gabriel sucked in a sharp breath when he saw the number.

Bryan nodded. "Yes. Alex and Jason are both level fives."

Alex was the telepath, and at that level, he could project his thoughts into another's mind as well if he wished it, though the file held no mention of the young man doing so. Gabriel jolted in remembrance. There had only been one other person that he'd ever known who could do more than just listen. He shoved those thoughts away, refusing to think of the worst moments of his life. All that mattered was getting the boys back.

Jason, the telekinetic, appeared to be as strong as his brother, if not stronger. There were several eyewitness accounts of Jason practically lifting a car by himself to save a little girl who'd been struck by the vehicle and pinned beneath the wheel. He'd brushed it off as an adrenaline rush, but the agency knew better.

Gabriel looked back up at his boss and said, "We'll leave in three hours."

"Good. Contact me the instant they are in your custody.

Use the safe house in Mineral Point. Lay low until we contact you." Bryan looked at his best agent. "Be careful, Gabe."

Standing, Gabriel nodded abruptly. He spun on his heel and strode out of his boss's office. The Agency for Deviant Assistance offered guidance and help to gifted humans such as the twins. It was the only safe haven for anyone with special abilities. No one understood how the abilities developed, but the tension grew thick between the humans without gifts and the humans who possessed them. Ten years ago, a third of the population on Earth began to exhibit signs of strange behavior. The first incident pertained to a man who could levitate things around him when upset or angry. Within a month's time, there were over five hundred documented cases of similar events happening all over the United States. Eventually it became known as a worldwide epidemic.

Normal human beings grew afraid of what these gifts could do to them or their families. Angry mobs broke out a year after the first occurrence. Gabriel had been twenty-two by the time the first Deviant murders occurred. They were dragged out of their homes, butchered, shot, or hung. At first, the police attempted to stop the incidents, but as the population of Deviants rose, they too grew afraid of what could happen to their families and loved ones. Soon it was an all-out war between Deviants and Normals. Deviants were forced into hiding, living in underground tunnels or abandoned homes. Fear of discovery and the knowledge that they were one misstep away from death left any Deviant shivering in the cold nights.

Gabriel remembered being one of those people. He'd been twenty-three when his own abilities surfaced. There'd been another murder of a Deviant, Paul, a friend of Gabriel's from college. He'd been forced to watch as they brought him to the ground, strung the rope around his neck, and tied it to the back of a car. They had driven around and around the block, dragging Paul behind. Gabriel could still see the bloody mess Paul was by the time the bastards stopped. He would never forget the nightmare that time became, or the rage he'd felt for an innocent life lost, which caused his own abilities to manifest. He hadn't been able to stop what happened next. It sent him running for his life as he tried to stay one step ahead of the humans who'd murdered his friend.

Five years of brutal slayings and destruction took place before the government stepped in and stopped the fighting. Known Deviants were sent to concentration camps in unpopulated rural areas, but it didn't stop the Normals from trying to destroy them. In Gabriel's opinion, it just made it all the easier for them to find the Deviants. Rogue groups of raiders hit the camps every chance they had.

A couple of months before the government tried to restrain the ever-heightening situation, Bryan Sorensen created the Agency for Deviant Assistance in memory of his child. Bryan's son, Jamie, had exhibited signs of being a strong level five telekinetic. He attempted to keep Jamie's abilities hidden, but a neighbor witnessed the child levitating his toys and, out of fear, turned the information over to a group of known Deviant hunters. At the time, Bryan was a successful attorney and a clear advocate for Deviants. He'd returned home from his office one day to find his wife and son dead on the kitchen floor. They'd shot his wife in the head when she tried to protect Jamie. To honor his family's memory, he'd created the agency to assist any Deviant who needed a place to stay or to learn how to control their abilities enough to prevent discovery.

Bryan inherited an old farmhouse when his grandfather passed away, and after it sat empty for two years, he'd decided to put it to good use by making it the headquarters of the agency. Investing thousands, he'd renovated the farm-house and added on additional rooms, as well as converting the run-down barn into a training facility. He'd also had the same private construction company build a garage big enough to house the agency SUVs, and eventually the heli-copter they used for their missions. The agency, Gabriel's home for five years, now accommodated up to thirty-five Deviants at a time, including the three five-member teams. Most of the Deviants were only there a matter of a month or two before being ensconced in a new life with a new identity.

Gabriel's hands clenched into fists as he strode into the common room. Jackal lounged on the couch with his girl, Teresa, while arguing with Lizard and Tank about the greatest football player of all time. Chris, the resident computer techie and genius, sat surfing the Internet, and looked up at him as he entered the room. He saw the serious intent on Gabriel's face and sat straighter in his chair. "What's going on, Gabe?"

"Jackal, find Bear," he ordered. Jackal was on his feet and out the door before he'd even finished speaking. Gabriel's usual team consisted of the four Deviants, and Chris, a Normal, was the pillar of support they relied on heavily. They were the only people Gabriel would trust with his life and the life of any Deviant on the planet, aside from Bryan. In their past four years together, Gabriel had never run a mission without them.

Chris Reed, a clear advocate for Deviants, provided the gear needed to complete a mission. He usually stayed at the farmhouse, the ADA headquarters, directing them via radio with the blueprints of whatever building or compound their targets were being held in. Gabriel depended heavily on his intel and trusted his knowledge without question. Despite his supergenius status, Chris didn't give off the "nerd" vibe most people associated with computer wizards and Internet geeks. Six foot one, he had a stocky build with well-defined muscles, blue eyes, and his head was almost completely shaved.

Bailey "Jackal" Ferris was a level four Deviant. Nicknamed the Jackal due to his cunning and speed, he had the ability to outrun just about anything and the strength to match. Jackal had been the only survivor of one of the concentration camps attacked in the middle of the night. He'd barely survived the blast that left him in a coma for two months. Bryan offered him a position at the ADA when he woke up, and Jackal had been there ever since. Jackal topped off at five foot nine with dark-green eyes, shoulder-length brown hair that he kept tied back, and a lean physique, which Gabriel supposed added to his speed and agility.

Vinnie "Lizard" Thomas, another level four, had also been in one of the concentration camps the Normals had raided. His ability to camouflage himself within his surroundings was the only thing that kept him alive. He'd seen his mother and father shot to death right in front of him. When he'd learned of Bryan's agency, he'd sought him out and offered his services. Lizard despised Normals with every breath he drew. Six foot two, shockingly white blonde hair, eyes as blue as the sky, and around two hundred pounds of toned muscle made an impressive package. One ear was lined with multiple piercings, while several tattoos littered his body, the most obvious one a lizard.

Jorge "Bear" Vallejo, a massive mountain of a man at six foot eight, earned his nickname due to his impressive size and his strength. Bear was able to lift a car with one hand while shooting a gun with the other. His mother tried to smother him in his sleep at the age of twelve. His strength saved his life. The silent type, he barely strung more than two words together at a time. When he wasn't running missions with Gabriel, he spent his time lifting weights and working on cars. Of Hispanic lineage, obvious in the dark olive-toned skin, black hair, and dark brown eyes, Bear had a temper that simmered to a boil before it exploded. Raised in Spain, he spoke Spanish fluently, but when he'd arrived in America, he'd made it a personal challenge to learn English just as completely. Bear tested at a level three, although many believed he should have qualified as a four.

Last but not least in Gabriel's lineup was Jackson "Tank" Beauvard, also a level four. Tank did exactly what his name signified. A solid wall of muscle that could tear through buildings like they were paper, he was practically indestructible. Not even bullets could penetrate his skin. He'd come to Bryan a few years back, when his sister had been kidnapped by a group of Deviants known for their hatred of Normals. Tank stood at six foot six, dark-skinned with short black hair and dark-brown eyes. He'd been the last Deviant to join Gabriel's team two years ago. They were still searching for his sister.

As soon as Bear entered the room, Gabriel launched into their newest mission. He handed the folder containing the information about the Ryker twins to Chris. "Twin brothers, Alexander and Jason Ryker, were abducted forty-eight hours ago and taken to a compound in Vermont. Both of them are level fives. We'll be staying at the safe house in Mineral Point for a while. Be prepared to move out in three hours. We're going in under the cover of darkness. Chris, we need a layout of the compound and where the boys are possibly being held. Tank, I'm going to need you as lead on this mission." The others looked at Gabriel in surprise. "It's Vincetti."

If a pin had hit the floor at that very moment, it would have been heard for miles. Tank's eyes grew hard, and his jaw clenched. Lizard growled low in his throat, and Teresa let out a small squeak when Jackal's hands tightened on her arms.

7

"Sorry, baby," Jackal murmured, immediately letting her go and massaging the bruised flesh.

Gabriel knew every person in the room had a reason to hate Vincetti and the monsters who worked under him. He gave a grim smile. "Let's move, people."

The next three hours passed in a flurry of activity. Tank prepared the helicopter, while Lizard and Jackal loaded up the weapons they would need. Bear gathered together everything necessary for their time at the safe house. A heavy tension hung over the occupants of the farmhouse as the hours ticked by like mere minutes. The usual chatter and joking around was absent from the five men getting ready to enter the compound of their strongest enemy.

Gabriel headed up to his room in the agency to change and fortify himself for what was to come. He pulled a pair of black jeans up over his muscular legs, buttoning them before tugging on a black T-shirt with a black nylon weapons vest over it. Picking up two matching daggers, Gabriel slipped them into two of the slots in the vest before grabbing his gun and ensuring it was loaded. The noise of the gun cocking echoed in the silence of his suite. He shoved it into the holster and snatched up a black duffel bag sitting in the bottom of his closet to stuff a few changes of clothing into.

When he realized his hands were shaking, Gabriel gripped the edge of the dresser tightly and looked into the mirror. Haunted amber eyes gazed back at him from his reflection. A tension around his mouth turned the skin white, no matter how hard he tried to force it away. Memories bombarded him, as fresh as the day they'd happened, and he breathed deeply, repressing them as fast as they came. He could do this. He had to do this. Those boys' lives depended on it. Shoving away from the cabinet, Gabriel seized his bag and stalked out of his suite. Nothing would stop him this time.

Exactly three hours after Bryan had given him the assignment, the team headed out. It would take them a few hours to arrive in Vermont, and Gabriel sat tensely in the passenger seat of the black SUV with Lizard at the wheel and Bear in the backseat. "You okay, Gabe?" Lizard glanced over at him in concern.

Gabriel could only offer a hard smile in answer to Lizard's question. With his jaw clenched so tightly, he'd be surprised if he didn't crack a tooth. Tank and Jackal followed behind in a similar black SUV towing a trailer transporting the chopper. They would stash the trucks and take the helicopter within a few miles from the compound. From there they would approach on foot. Getting into the compound would be the easiest part. Gabriel worried about getting out.

The six hours it took to get to Vermont were the longest Gabriel had ever felt. His mind kept returning to the image of the two boys, and knowing anything could be happening to them right at that very moment. His fingers dug into his thigh in frustration. He hated feeling helpless. It reminded him too much of the day Paul was killed and he'd been unable to stop those men. Just inside the Vermont state border, Chris's voice came over the bud in Gabriel's ear, disrupting his thoughts. "The targets are most likely being held in the back of the compound, boss. It appears that the place was originally a prison, shut down about twenty years ago."

"Good work," Gabriel barked. "Is there a way in?"

"There's a section on the east side of the complex that shows a storm drain leading into the compound. Not sure if they've blocked it off or not, but that's the best place to start." Static crackled over the speaker for a split second before Chris continued, "If you go in on the east side, head north about half a click and you'll see an entrance into the building. Inside, there is another access door to the old jail cells."

Gabriel looked down at the small gadget in his hands as Chris transmitted the blueprints with the details he'd just given. He studied the layout, memorizing every building and room shown on the screen. It looked like there was every possibility of getting back out the way they came in if they could shut down the camp surveillance and alarms. "Is there a way to deactivate the security systems on your end?" he asked in a flat tone.

"Already on it, boss. Just give me the word, and with the press of a button you're good to go," Chris replied with confidence ringing clearly in his voice. He'd already thought that far ahead, and, after getting the blueprints, he'd started hacking into the system.

"Almost there, Gabe," Lizard stated quietly. His hands tightened on the wheel as they approached the target zone for stashing the trucks. The helicopter would draw too much attention if they took off inside a town or city, so the vehicles would need to be stashed as far into the trees as possible.

In a matter of thirty minutes, the team was in the air and on their way to the compound. Gabriel's face became grimmer the closer they got to their destination. Tank took lead the moment they were on the ground, and Gabriel followed closely behind. Lights shone from the compound, and they could see several guards patrolling the yard. They observed radio silence when they were two clicks from the fence. Gabriel sent the single beep over the radio to let Chris know to disable the systems. They would have to move quickly, because it wouldn't take long for the guards to realize something was up.

The storm drain had a padlocked grate over it, but other-wise the drain remained intact. Bear reached out with one hand and crushed the lock, tossing the pieces to the ground. The gate swung open with a small squeal, and Gabriel's eyes darted to the guards, holding his breath as he waited to see if they'd heard the noise. He carefully released it when they continued on their paths. He pointed at Lizard and Jackal before motioning for them to stay put. Lizard scowled but nodded.

Tank hunched over and stepped inside the drain, almost having to bend in half due to his height. Gabriel followed, with Bear taking up the rear. They stopped just inside the entrance to wait for the spotlight to sweep past their hiding place. The moment it passed, the three figures stealthily raced across the yard and flattened against the side of the building. Making their way north, they located the door Chris directed them to, and Bear made short work of the door handle, twisting it harshly.

Sweat built up on their skin, and Gabriel felt as though the tension would send him to his knees. They'd made it this far without a problem, but they still had to locate the boys. The dim hallway they entered beyond the door made Gabriel wary of whom they might run into. The three could see the other door just ahead of them, and they crept forward, all senses on alert. When they reached it, Gabriel motioned for Bear to wait. He closed his eyes and pushed outward, "feeling" for any presence of life on the other side.

Gabriel flicked his gaze toward Bear, tipping his head to indicate for him to open the door. The cells that lined the hallway had been modified from the original wrought iron bars to what looked like reinforced plexiglass. Horror slammed into Gabriel as he saw several cells were already occupied. Tank looked at him, a pleading expression in his dark eyes, but Gabriel shook his head. They couldn't take them all. A low growl rumbled in Tank's throat, and he swung back around to continue down the corridor. Gabriel knew how Tank felt. His jaw was a rigid line as he ignored the Deviants they passed.

The twins were in the second to last cell they reached.

11

Gabriel could see one boy sitting with his brother's head in his lap. More than likely they were keeping Jason sedated until they had a firm hold on him being able to use his abilities against them. Alexander looked up at them in surprise as they approached the cell, and fear shimmered in his eyes when he saw it wasn't their usual guards. Gabriel saw Alexander clutch his brother tighter, and tried to reassure the teenager with a tight smile and a tip of his head. They were there to rescue them, not hurt them. Understanding dawned in those bright green eyes Gabriel couldn't look away from. The boy was, no doubt, reading his mind, and their intentions were evident to him.

He finally managed to tear his gaze away from that intent stare and looked for an access panel. There was a keycard slot and pad on the wall. Gabriel pulled a small device from one of the pockets on his vest which contained a keycard. Punching in a couple of sequences, Gabriel slid the card through the slot decisively. The light stayed red, and he almost punched the wall in frustration. Tapping the piece in his ear, Gabriel fairly snarled over the radio, "Need a little help."

Chris sounded surprised when he responded, "Problem, boss?"

"The keycard didn't work." Gabriel motioned for the other two to keep a lookout while he stared intently at the device on the wall. "It requires a code. Find it."

The radio fell silent as Chris zipped through program after program, hacking into the security system at the jail until he located the necessary information. "Cell number?"

Gabriel glanced around the cell walls but didn't see any identifying numbers. Agitation glittered in his gaze, and he looked at Tank and Bear. They'd been in there too long. The longer they remained in the compound, the more likely they would be discovered and possibly captured. "Be ready for anything."

Bear's eyes widened a fraction at the realization that Gabriel intended to use his abilities. In four years, the team had only seen him use them a handful of times. The three of them stepped back from the cell. Taking a deep breath, Gabriel concentrated on the plexiglass door. The glass shuddered before a powerful boom reverberated against the cement walls and it fairly exploded into pieces that scattered across the corridor floor. Gabriel pushed inside the cell in the breath of a second. He hauled Jason up into his arms, tossing him across his shoulder. "Let's go," he commanded quietly.

The moment Alexander stood from the bed, a piercing alarm sounded throughout the complex and red lights started flashing everywhere. Gabriel swore profusely. "Go, go, go!"

Tank started at a fast clip down the corridor while Gabriel shoved Alexander in front of him, followed by Bear at the rear. Several of the Deviants were pounding on the glass, begging them to release them. His stomach clenched as he swallowed the bile rising in his throat. There was no way to save them all.

Gun shots rang out across the yard when they broke out of the building. Lizard and Jackal were keeping them busy, firing as they ran to cover the four of them. Gabriel felt a bullet slam into his shoulder and suppressed a loud roar at the pain tearing through him. "Jackal, Lizard! Let's go!" he shouted through clenched teeth.

It felt like they were miles from where they had entered the compound. He was only able to take a deep breath when the drain appeared up ahead. Gabriel sheltered Alexander with his body as he practically pushed the boy into the storm drain. The others raced behind them, firing on the guards chasing after. Bullets thudded into the tree trunks a hairs-breadth from hitting their targets as they raced into the cover of the trees. The sound of the alarm echoed through the forest. Gabriel stumbled briefly under the weight of the boy across his shoulder. He could feel the warm, sticky blood flowing down his free arm. Tank stopped Gabriel briefly, yanking Jason from him. "I've got him, boss."

He grabbed at his shoulder, trying to stem the flow of blood as best he could. Shouts could be heard behind the team, but farther back now. It wouldn't be long before they reached the helicopter. Jackal had raced ahead of the group to start the engine, and they could hear the blades long before they saw the chopper. Lizard jumped inside, reaching out and pulling Alexander into the seat next to him. Bear slipped into the passenger side as Tank hefted Jason in and turned back to Gabriel, offering his hand to him. "Come on!"

A bullet pinged into the metal side of the helicopter, and Gabriel whipped around, holding up his hand. The gun exploded in the guard's grip, and he screamed as the shrapnel dug into his skin. Gabriel clasped Tank's wrist, allowing the man to tug him into the chopper. Jackal took off as fast as safely possible. Gabriel watched the field flood with men below them. They were still firing at them, but they were too far out of reach for the bullets to hit anything with accuracy.

When they were finally heading toward the safe house, Gabriel slumped back and sighed, still holding his shoulder tightly. He felt eyes on him and rolled his head against the seat to see the boy staring at him. Unable to take the strong emotions ripping through him as he gazed at the teenager, Gabriel closed his eyes and attempted to ignore him. He'd learned a long time ago how to block out a telepath, and closed his mind to the boy.

Lizard let out a profane word when he finally saw the

blood covering Gabriel's shirt. He shifted into the seat next to his friend and shouted, "Why didn't you say you were hit?"

Gabriel felt pretty certain his face was pale from the pain and loss of blood, but he managed a cocky, though somewhat shaky, grin. "You know me, Lizard. I can take a hit and keep on trucking."

Glaring at the stubborn bastard, Lizard reached out and stripped the weapons vest from Gabriel's chest before ripping the shirt down the middle. He worked carefully to pull Gabriel's arm from the short sleeve, but Gabriel still let out a hiss as the fabric pulled at the bullet hole. Lizard popped the end of a flashlight in his mouth as he examined the wound. Gabriel knew the bullet had gone all the way through, but figured it would need stitches. Lizard tore open the first aid kit from under the seat and wrapped the wound up as best as he could. "You're going to need stitches," Lizard yelled to be heard over the loud blades.

Gabriel grimaced but nodded, tipping his head back into the headrest. God, he hated needles.

2

ALEX

ALEX had been cradling his unconscious brother in his arms and trying to close his eyes in an attempt to sleep when the three strangers had come up to his cell. Panic struck through him when he hadn't recognized them. They weren't his usual guards, and he feared they'd finally come to do whatever they planned on doing with the two of them. But when he'd met those dark amber eyes, somehow he'd felt that they weren't dangerous. His dread had faded completely when he'd read the stranger's thoughts of how they had come to rescue him and Jason.

Astonishment speared through him when he saw the kind of power the stranger had. The door literally shattered into pieces. He'd been in awe when he saw the other two hulking figures enter the cell. They were huge! They almost seemed to dwarf the amber-eyed man. He'd reluctantly released Jason when the stranger yanked him across his broad shoulders. What struck him harder than any fist from his guards had been the husky voice coming from the man carrying his brother. "Let's go."

It sent shivers of electricity down his spine. He'd almost

gasped at how his body tingled when he felt a strong hand push him forward. A scream had lodged itself in his throat when he felt a bullet whizz by him the moment they'd exited the building. He huddled as close as possible to the amber-eyed stranger, almost stepping on the heels of his boots. Two other men joined them when they were halfway through the compound yard. Alex almost yelped when one of them appeared as though from thin air.

He heard the bullet slam into the man one of them called boss. It wasn't until they were inside the helicopter that he saw how badly the man was bleeding. His heart beat fiercely at the realization of how the bullet could have hit him or his brother. Shame almost overwhelmed him at the relief that it hadn't been them. The man could have been killed if it had gone several inches lower. Alex couldn't stop staring at him.

The man was breathtakingly gorgeous. Dark hair kept in a military-style fade, with strong chiseled features and a beautifully muscled body caused Alex to feel hot all over, and not from the run through the woods. A small scar across his brow made him appear even more dangerous. The amber eyes reminded Alex of the honey maple syrup his grand-mother used to make. He was obviously in pain and being stubborn about it. When the broad expanse of tanned skin was revealed as the other man removed his shirt, Alex had to bite back a gasp at how strongly his body reacted. A strange warmth settled between his thighs, and he felt his dick growing hard. He dropped his hands into his lap to cover up his body's response.

When those honeyed eyes met his, Alex's gaze flitted away for a moment, only to come back to them. The man closed his eyes against Alex's perusal, and Alex tried to reach out, to see what thoughts the man held, only to hit a wall. Surprise widened his eyes by a fraction, and his breath caught. He'd never met anyone he couldn't read. How could the stranger block him so completely? Then he started to wonder who the men were and why they'd rescued him and Jason. Were they like the others? Did they want to use them too?

It seemed like forever before the helicopter started to descend. "Gabriel?" The one called Lizard reached out and touched a broad shoulder. "We're here."

Alex watched the man's eyelids lift. His eyes were glazed with pain, and his hand shook as he ran it over his face. "Send Jackal and Bear to get the vehicles. I need to call Bryan."

"Let me do that, boss," the dark-skinned mountain rumbled before climbing out of the helicopter. Alex saw him pull a cell phone out of his pocket and hit a button. It wasn't a long conversation, and the man returned in less than a minute, but chose to stand outside rather than get back into the helicopter.

"Who are you people?" Alex couldn't contain his outburst, and the man named Gabriel pinned him in place with a sharp look.

Lizard grinned and stuck out his hand. "I'm Lizard. This big guy here with the bullet in his shoulder is Gabriel." He pointed at the dark-skinned man. "That's Tank. Bear's the wall of muscle over there, and the one who just left was Jackal. We're from the ADA."

Alex frowned at Lizard. "ADA?"

Surprise flashed over Lizard's face. "You've never heard of the ADA?"

Shaking his head, Alex asked, "What is it?"

"The Agency for Deviant Assistance," Gabriel bit out. "How is it that you've never heard of us? Every Deviant should know who we are."

A flush dusted Alex's cheeks, and he looked down at where his hands lay in his lap. "Up until a year and a half ago, we lived on our grandmother's farm. We were homeschooled and have never met any others like us. Until we were kidnapped."

Alex and Jason had been raised by their grandmother from the time they were five, when they started to exhibit powers. Their mother freaked out and tried to drown them. If their father hadn't returned home from work early, she probably would have succeeded. To keep them safe, their father sent them to live with their grandmother. They were almost never allowed to leave the farm for fear of being discovered. Alex still remembered waking up every night from horrible nightmares.

"The ADA is to help Deviants like you," Lizard explained. "We offer support financially, as well as educating Deviants on how to control their abilities. We also do what you saw tonight, kid. Rescue ones who have been abducted."

"But what about all of the others there? Why didn't you rescue them?" Alex demanded.

Lizard's eyes shifted away from Alex in guilt. "We were only sent to rescue you and your brother. We didn't have the equipment to rescue everyone else."

"Why us? Why were you sent to rescue me and Jason and not the others?" Alex couldn't believe what he was hearing. If they were there to help Deviants, why didn't they help all of them? It wasn't right!

Gabriel growled at Lizard when the man went to open his mouth. "We don't know why the ADA chose to rescue you. We only do what we're told."

Alex gaped at Gabriel in shock. The man had just lied to his face. He could tell without reading the bastard's mind. Alex didn't like to invade others' thoughts without invitation, but considering this concerned his and Jason's safety, he felt no such compulsion. He reached out to Lizard and picked up the stray thought of level fives and surprise over Gabriel lying. "Level fives?"

Swearing, Gabriel glared at him. "Reading someone's mind without permission will get you killed, kid."

Embarrassment would have swamped Alex if it had been any other situation than the one he currently found himself in. "It can also keep me alive. I don't know you or anything about you. How do I know you aren't lying to me and looking to use me like they were?"

Lizard stifled a laugh. Alex glanced at him and saw a twinkle in Lizard's eyes. Gabriel swung himself out of the helicopter. Alex watched the muscled back ripple as the man staggered to lean against a tree. "Been a long time since someone challenged Gabe," Lizard mused. "Nice to see something can get under his skin every once in a while."

Alex looked toward Lizard. He liked the man sitting across from him. He sensed Lizard was a good person, friendly. "Why were you sent to rescue us?"

Sighing lightly, Lizard lifted a shoulder. "All that Gabriel told us is that you and your brother are level five Deviants. There are only five levels, kid. You and your brother are extremely powerful, and if the wrong person got hold of you, they could use your abilities for the wrong purpose."

Shock spread through Alex. He didn't even want to think of what would have happened if he and his brother had remained with those people. "Are we free to leave, then?"

Uneasiness flitted over Lizard's face. "Ah… I think you should talk to Gabriel about that one. We're supposed to stay at a safe house for a while. Just until the men who had you have stopped looking for you."

Alex bit his lip and glanced at his brother. Jason wasn't going to like this at all. His brother tended to get angry pretty easily, which was the whole reason they'd been discovered. Jason had lost his temper in a restaurant and caused all of the lightbulbs to implode. They'd run for their lives when one of the men pulled out a shotgun. He could still hear the loud explosion of the gun going off and the shatter of glass as the bullet blew out the window of the front door. He reached out and brushed a stray strand of dark hair back from Jason's cheek. "Will they be able to teach him how to control it?"

"That's what we're here for, kid," Lizard replied quietly, gently touching Alex's forearm. "We aren't here to hurt you. Gabriel must have had a reason for not explaining everything. He's a good man and would never let anything happen to you."

A trembling smile graced Alex's face for a split second before he looked back out at the man in question. The smile died when he saw Gabriel had slumped down to the ground and leaned limply against the tree. "Is he okay?"

Lizard followed Alex's gaze. "Fuck," he swore, hopping out of the chopper and rushing to Gabriel's side. "Where the hell is Jackal?"

Gabriel had passed out, apparently. Alex saw the concern everyone displayed for the big jerk, and it made the tension in his shoulders relax slightly. If he wasn't a good man, they wouldn't care so much about him. Now he would just have to get his brother to listen to him when he woke up. Alex found it unlikely Jason would be okay with the situation, and he wouldn't hesitate to use his powers before asking questions.

The man named Jackal drove up a short while later in a black SUV, followed by a second SUV pulling a trailer that Alex assumed was for the helicopter. Jackal leapt from the vehicle in a blur of action. "What happened?" he demanded as he rushed to Gabriel's side.

"He passed out. I think he lost a lot of blood before we realized he'd been hit," Tank outlined in a deep voice.

Jackal growled, his eyes flashing. "Fucking Vincetti. I am going to gut that motherfucker one of these days. Tank, get

Gabriel in the truck. Lay him out in the back if necessary. Bear, get the twins. Lizard and I will grab the supplies from the helicopter. Then you and Lizard follow us to the safe house once the chopper is loaded."

Before Alex could even ask where they were going, he found himself seated in the SUV next to Jason as they loaded Gabriel in the back of the truck. Alex turned in his seat as best he could to look at Gabriel. The man's face appeared several shades lighter than before, and sweat gave a slight sheen to his skin. "Is he… is he going to be okay?" He couldn't stop himself from asking.

Tank patted Alex's shoulder with one large paw. "He'll be fine. We just need to get to where we can take a look at his shoulder."

Thirty minutes into the drive, Alex finally worked up the courage to ask, "Why does this Vincetti person want us so badly? Who is he?"

No one answered for several minutes. Jackal spoke first. "A ruthless son of a bitch who wants to control Deviants for his own personal gain."

"Is he a Deviant?" Alex asked curiously.

"He's a level three, not very powerful, though. He has the ability of manipulating others. It's how he controls so many Deviants. The control doesn't last long, but he uses other forms of torture and violence to force them to follow him."

"Why is he after us?"

"Who knows, kid? Power? Money? Last we knew, he'd begun selling off some of us to Normals, governments, or whoever the highest bidder was for profit. Being a telepath or telekinetic would come in handy in the right, or rather wrong, hands."

Alex shivered at the thought of being forced to use his ability to hurt others or to help someone commit crimes. He bit his bottom lip and stared out the window, lost in thought, for several moments before speaking again. "Why hasn't he been stopped?"

"There's the million-dollar question, kid," Jackal said. "No one gets near him. The Deviants he has guarding him are too powerful and no one can get the drop on him. Not even the US government has been able to stop him."

"You guys are Deviants. How is it you haven't been able to stop him?" Alex asked.

Jackal turned in the front seat to pin him with a fierce look. "Everyone in this car, on this team, has cause to hate that prick for one reason or another. They'd give everything they have to stop him, but it's not that easy. Like I said, he surrounds himself with some very powerful Deviants who, under his manipulation, would do anything to keep him safe."

Alex dropped his gaze away from Jackal's. "I'm sorry."

Relaxing back into his seat, Jackal replied, "No worries, kid. Why don't you try to get some sleep? It's going to be a long ride to the safe house."

Silence reigned for the duration of the drive. They reached the safe house as the sky began to lighten: a large two-story structure that looked like it needed a good paint job. Several of the shingles were hanging by a nail, and one of the shutters was missing completely. The yard even needed to be mowed, as weeds were growing everywhere. There wasn't another house for miles, from what Alex could see, and a thick set of trees surrounded the backyard. He swallowed hard as memories of his grandmother's farm hit him. He missed it fiercely.

Alex scurried after Tank as the hulk of muscle carried Jason into the house. Bear followed, holding Gabriel. They disappeared into one of the bedrooms on the first floor as Tank headed up the stairs. The inside appeared to be in better shape than the outside. A layer of dust covered gleaming wood flooring, and a true cherry oak wood banister lined the stairs. One Alex could just picture his brother sliding down. The furniture had covers over it, and he could see the house hadn't been used in quite some time. Tank called back to him, "Do you want to share, or do you want your own room?"

"I think I should share with Jason, at least until he wakes up," Alex replied cautiously. Truth was, he didn't want to be separated from the only person he knew and loved in the messed up and confusing situation they found themselves in.

Tank grunted carelessly and shouldered his way into a large bedroom. He tossed his chin at an armoire against the far wall. "Grab some sheets, kid."

Alex did as suggested and quickly made up the bed. Tank set Jason down gently on the sheets before stepping back. "You hungry, kid?"

"Oh, no. I couldn't eat right now," Alex said, internally shuddering at the thought of trying to keep anything in his stomach after what they'd just been through.

"Bathroom's there." Tank pointed at the closed door to his right. "Get some sleep. We'll go into town tomorrow to get you some clothes."

"Oh, thank you." Alex watched in wonder as the mountain flushed and nodded. He smiled as the man left the room, but the smile slowly faded as he sank down onto the edge of the bed next to his brother. Had they been taken from the frying pan and dumped into the fire? He still didn't entirely trust these people. There'd been snippets of things he'd picked up, but after Gabriel had pricked his conscience about listening in on people's thoughts without permission Alex hadn't felt right about it.

Sighing, he moved further onto the bed and slid down, yawning. He'd barely slept in almost three days. They'd kept his brother sedated the entire time, so Alex had nothing left except to think. Every time he'd dozed off, a strange noise would cause him to jerk awake. Both of them still wore the same clothing from the day they were kidnapped, and it had made for an uncomfortable couple of days. If he wasn't so tired, he'd have gotten back up to strip them off in distaste. Alex couldn't keep his eyes open any longer and in minutes fell into a deep sleep.

He couldn't be sure of how long he slept, but the next thing he became aware of was Jason shouting and the crash of glass. Alex sat up, gasping loudly. "Jason!"

Jason stood in the corner of the room, a wild look on his face, currently levitating whatever wasn't nailed down and lobbing it at the dark-haired male who stood in the doorway. Gabriel growled, "I'm not going to hurt you, kid, so cut it out."

Blood dripped down one muscular arm, and there were several scratches lining his face, most likely due to stray glass. Alex stood from the bed and jumped in front of Gabriel, holding his hands up toward his brother. "Jace, stop."

His brother stared at Alex in astonishment. "Get out of the way, Alex."

Alex shook his head furiously. "No, Jace. They aren't going to hurt us. They rescued us."

A scowl marred Jason's features. "Rescued us? Alex, have they brainwashed you? They kidnapped us."

"Jace, these aren't the same people. Gabriel and his friends got us out of that god-awful place. Please calm down and listen to me, to Gabriel." Alex pleaded with his brother. He felt Gabriel's surprise at Alex's defense of them. He also knew that, if he'd wanted to, Gabriel could have stopped Jason, but he hadn't. Gabriel allowed Jason to use his abilities against him, never lifting a hand to stop him.

Jason remained tense, but let the mirror he'd been about

to throw settle down to the floor, leaning beside the dresser. "Where are we?"

"You're in a safe house in New York," Gabriel replied, placing a firm hand on Alex's shoulder. "The ADA became aware of your abduction, and we were sent in to rescue you."

"ADA?" Jason frowned, his lips pursed.

Alex couldn't have been more acutely aware of the heat radiating from Gabriel's hand into his shoulder. He wanted nothing more than to lean back into the other man's body, but he was pretty sure Gabriel would not welcome the contact. "The Agency for Deviant Assistance," Alex explained.

Gabriel's hand tightened on his shoulder when Alex attempted to take a step toward his brother. Alex reached up and gently took the man's hand in his. He couldn't believe Gabriel thought his own brother would hurt him, but he supposed the amber-eyed Deviant couldn't know Jason would never intentionally hurt him. He squeezed Gabriel's hand slightly before letting it go and moving closer to his brother. "It's a place to help people like us, Jace. These men helped us, and they can even show us how to control our abilities better."

Jason grew agitated again at Alex's words. "Sounds just like the men who kidnapped us, Alex. How are they any different?"

From the corner of his eye, Alex could see the mirror rising from the floor again. "Jason!" he snapped. "If they were here to hurt us, they would have done so already, and they wouldn't have allowed the sedative to wear off. You'd still be unconscious."

The fear and anger in Jason's eyes wavered as his gaze bounced between Alex and Gabriel. "If you're hungry, there's breakfast in the kitchen," Gabriel said in a bored tone, turning and leaving the room.

Alex ignored the somewhat bereft voice in his head when Gabriel left. He figured Gabriel wanted to give them time to talk and to show Jason they weren't prisoners. Reaching out, he lightly took Jason's hand and led him to the bed. "I heard their thoughts, Jace. They aren't going to hurt us."

"How can you believe them, Alex?" Jason demanded, running a hand through his thick, shoulder-length dark hair. "How do you know they aren't trying to trick us and make you think they're here to help us?"

"I trust my instincts, Jason." Alex looked down at where their hands lay entwined on his thigh. "I'm tired of running, brother. Ever since Grams died and you lost control of your power in the diner, we've done nothing but run. I want to be able to have a home and to stay in one place for more than a week. I believe these people can help us."

Jason studied Alex for a long time. Alex knew his brother felt responsible for the danger they'd been in for the last year and a half. He felt bad trying to play on Jason's guilt, but he really was tired and felt nothing except a sense of rightness around the Deviants he'd met. "They're like us, Jason. They have abilities too. Gabriel... Gabriel has a power I've never even imagined."

"Gabriel, huh?" Jason looked at him, a knowing gleam in his eyes causing Alex to flush. His twin knew he'd never shown an interest in girls while they were growing up. None of the girls on their infrequent trips into town ever caught his attention. Rather, the other teenage boys captured his eye. They'd never revealed Alex's preference to their grandmother because, according to the Bible she'd read from every Sunday, it was a sin for him to love another man. Alex didn't understand why it would be wrong. Wasn't love just that? Love? It shouldn't matter what form it came in as long as it was right and true.

Alex cast his eyes away from his twin. "Even if he was into men, he'd never be interested in a freak like me, Jace."

Jason scowled at his brother's words. "He'd be stupid not to be interested in you, Alex. And you're not a freak!"

"Aren't I? Who wants to be around someone where they can never have a private thought? Someone who would always be able to know what they're thinking?" Alex pushed away the thought of how effectively Gabriel had cut him off earlier. It wasn't as if the gorgeous amber-eyed man would be interested in a skinny nobody, let alone a skinny nobody who happened to be another guy. "Can we at least give it a try here, Jace? If there is even a hint they aren't what they say they are, we can leave."

His twin didn't speak for a long moment before nodding. "Fine. We'll stay for now."

Alex grinned brightly at his brother. "Thanks, Jace."

"Now, the man mentioned food, and I am starving!"

Alex realized it was indeed early morning outside. He must have slept the entire twenty-four hours! His stomach growled loudly, and he blushed. "I guess I am too."

Jackal, Tank, and Bear were already seated at the table with huge, heaping plates of eggs and bacon when they went downstairs to the kitchen. Alex breathed the smell of food with pleasure. Lizard stepped out of the kitchen with three more plates balanced on his arms. He smiled at Alex widely. "Good morning, Alex. Ah, you must be Jason. I'm Lizard."

An eyebrow went up at the name. "Lizard?"

Alex took a seat beside Jackal and placed a paper towel across his lap. He couldn't keep his eyes from flitting around for a glimpse of Gabriel, who didn't seem to be present.

"He's cleaning up after his recent battle," Jackal said drily.

"How did you—"

Jackal cut Alex off. "It's pretty obvious who you were

looking for. You aren't exactly skilled at hiding your interest, kid."

Red dusted Alex's high cheekbones, and he cursed his easy tendency to blush. "Is he... is he okay?"

Jason plopped down in the chair beside him. "Yeah, sorry. I tend to act first and ask questions later."

Tank shrugged. "We expected it, kid. Any one of us would have done the same thing in your place."

"It's Jason, not kid," Jason growled. Jason hated being treated like a child.

Alex set his hand on Jason's forearm to stop his brother from getting upset further. "Relax, Jace. He didn't mean anything by it."

Scowling, Jason slouched further into his chair but didn't say anything else. Alex almost breathed a sigh of relief, except it caught in his throat when Gabriel stepped into the dining room. He couldn't stop his eyes from sliding down the man's large, muscular frame. No one had ever mesmerized Alex so completely. "Are you okay?" he asked, watching Gabriel sit down across from him.

Gabriel nodded. "Fine. Surface scratches." He turned his attention away from Alex to Tank. "Are the vehicles topped off?"

Tank grinned at his boss. "Ready and waiting, boss."

"Hurry up and eat," Gabriel directed at Jason and Alex. "We'll be heading into town in ten minutes to get you both some clothing. We'll be here a while."

"How long's a while?" Jason demanded, sitting up straighter. "We have a life, you know."

At the same time, Tank spoke up, "Are you sure that's a good idea, boss? Taking them into town? What if someone spots them?"

Cocking an elegant eyebrow at Jason, Gabriel replied, "Not much of one, if your files are any indication." Directing his attention at Tank, Gabriel stated, "It's highly unlikely Vincetti will know where to look right now, as I'm sure he's still ripping into whoever didn't manage to stop us. We're in the middle of nowhere with a population of roughly two thousand and not exactly going to draw attention to ourselves at a Walmart. It'll be easier for them to get everything they need if they go. We won't be returning to town again. Jackal will accompany them to make sure they don't do anything stupid."

Files? The ADA had files on them? Alex wondered what exactly the files contained about them. Did Gabriel know he preferred men? Was that why Gabriel seemed to dislike him? "What the fuck!" Jason exclaimed.

"Jason," Alex admonished gently, nudging his brother in the ribs with his elbow. "Don't use that kind of language."

"Fuck that! Files? Why would they have files on us?" Jason demanded.

Gabriel continued to butter his toast, giving off an aura of carelessness, but Alex saw the slight tension in his shoulders. "The ADA has files on every known Deviant. For your protection as well as our own."

"I want to see these files." Jason's hands fisted on the table, and Alex knew what happened when his brother got angry. He could already see several of the dishes on the table shaking, shifting on the table in response to Jason's emotions.

The others must have picked up on it as well. Tank stood up, towering over Jason. "This is why you were discovered in the first place, dude. Because you can't control yourself and your powers. If you have a prayer of having a life, you need to listen to Gabriel."

"I don't have to listen to anyone," Jason snapped at Tank, standing to face off with the giant.

Alex saw Jackal's mouth parted in astonishment. Apparently it was a rare occurrence for anyone to stand up to

Tank. His size alone would probably make the strongest person shake in their boots. Tank smirked at Jason. "You think you could take me, kid?"

"Jason, no!" Alex jumped up, grabbing his brother by the arm. "Stop it. You promised."

Gabriel stood abruptly, shoving his chair back. It scraped sharply over the wood floor, drawing each of the men's gazes. "Enough. We risked our lives to break you out of that hell hole. If you think you'd be better off with someone like Vincetti then you can just walk out that door and go right back to him. As far as I can see, you need to check the attitude and listen for a change. Otherwise you may end up dead or worse."

Worse than death? Alex trembled at the possibility of anything being worse than death. His brother's muscles were taut beneath his hand, and he knew it wouldn't take much to make Jason snap. He looked up at Gabriel, becoming ensnared in the haunted look shimmering in the man's amber eyes. "How is being here any better than being held prisoner by this Vincetti?"

Jason's question pulled Alex's attention away from Gabriel. He saw Bear's hand come out and land on Gabriel's shoulder. "Don't, Gabe."

Whatever Bear meant must have registered with Gabriel, and the man grimaced, straightening. He glared at Jason before wordlessly stalking out of the room. Bear reached out and cuffed Jason on the back of the head, shocking Alex's brother into silence. "Stupid, pup. You have no idea what fate Gabriel has saved you from. Pull your head out of your ass and look around. Are you in a cell? Are you drugged and unable to fight? Are you handcuffed, tied, or restrained? That alone should show you that you're far better off here than there."

Alex would have laughed at Jackal's expression if the situation hadn't been so serious. His eyes appeared huge as he stared up at Bear in shock. Jackal spoke in a hushed tone to Lizard the moment Bear swept from the room. "I think that's the most I've heard him say in three years."

His brother didn't speak and sank back into his seat. Alex sighed and sat down again too. "You promised to give it a chance, Jace. Why must you always let your anger get the better of you? Didn't Grams tell you that it's going to be your downfall? Now look where we are. Kidnapped, held prisoner, and now in a house full of strangers. "

Jason didn't respond. He just stared down at his plate. Alex shook his head and stood. "I need to use the bathroom."

Exiting the dining room, Alex heard a low murmur coming from the living room and trod softly, inching closer to listen. "Damn it, Bear. I can't do this!"

"Yes you can, Gabe. Bryan asked you to handle this because he knew you would be the only one who could. Remember that by helping these boys you're helping Rafael."

Gabriel's voice came out in a low snarl. "Rafael's dead."

"You think I don't know he's dead, Gabe? I know it just as well as you do. I was there too!"

A hand wrapping around his wrist startled Alex and he jumped, stifling a squeak. He turned around to find Lizard glaring at him. "Eavesdropping, kid?"

"N... no," he stuttered before hanging his head. "Yes."

Lizard yanked him away from the living room, shoving him toward the bathroom. "The bathroom's that way."

When he came out, he found Jason waiting for him by the front door. Jackal tossed Alex a pair of sunglasses and a baseball cap. "Put those on and let's go. Gabriel's already in the car."

Alex slid the glasses on and jammed the cap onto his head, covering his short, silky hair. The thought of eating breakfast long gone, he followed Jackal out of the house and to the SUV. Embarrassment still twisted his stomach at having been caught listening in on a private conversation, and he didn't speak during the entire ride to town. He missed every bit of scenery flying by, lost in his thoughts of the conversation. Just who was Rafael? And why did it seem to hurt Gabriel to talk about him? Jealousy spiked through Alex when a thought occurred to him. Maybe Rafael had been Gabriel's lover. He brushed the idea aside. Why would he assume Gabriel held any interest in men?

The SUV came to a stop in front of a Walmart, disrupting Alex's mental musings. "Get what you need," Gabriel ordered, opening the glove compartment and pulling out a bundle of bills. "Enough for at least six weeks."

Jason went to protest the amount of time, and Alex tried to object to the ten one hundred dollar bills shoved into his hand. "Go," Gabriel barked, effectively stopping anything they would have said.

Alex reluctantly stepped down from the vehicle and followed his brother into the store with Jackal behind him. Gabriel stayed in the truck, calling someone on a cell phone. He glanced down at the amount of cash in his hands. They'd never be able to repay that kind of money, and he felt uneasy using it. "This is too much," he said shakily to Jackal.

Jackal waved his hand. "Don't worry about it. The ADA is funded by many Deviant advocates, and there's plenty to spare. Just do what Gabe said and get your shit. Make sure you get everything in this trip because we won't be coming back to town for a while."

He saw his brother already throwing jeans and T-shirts over his arm. Haltingly, he pulled two pairs of jeans in his size off the rack. Jackal grunted, grabbed five more pairs and stuffed them into Alex's hands. "I'm going to go grab a cart. Don't move from this section," Jackal instructed, loping off to find the basket.

It didn't take more than five minutes for Jackal to return. "Put them in the cart and get the rest."

By the time they headed to the registers, the cart was full to the brim, almost overflowing. Shoes, socks, boxers, jeans, T-shirts, and a couple of jackets were piled on top of each other. Jackal tossed in deodorants, shampoos, conditioners, razors, shaving cream, and a few other hygiene items as well. The total stopped Alex's heart. "Nine hundred and seventy-two dollars and sixty-five cents," the cashier stated calmly, obviously not unused to seeing such an extravagant amount of money spent.

3

GABRIEL

"**S**ORENSEN."

"It's Gabe."

"Everything okay?"

"Everything's fine." Gabriel watched the slim back disappear into the store, his gaze hungrily roaming over the lean muscles bunching with each step.

"Bear reported you were injured. What happened?" Bryan's voice held a concerned note.

Gabriel gave a brief rundown of the mission, including a clipped mention of being shot. He didn't want anyone making a big deal out of it. It wasn't the first time he'd been shot and probably wouldn't be the last. Lizard's sewing skills were testament to how many times someone on the team had been injured enough to require medical attention beyond a Band-Aid. They kept a small medical supplies kit on hand in case a mission got rough. "I owe you a vacation after this," Bryan replied.

"I've been shot before. It's nothing."

"How did the twins react?"

"As expected. Suspicious. The telekinetic is a hothead. We

may have trouble with him later." Gabriel glanced at his watch. They'd been in the store for twenty minutes already. He didn't like being in such an exposed position. If the three of them didn't appear in another ten minutes, he'd give Jackal a call on his cell.

"Where are they now?"

"Shopping. They needed clothes. Jackal's accompanying them."

Bryan fell silent for a moment. Gabriel could almost picture the man, only a handful of years older than himself, standing, looking out of the window behind his desk, a serious expression on his face. He knew the other man couldn't help but think of his own son, who hadn't even had a chance at a life. "Are they as strong as the reports say?" Bryan finally asked.

"Yes. I can attest to the fact that Jason's powers as a tele-kinetic are very strong," Gabriel said dryly. He looked down at his arm. The white bandage stood out starkly against his tan skin. "I've only had brief contact with Alex, but the only reason he trusted me at the compound was because I allowed him to read my mind."

He knew Bryan would be surprised he'd lowered his shield enough for Alex to access his thoughts. Gabriel learned a long time ago how to block out a telepath, an ability which had saved his life. "Keep me posted, Gabe. I don't have word yet on what Vincetti is doing since the boys were taken. As soon as I know something, I'll contact you."

Gabriel cut the call after a grim farewell. He lifted his gaze to the storefront and saw Jason step out of the auto-matic doors. Jackal followed closely behind, pushing an over-loaded cart and talking to Alex. The smile Alex gave at something Jackal said went straight to Gabriel's gut, wrenching it hard. Scowling, he shoved the pang of attrac-tion deep inside, refusing to acknowledge it. He jabbed the auto release button, opening the tailgate of the SUV. Snatches of conversation reached his ears, but he tuned it out, rubbing his eyes with his thumb and forefinger. Even if his past didn't hold the horrors it did, he knew a young, vibrant man such as Alex would never want an old, beat up son of a bitch like him.

"Gabe?" a soft voice right near his ear jerked Gabriel out of his personal torment.

Somehow the three men had finished loading the back of the SUV and gotten into the vehicle without him even noticing. Alex had spoken directly into his ear. "Sorry," he grunted, starting the car.

The entire ride back to the safe house, Gabriel could feel Alex's eyes on him. From time to time he glanced into the mirror and caught Alex's gaze in his. It unsettled him, the intensity of Alex's interest. He sensed that it shocked Alex how easily he'd been able to block him out, and Gabriel couldn't help but worry for the younger man. Telepaths were able to hear others' thoughts, to listen to their private emotions and things which shouldn't be known to anyone else. There were some who'd learned how to turn being telepathic against a Deviant. Alex clearly had never been exposed to someone who knew that particular type of torture. Gabriel clenched his hands on the wheel in an effort to control himself. Memories bombarded him, and he stifled a growl of rage and pain.

"Did Bryan have anything to report?" Jackal questioned. "Gabe?"

Giving a mental shake, Gabriel loosened his grip slightly, his knuckles fading from white to tan once more. "No. His informant hasn't contacted him. He's pretty sure he'll hear something when it's safe for his contact to get in touch."

Jackal nodded in understanding. "So no idea how long we'll be here?"

"No. I don't want to risk taking them back to the agency until we're sure Vincetti won't look for them there. Bryan wanted us to return in a few days, but with how badly Vincetti wants them, I don't want to put everyone else in danger." Gabriel knew Jackal asked because he missed Teresa. The nightmares of his past haunted Jackal as surely as the ones in Gabriel's past haunted him, and Teresa offered a safe harbor to his friend. Someone who could take away that pain and torment just by being there, holding him. "If it's going to take more than a couple of weeks, I'm sure the rest of the team can handle it."

"I'm not going anywhere, boss." Jackal rejected Gabriel's offer to let him go home sooner. "I'll see this through to the end."

Jason spoke up from the back seat. "We are here in the car, you know."

Gabriel waved his hand at Jackal when his team member started to snap back at the teenager. "We're aware of that, kid, but we are also the ones here to keep you safe, which doesn't mean you'll be privy to everything we speak of or plan on."

"I think we should have some say!" Jason protested.

Clenching his jaw, Gabriel prayed for patience, something he had very little of in the first place. "When I think we need your input, I'll ask for it. Until then, sit back and shut up."

"Don't fucking speak to me like I'm a little kid," Jason snarled.

"Then don't act like one, and I won't have to treat you as one." The safe house came into view, and he could see Tank in front of the house running a lawn mower. Gabriel smiled. Such a mundane activity in a dangerous situation seemed incongruous.

Alex stalled anything Jason would have said by asking,

"You said that you can teach us how to control our abilities. When are we going to start?"

There were no telepaths or telekinetics in Gabriel's team. Despite having experience in both, he didn't relish the thought of trying to teach either of the twin brothers anything. He never used his own ability unless in dire circumstances, and spending that much time around Alex when he felt such a strong attraction to the teenager was a bad idea. "When we get back to the agency."

"Why not now?" Alex demanded, shifting closer to the front seat.

The heat from Alex's body seeped into Gabriel's shoulders through the thin T-shirt he wore, causing another spike of awareness to shudder down his spine. His voice had a harsher tone than he intended when he answered. "Because we do not have any telepaths or telekinetics here to teach you."

Alex sat back against the seat, hurt shining brightly from his gaze. "But I thought you had telekinetic abilities."

Unable to suppress it, Gabriel growled low in his throat, furiously putting the SUV into park in front of the house and wrenching the engine off. He didn't speak as he thrust open the door and exited the vehicle. "He's not telekinetic," reached his ears a split second before he slammed the door.

Gabriel strode into the house and straight up the stairs to his room. Very few had ever seen Gabriel use his gifts. The other night when they'd rescued the twins was the first time in six months that he'd utilized them. If he could get out of a situation without them, he did. They'd brought him nothing except trouble since the day he'd discovered his abilities. As far as everyone else in the ADA knew, Gabriel registered as a level four Deviant. He'd asked Bryan not to register him as a level five as a favor. Not even his team knew the depth of his power.

Needing to run off some of his frustration and anger, Gabriel shed his clothing and yanked on a pair of sweatpants, T-shirt, and sneakers. When he reached the bottom of the stairs, Alex came in the front door carrying three bags in each hand. Alex stopped, staring at Gabriel. He opened his mouth to speak, and Gabriel brushed by him, ignoring him. The instant his feet hit the dirt path, he took off running.

Nothing soothed Gabriel more than mindless exercise. It cleared his head and eased his soul. His breathing came deep and steady. His sneakers tapped out a regular rhythm, pounding out a staccato beat. Trees flashed by him, bright green leaves a blur. Sweat built along his skin, giving it a glistening sheen in the sunlight overhead. The silver cross around his neck tinkled with each movement, a gift from his father years ago.

By the time he'd gone at least five miles, his lungs burned and his muscles felt warm, blood pumping through his veins heatedly. But his mind had cleared, leaving behind the certainty that this assignment may very well dredge up more of the pain he'd lived and breathed for almost six years. Stopping, he bent at the waist and gasped, dragging air into his tortured lungs. His shoulder twinged from the exercise, still tender after being shot, but he'd been a fast healer since he'd broken his first bone as a child, perhaps because he was a Deviant or maybe because he was a level five. The wound had already closed over, leaving a bone-deep ache that would last for several weeks and another scar on his tanned skin. Lizard had removed the stitches practically the next day. He'd dealt with worse and knew he'd survive. Much worse.

Only Bryan knew everything he'd gone through. Bryan had been the shoulder he'd leaned on and the arm supporting him in his weakest moments. Gabriel straightened, tilting his head back to look up at the dazzling blue sky above. Bryan was the one man Gabriel had let close enough to be his lover for three years, before Bryan called a halt to it a year and a half ago. Sometimes, late at night, Gabriel missed the warm body next to his. He missed the touch of the man's skin over his and the hard thrust of Bryan's cock inside him. But he knew it wasn't because he loved Bryan. They had drowned in each other for three years to fight off the loneliness and sorrow they both felt.

He remembered the first time they'd given in to it. Six months after Gabriel's arrival at the ADA, Bryan invited him into his room to talk and drink. The full bottle of scotch slowly emptied while the small spark of lust between them ignited. Gabriel could barely recall who'd made the first move, but the memory of Bryan's soft lips hungrily pressing down on his hadn't faded with time. Bryan had apologized the next morning, telling Gabriel that he never should have done it, but Gabriel stopped him, knowing they'd both needed an outlet for their loneliness. After talking it out, they had reached an agreement to continue the affair, and over the course of the three years, Gabriel lost count of how many times they'd fucked each other senseless.

Only, Bryan had abruptly called endgame to it out of nowhere. He'd never given Gabriel a specific reason why, merely stating that it was time for them to stop. Gabriel respected Bryan too much to cling like a jilted lover, but he couldn't deny it stung. It took him several months to break the habit of touching Bryan whenever they were around each other. The others in the agency had known of their relationship, so he'd always been able to hug, caress, and kiss Bryan without fear. Sometimes he still found himself overwhelmed by the urge to touch his boss when he knew the other man was upset.

The sound of a vehicle approaching brought Gabriel back to the present. He started jogging, keeping his keen senses open. A black pickup truck slowed for a brief moment as it passed him and then continued on at a normal speed. He memorized the license plate number before turning back toward the safe house. His stride smooth, he picked up the pace. Suddenly he needed to be back, needed to make sure that everything was secure and the others were all right. He cursed himself for not bringing a radio or cell phone along with him. The back of his neck prickled, sending the certainty that the people in the vehicle weren't out for just a pleasure ride rushing down his spine.

His suspicions were confirmed seconds later when the roar of a speeding vehicle reached his ears. He leapt to the side a mere breath away from the car running him down. Tires squealed as the truck came to a stop, cutting him off. Three men leapt down from the cab, surrounding him quickly. Cruelty glittered in their eyes and twisted their faces. "Deviant," the one who appeared to be the leader spat out.

Gabriel almost let out a breath of relief when he realized they weren't from Vincetti. It didn't explain how they had known what he was just by looking at him, though. "I don't know what you're talking about," he growled, shifting on the balls of his feet, trying to keep all three of them within sight.

"We saw you and those other freaks at Walmart," the leader snarled. "The dark-haired one that can move shit with his mind."

Jason, Gabriel grunted mentally. Stupid kid. He should have known better than to let them go into the store without him. "What makes you think I'm not strong enough to handle the three of you?" he asked casually, rolling his shoulders.

The taller blond snorted derisively. "One of you freaks against three?" He slammed his fist into his open palm, grinning evilly. "Besides, my buddy here has something even you freaks can't stop."

Swearing silently, Gabriel tensed when he saw the gun

the third Normal pulled from his jacket pocket. This situation was getting uglier by the minute. "We're not here to cause trouble. Just leave us alone. We'll be gone soon."

"You're right. You will be gone soon because we don't tolerate freaks like your kind here," the leader barked. "Get in the truck."

"Fuck you," Gabriel replied smoothly, his entire body on alert.

"Wrong answer," the blond said, reaching into the back of the pickup truck and pulling out a baseball bat.

Reining in his temper, Gabriel gave an icy smile of calm at the one holding the bat. "If you're so sure I'm a Deviant, do you really think a baseball bat will make a damn bit of difference?"

"Maybe not," the leader laughed. "But even you can't stop a bullet. Now get in the truck."

Gabriel weighed his options. He could make a run for the trees behind him and risk taking another bullet, or he could get in the truck, which would certainly lead to his death. The third option left him in a cold sweat, but the third option seemed to be the only one that wouldn't lead to his own injury. Concentrating his gaze on the gun in the leader's hand, Gabriel threw out a burst of his power, watching in detached satisfaction as the Normal let out a screech and the gun dropped to the ground, nothing but a puddle of melted metal.

The blond struck out with the baseball bat, catching Gabriel in his side. Gabriel grunted at the pain, staggering under the blow. "Freak!"

The bat connected again, this time with Gabriel's temple. Gabriel could feel the skin split, and blood rained down the side of his face. It took every ounce of willpower he had not to pass out, but he did drop to his knees. Rage exploded inside him, and he threw out another burst of power, the bat shattering into splinters in the Normal's hand. The blond shrieked as the third man slammed his fist into the side of Gabriel's face. "Fucking piece of shit," the blond snapped, striking out with his booted foot.

He managed to grab hold of the bastard's foot, wrenching it to the side. The bone cracked loudly, snapping like a twig under a footstep. Gabriel smiled when the blond screamed in agony and dropped to the ground. Finally unable to contain it any further, he unleashed the extent of his abilities. His loud roar echoed through the trees surrounding them. The two Normals still standing were flung off their feet, thrown back about fifty feet and landing with a harsh thud. Gabriel's conscience shut down, survival the only instinct. After quickly getting to his feet, he picked up the blond, tossing him carelessly into the bed of the truck. "It didn't have to be this way," he said harshly, stepping over to the leader, who cowered from him.

"Get away from me," the leader howled, crab-walking backward.

A stony expression was the only response Gabriel gave as his eyes narrowed in on the Normal's right hand. The bones inside the man's hand literally shattered, and the screams the leader let out could be heard for miles. "You think that Deviants are filthy? Freaks?" Gabriel demanded angrily, this time training his gaze on the man's left leg. "Who are the ones attacking someone unprovoked? Who are the ones threatening to kill someone just for being something they didn't ask to be?"

"I'm sorry," the leader pleaded, cradling his hand to his chest. "Please... don't kill me!"

"Why?" Gabriel asked, a humorless smirk curving one corner of his mouth. "Weren't you going to kill me? So why should I spare your life?"

Gabriel heard a noise behind him and realized he'd

forgotten about the third man. He swung his head around in time to see the shorter Normal rushing at him to tackle him. Smoothly sidestepping, the man flashed past him, landing in a heap beside the leader. "Tsk, tsk. That doesn't reassure me that you want to live through this."

"We'll go! We'll leave you alone, I swear," the leader cried.

Reaching up, Gabriel touched the wound on his temple, swiping at the blood still trickling down. "I think you're lying."

"No! We will!"

The blond on the ground beside him growled. "What the fuck is wrong with you, Vic? He's a filthy Deviant. Don't beg him like a pussy."

"Shut the fuck up, Zeke. He fucking shattered every bone in my hand with just a glance," Vic spat out.

This time Gabriel concentrated on the one named Zeke's shoulder where it connected with his arm. A small thrust of his power and Zeke writhed on the ground, clutching at his shoulder and crying out. "Stop! Stop! Please!"

"If you come near me or any of the others with me again, I will kill you next time. Do you understand me?" Gabriel towered over the two men on the ground, his eyes glittering furiously.

"Yes! Yes. We swear we won't," Vic simpered, still cradling his hand which had already begun to swell and turn purple.

"Get the hell out of my sight before I change my mind," Gabriel shouted.

The two men struggled to their feet, stumbling as they rushed to their truck. Gabriel hoped he hadn't made a mistake in letting them go, but he wouldn't use his powers to kill unless he absolutely had to. He'd sworn he would never do it again. His gaze remained on the truck's taillights until he could no longer see them before he started walking back. Pulling the shirt over his head, he pressed it to the still bleeding wound on his temple, stemming the flow as best he could.

Surprisingly, he didn't have to walk for more than five minutes before the black SUV came screeching to a halt in front of him. "Gabe!" Lizard jumped out of the driver's side, rushing to his aid. "What happened?"

Gabriel leaned heavily on Lizard and grunted. "Stupid Normals. Three of them saw Jason use his ability."

"Fuck," Lizard swore, helping Gabriel into the passenger seat. "Where are they now?"

"Gone. And before you ask, no, I didn't kill them, but I'm not so sure we'll be able to stay at the safe house." Gabriel ran a hand over the uninjured side of his face.

Lizard didn't say anything. His hands tightening on the steering wheel told their own story. "How did you know where to find me?" Gabriel asked tiredly, his words slurring slightly.

"Alex. He kept insisting something was wrong. He wouldn't relax until I agreed to come out to look for you." Lizard looked over at Gabriel in concern. "Maybe you need a hospital, Gabe. You could have a concussion."

Surprise shafted through Gabriel for a second. Alex had known he was in trouble? Frowning, Gabriel shook his head. "No. I'll be fine. I just need to lie down for a while."

"Gabe—"

"Shut up, Lizard. I'm fine. A hospital would be a very bad thing right now, and you know it." Gabriel rarely raised his voice with any of his team members, but his patience had worn out. His head throbbed like a son of a bitch, and he just wanted to forget what had happened. He loathed using his abilities against another human being. Although it came down to survival, it still left an acrid taste in his mouth. The twisted side of the whole situation was that he'd enjoyed it.

The screams of pain from the Normals made his blood sing out and adrenaline rush through him.

Lizard didn't speak the rest of the way. He did sprint around to help Gabriel out of the truck. The others in the house let out foul words and gasps of shock at the sight of their boss. Alex was instantly beside him, hooking his free arm around his shoulders. "I'm fine." Gabriel brushed off their concerns, trying to pull away from Alex.

Alex stubbornly held onto Gabriel, glaring up at him. "You're not fine. You are far from fine, and, since you won't let Lizard take you to a hospital, you're going to let me take care of that wound."

A frown flashed over Lizard's face that Alex caught. "Sorry, Lizard. I wasn't trying to hear your thoughts. Sometimes when emotions run high I can't filter them out."

"It's okay, kid," Lizard mumbled.

The two of them forced Gabriel down the hallway to the bathroom on the first floor, where they pushed him down onto the lid of the toilet. "I don't need help," Gabriel groused, but didn't move from where they'd put him.

"Yes, you do," Alex stated calmly, taking out bandages and antiseptic from the medicine chest over the sink. He grabbed a small washcloth and poured some of the antiseptic on it. "This is probably going to sting."

"Just do it." Exhaustion littered Gabriel's tone and face. His eyes were almost closed as he sat there. He could feel the heat of Alex's body when the man stepped close, and his cock responded to it despite the stinging pain of the peroxide. When Alex's breath whispered over the cut, soothing the burn, Gabriel clenched his jaw, and his hands became fists on his thighs. His body wanted nothing more than to reach out and snatch the light the other male offered, but his heart and head stopped him.

The crinkling of a package brought Gabriel back to

himself. Alex opened several butterfly bandages and carefully applied them. "Without stitches, you're going to have a scar," Alex told him softly.

Gabriel couldn't tear his eyes away from the lean chest in front of him. His fingers itched to reach out and shove the T-shirt the younger man wore up and explore the smooth skin underneath. He knew deep inside that Alex would be like a drug. The first taste would leave him addicted and doing everything he could for more. His breathing grew heavier the longer Alex stood so close to him. Heat built in between his thighs, reminding him it had been a while since he'd been laid. *Stop it*, he ordered himself, closing his eyes. Only, taking away his sight left him even more aware of the sweet scent of Alex's skin, and Gabriel abruptly shoved Alex away from him, standing. "Enough."

Alex stared at him in surprise, his hands gripping the counter he'd been thrust into. "I'm sorry. Did I hurt you?"

Snorting, Gabriel coldly said, "You couldn't hurt me if you tried, kid. Now get out."

"But—"

"I said get the fuck out." Gabriel wrenched open the door and pointed. He couldn't touch Alex, because he knew if he did, he'd snap. He'd yank that beautiful body up against his and fuck him where he stood.

Hurt flashed in Alex's eyes, stinging Gabriel deeper than the antiseptic, but he drew his cloak of indifference around him. He couldn't afford to care. Alex carefully slipped past him and out into the hallway. Before the teenager could turn around, Gabriel shut the door with a harsh bang, leaning his forehead against it. This assignment would be the hardest one he'd ever done.

4

ALEX

Lex stared at the wood of the bathroom door for the longest time, wondering what he'd done to make Gabriel so angry. He remembered being in the living room, watching television with his brother and the others, when a sudden surge of panic went through him. Sitting up straighter on the couch, he'd tried to search out where it came from. The certainty that Gabriel was in trouble flooded him. "You okay, kid?"

He'd looked to see Lizard watching him closely. "Something's wrong."

Lizard frowned. "What?"

"Gabriel's hurt."

Those words grabbed everyone's attention. "What the hell are you talking about?" Jackal demanded.

"Please, you have to go find him," Alex begged, his heart pounding in his chest. Pain exploded in the side of his head, and he grabbed at it, crying out. Jason immediately wrapped an arm around Alex's shoulders.

"Listen to him," Jason snapped. "He's telling the truth."

"What is going on?" Tank rumbled from the doorway. He

looked around to see what caused Alex's cry, but could see no immediate danger.

"He says Gabriel's in trouble," Lizard explained, shrugging.

Tank studied Alex for a moment, saw the absolute certainty in the man's eyes and nodded. Alex breathed a sigh of relief. "Lizard, go. He went for a run earlier."

Lizard immediately stood, grabbing the keys to the SUV off the front table, and hurried out the door. Alex looked up at Tank. "Thank you."

Shrewd dark eyes assessed him a bit longer, causing Alex to flush under the scrutiny. Jason had leaned back into the couch again next to him. Alex tried to relax, but worry weighed heavily on him. Unable to contain his restlessness, he stood and started pacing. Jason sighed at him. "Alex, chill. I'm sure the man is fine."

Alex didn't answer his brother and just continued pacing. It took everything he had not to rush outside the instant he heard the tires on the gravel drive. But he couldn't contain his gasp at the blood covering Gabriel's shirt and face or stop himself from hurrying over to the man's side to help him. Nothing prepared him for the warmth that shafted down into his belly at the feel of the muscular arm on his shoulders. He choked back a moan of arousal. He'd never really had physical contact with another man, aside from his brother, and it felt better than anything he'd ever imagined.

Forcing himself to concentrate, he helped maneuver Gabriel down the hallway to the restroom. The heat from Gabriel's body seeped into his as he worked at bandaging the injury on Gabriel's temple, and Alex wanted nothing more than to press closer to the dark-haired male, to feel his hard length against his. When Gabriel abruptly thrust him away, it caught him by surprise, and hurt tightened across his chest like a steel band. The band grew even tighter when Gabriel forced him from the room and slammed the door behind him.

A firm hand on his shoulder brought Alex out of his thoughts. "Don't take it personally, Alex. He's like that with almost everyone." Lizard gave him an encouraging smile that Alex couldn't find the energy to return.

"Did I... do something wrong?" Alex asked softly.

Lizard shook his head. "No. Gabriel is a solitary person. He doesn't let anyone near him. In the entire time I've known Gabe, there's only one person that I know of who's been able to get close to him."

Jealousy speared Alex, and his hands clenched. "Who?"

"Our boss, Bryan Sorensen. He's the founder and head of the ADA." Lizard guided Alex away from the bathroom and back out to the living room. "Have you ever been trained to fight?"

Alex shook his head, his brow furrowed. He'd never needed to since he'd lived on the farm all of his life. He'd also never been interested in learning. "Come on. We can start your training there. Since none of us have your abilities, we can't teach you how to control it, but we can show you some things that just might save your life."

Jason looked up at them when they entered the living room. His gaze narrowed in on Alex instantly. He could see the concern in his brother's eyes, and he tried to smile to show Jason he didn't have to worry about him. "You too," Lizard said, pointing at Jason. "Come on. We've got some training gear with us."

"What's going on?" Jason questioned curiously as he got up to accompany them.

Lizard explained to Jason about showing them some defensive moves and starting their training. The better part of the afternoon was spent with Lizard, behind the house. Both of the twins were covered in sweat and aching from being tossed over Lizard's shoulder countless times. Alex stripped off his shirt, swiping his face with it before throwing it onto the porch railing. "Again," he demanded of Lizard, crouching like the Deviant had shown him.

This time Lizard was the one on the ground, staring up at Alex and sucking in air from the impact. He grinned as he accepted the hand Alex offered him. "I think you're going to do just fine, kid."

Alex felt happy at the small accomplishment. He'd consciously made the decision to do whatever it took to gain Gabriel's attention. If one person could get close to the big, imposing man, then so could he.

"I don't see why I have to do this," Jason whined petulantly, an unbecoming pout on his lips. "I can lift a damn car with just my mind. What do I need to learn how to fight for?"

"Because you might find yourself in a situation where you can't use your abilities or they won't be able to help you." Gabriel's voice came from the porch, and Alex immediately swung around, catching sight of the dark-haired man who'd captivated him from the moment he'd seen him.

Jason scowled at Gabriel. "I could just pick the bastard up and throw him like that too."

"Perhaps," Gabriel replied blithely, coming down the steps to where they stood. His chin was level with Alex's gaze, and Alex suppressed a visible shudder at Gabriel's proximity. "But there are Normals and Deviants out there who have learned how to fight abilities like yours and Alex's."

He couldn't stop a shiver the second time. It wracked his lean frame at the sound of his name on Gabriel's lips. Alex suddenly felt extremely exposed without his shirt on and wished he hadn't taken it off. "Pfft. You seriously think someone can prevent me from doing what I want?" Jason demanded, crossing his arms over his chest.

Alex knew his brother probably sounded arrogant to

anyone who could hear him, but he knew Jason also hid a lot of his fears behind a façade of confidence. It was his brother's defense mechanism when he felt cornered. He'd seen Jason use his powers as a shield since their mother's betrayal and had known it would one day get them in trouble.

"I know they can," Gabriel said assuredly. "I've seen it. I've trained some of the best at it."

Jason's arms dropped to his side as he concentrated on Gabriel, and Alex stepped in front of Gabriel, glaring at his brother. Gabriel was still injured. "Jason, no."

Gabriel's hands wrapped around Alex's upper arms and carefully moved him to the side. "It'll be fine, Alex."

Alex froze at the fire licking along his body where Gabriel's palms scraped over his skin. He sucked in a sharp breath, catching Gabriel's attention. Gabriel looked down at him, frowning. "You okay?"

"I'm fine," he coughed out, pulling away from the older male. He blushed when he saw Lizard staring at him with a knowing smirk.

Gabriel rolled his shoulders, and despite the fact that his body looked loose, casual even, Alex could see the alertness in the other man. His gaze bounced between Jason and Gabriel, waiting to see what would happen. Projecting his thoughts outward to his brother, Alex demanded, *"Be careful, Jace. He's hurt pretty badly from whatever happened earlier."*

"Yeah, yeah, bro. I'm not going to mess him up... much." Jason's laugh echoed in Alex's mind, and he glared at Jason in warning. He knew his brother didn't like being challenged and believed no one could stop him, but Alex sensed Gabriel had a lot of experience on handling Deviants and their abilities.

"You ready, old man?" Jason taunted, his eyes narrowing in on Gabriel once more.

A serene smile graced Gabriel's lips briefly, and he gave a careless tip of his head. Alex tensed when he felt his brother's power flare out, but what shocked him was Gabriel seemingly sidestepping away. What the hell? Jason stared in shock and anger. Alex knew that look and knew Jason intended on throwing out every ounce of strength he had. Gabriel danced to the side a bit, and at one point even took a hit full on. Finally, Jason collapsed in a sweaty heap, his breathing ragged. "What the fuck?" Jason gasped out while grabbing at his head.

Lizard chuckled from where he stood, his arms crossed over his chest. "You never asked what Gabriel's abilities are, kid."

"What can you do?" Alex burst out, dying to know something about the other man.

Gabriel tensed, a curtain falling over his expression. Lizard lifted an eyebrow at Gabriel. "Come on, boss. You know you're going to have to tell them sometime."

Growling at Lizard, Gabriel explained stiffly, "I can manipulate molecules and the molecular structure of things."

"What the hell is that supposed to mean?" Jason snapped up at him from where he sat.

"It means that he can literally change the density of his body to make it so heavy you can't lift him," Lizard finished for him when Gabriel stayed silent.

Jason's eyes widened in shock. "You can do that?"

"Yes," Gabriel said tersely.

Alex was filled with awe at how powerful Gabriel actually was. It explained what had happened to the door of their cell at the compound. "That's... amazing," Alex breathed out.

"Enough for today," Gabriel stated flatly, spinning on his heel and stalking back into the house.

He went to follow Gabriel, wanting to ask him all kinds of questions about his abilities, but Lizard stopped him, grabbing his elbow. "Leave him be, Alex."

"But—"

"Gabe doesn't like talking about what he can do. I don't know why, but it's a touchy subject for him. And to be honest, this is the first time we've seen him use his abilities when it wasn't a life or death situation. I'm surprised he did it, in fact." Lizard squeezed Alex's elbow reassuringly before letting go.

Jason interrupted what Alex had been about to say. "What level is he?"

Lizard hesitated, glancing at the house for a brief moment. "Gabriel's registered as a level four."

Alex noticed the way Lizard phrased his answer and frowned at the other Deviant. "But you don't think he is?"

"We're all pretty sure that Gabriel isn't a level four." Lizard left it at that. He didn't go into specifics or what anyone else thought. "He is right, though. I think we've had enough for the day. We may have to move locations soon."

"Why?" Alex asked.

"Because the Normals who attacked Gabe may come back, and we can't be here when they do."

Pausing in his tracks, Alex was horrified. Someone had attacked Gabriel? "Why did they attack him?"

Lizard hooked a thumb over his shoulder at Jason. "Because they apparently saw him use his ability in Walmart."

"Jace?" Alex swung his attention to his brother, silently demanding he deny it. Guilt clearly shone from his brother's face. "Damn it, Jason! After all Grams taught you, you still don't understand that you can't use your gifts in front of others!"

"Alex, I'm sorry. I didn't think anyone saw!" Jason protested, standing up and going to his brother. "My arms were full, and I didn't want it to fall."

Alex backed away from his brother, sadness enveloping him. "We almost died that day at the diner, Jason. And now Gabriel was almost killed because you can't learn to control yourself. One of these days, no one is going to be there to help us, and then what? When are you going to learn this isn't just about you? If you're discovered, so am I! Is it because you want me gone? Are you tired of dragging around your weak brother?"

"What?" Jason exclaimed in horror. "Of course not! How could you even say that?"

"Then stop being so selfish," Alex sniped. "I'm tired of having to deal with the messes you create."

"Alex...." Jason looked at him helplessly, his eyes turbulent. "I'm sorry."

Breathing in deeply, Alex shook his head. "We need to learn how to live in the real world, Jace. How to survive, because the farm is gone. Grams is gone. There is nothing there for us anymore, and I'm tired of hiding."

"Isn't it hiding by not being able to be who we are?" Jason challenged. "I hate not being able to be free to use my abilities because of ignorant people."

Tank came around the back of the house just then and stopped. "Are you two done fighting? I think they can hear you in California!"

Jason opened his mouth to retort, but Jackal interrupted them. "Come on. Let's see what Gabe has to say about whether or not we're going to another safe house."

Guilt shrouded Jason again, and his shoulders slumped. Alex knew he'd been harsh on his brother, but he couldn't seem to stop himself. Resentment had been building inside him for a long time now, and the recent events only tripled the feeling. If Jason hadn't lost control of his temper that day in the diner, they wouldn't have been fighting for their lives since. They'd still be living on the farm.

Alex trailed behind the group heading into the house. His brother fell into step beside him.

"I really am sorry, bro," Jason muttered. "I didn't mean for Gabriel to get hurt or to out what we are back home."

"I know you didn't," Alex replied tiredly. His head hurt. "You need to start thinking before you do something, Jason."

His brother slipped his arm through Alex's, pulling him into his side. "I promise I'll try, Alex. I don't want to lose you. You're all I have."

Smiling slightly, Alex leaned his head against Jason's shoulder. "Thank you."

Jason meant everything to him. His twin's words were the truth. They were all each other had, and they needed to protect one another as fiercely as they could. Alex didn't know what he'd do if anything ever happened to Jason.

The instant they entered the house, Alex focused on Gabriel, who at the moment was on the phone talking to someone. "No, Bry, they'll live. I can't guarantee they won't come back." Gabriel fell silent for a few seconds. "What? I'm not sure it's safe enough to do that!"

Alex saw Lizard watching Gabriel intently, obviously knowing something wasn't right. "Fine."

"I said fine, Bryan," Gabriel snarled into the phone. "Tonight."

Gabriel's hand tightened on the cell, almost hard enough to crush it, after he'd finished the call. "We're going back to the agency."

Voices went up in volume, protesting the advisability of that idea. "Enough," Gabriel barked. "Start packing. Bryan wants everyone to return to the farmhouse tonight. We're leaving in three hours. Make sure you have everything, because we can't leave behind anything that can lead anyone back to us."

The tension in the team of men was like a tangible being, hot and heavy on Alex's senses. His movements were sluggish while packing the new clothing they'd purchased for him into the garbage bags Tank had handed him. Jason paced the bedroom they'd used for the three days they'd been at the safe house once he'd finished his own packing. "I don't understand. I thought it wouldn't be okay to go back there yet."

"It didn't seem like their boss gave them a choice, Jace," Alex said without emotion, sinking down onto the bed and cradling his head in his hands.

The bed gave as Jason sat next to him, rubbing along his back. "Head hurt?"

Alex nodded. Whenever emotions inundated him from others or it had been a day where he'd overused his abilities, it caused a fierce migraine to grip him for hours. He tried to even out his breaths and battle the rising nausea. Sometimes it even came from just trying to block out everyone around him, to keep from hearing their thoughts and memories.

Jason abruptly stood. "I'm going to go see if they have anything you can take. Why don't you lie down, and I'll be right back."

Gratefully, Alex leaned back and curled up into a ball on the bed, burying his face in a pillow. Shudders of pain wracked his body. He'd pulled on a shirt when they'd come upstairs, and it stuck to his skin with sweat. He barely registered the door opening or the arms that slid around his body, lifting him up. Gabriel's deep voice caressed his ear: "Relax. Breathe in and clear your mind. Let it all go."

"Is this normal?" Alex heard Jason ask.

"Get out," Gabriel instructed Jason quietly.

"Hey! He's my brother, and I have the right to be here."

"This isn't about you. It's about him. Now get out."

Jason would have protested, but Alex made a small whimper of pain. "Fine, but I'll be right outside."

The door shut with a soft snick, leaving the two of them

alone. "You're going to be the death of me, kid," Alex heard Gabriel mutter under his breath.

"I'm sorry," Alex whispered. "You don't have to be here. I'm used to these."

"Just shut up and listen to my voice," Gabriel growled gently.

For the next fifteen to thirty minutes—Alex couldn't be sure exactly how much time passed—Gabriel spoke to him in a low tone, instructing him on meditating and breathing. When the pain finally dulled enough to be bearable, Alex managed to sit up without wanting to throw up. "Wow," he breathed.

"You should meditate regularly. Your mind may be strong, Alex, but it can't handle everything, and eventually it overloads, causing a migraine. This isn't something to mess around with. It can cause serious damage." Gabriel moved off the bed and over to the window, giving his back to Alex.

Alex could see the tension in the man's muscles and wondered what caused it. "Thank you, Gabriel. I don't know how I can repay you."

Gabriel turned his head to scowl at Alex. "Just try to keep a leash on your brother."

Guilt sliced at Alex when he remembered how injured Gabriel was, and awe followed quickly on its heels when he realized how Gabriel had ignored his own pain to help Alex deal with his. "Is it time to leave?" Alex asked after a long moment of silence.

Letting out a grunt, Gabriel replied gruffly, "You've got time, kid. Just… take your time."

He watched Gabriel leave the bedroom, his heart stuffed so tightly into his throat that he could barely breathe. The man didn't want anyone to know how much he actually cared about other people. It was all an act. The harsh exterior and the short, clipped words were just a cover. Alex smiled slightly and stood up from the bed, his hands still shaking a bit as he resumed packing the remainder of his clothing. Maybe Gabriel wasn't as impervious to him as he'd thought.

The vehicles were already packed up and ready to go by the time Alex made it downstairs with his bags. Jason's eyes narrowed in on him like a hawk, taking in the peaceful, happy expression on Alex's face. "You okay?" Jason questioned thickly.

"I'm fine, Jace. Gabriel really helped me." Alex glanced at the tall, dark-haired Deviant, unaware of the look on his face.

"Alex...." Jason trailed off and shook his head. Alex gave him a curious look which he just shrugged at. "It's nothing."

The team piled into the vehicles as soon as Alex's bags were loaded. Alex and Jason sat in the back of one of the SUVs, Gabriel and Lizard in the front. At some point during their stay at the safe house, he'd noticed that the trailer carrying the helicopter was gone. He supposed that it would be too noticeable if they'd kept it, but he couldn't help but wonder where they'd stashed it. "It's going to take a day to get back to the agency." Gabriel's voice interrupted his thoughts. "We're driving all the way through. I suggest you both get some sleep."

Settling back into the seat, Alex watched out the window as the trees and houses flashed by. His thoughts switched to the memory of Gabriel holding him, comforting him as he struggled to push the pain away. In a small way it reminded him of his Grams and the way she used to hold him as a child, but it had also been nothing like the way she held him. Her touch had never awakened every sense in his body, sending sharp tugs of desire deep into his gut. The sound of her voice didn't cause every tiny hair on his skin to stand on end, begging to be touched. Her body had been soft and feminine, while Gabriel's was all hard muscles and strength. His mind played images of pulling

Gabriel down on top of him and losing himself in the other man's taste.

Alex ran a shaky hand through his messy dark hair, shifting in his seat to cover his erection. He didn't know how to handle the feelings and emotions Gabriel stirred in his body. Having been raised on the farm and not allowed to really go anywhere, he hadn't been able to act on the attraction he had toward other men. The only touch he'd ever had was his own. Yet it didn't stop him from wanting the other Deviant. But what if Gabriel didn't want him? His mind whirled around and around, looking at it from every angle possible. There really hadn't been any indication that Gabriel wanted him. Then again, with no experience, how would he really know?

He wasn't sure when he actually fell asleep. He remembered staring at Gabriel in the rearview mirror and then slowly drifting in a haze. The sound of the engine cutting off woke him up. Sitting up, he swiped at his mouth to make sure he hadn't been drooling and looked around. Jason was slumped down in the seat next to him, deeply asleep. He caught sight of Lizard's back as the man strode to the window of the little gas station. His attention settled on Gabriel in the passenger seat, and he leaned forward, gazing at Gabriel's face, slackened in slumber. The man's beauty literally stole his breath. He traced the elegantly arched eyebrows, high cheekbones, and lean nose slowly with his eyes before allowing them to rest on Gabriel's firm lips. He wanted nothing more than to be able to taste the older man, to have the right to kiss him and not care who watched them.

"Hey, kid," Lizard hissed through the window. "He just fell asleep, let him alone."

Jerking back, Alex flushed and opened the door, quietly stepping down from the vehicle and stretching. He moaned a little as his muscles protested the long hours sitting down in one spot. His stomach gave a loud growl, and he smiled sheepishly at Lizard. They hadn't stopped to eat, and, after the upset from earlier, Alex really hadn't had much of an appetite. Lizard grinned at him and pulled out his wallet, handing him a bill. "Here, kid, go get something to eat. Grab enough snacks for everyone, okay?"

Alex nodded in understanding, heading toward the little convenience store. There was only one other car in the lot aside from the two SUVs, and he could see the occupant of the car watching him closely. A shiver of uneasiness trickled down his spine, much like a drop of sweat. He shook it off, but the stranger never looked away from him, even after he'd entered the building.

Inside, he picked up a little hand basket and started hurriedly tossing a bunch of different things in it: chips, cookies, crackers, and drinks. Things were practically falling out of it as he set it on the counter. The clerk lifted an eyebrow, but began slowly ringing the food up. Alex glanced at the television on the wall behind the counter, and his eyes widened as he saw pictures of him and Jason on the screen. His breath caught when he read the caption about them being wanted Deviants for some crime they hadn't committed. "You okay, son?" the clerk asked.

"Uh... yeah, I'm fine. How much?" Alex choked.

"Thirty-three seventy-two."

He handed over the fifty Lizard had passed him, and anxiously danced foot to foot waiting for the change. The instant the money was in hand, he grabbed the bags and darted out of the store, racing to the SUV. Lizard saw his panic and straightened, alert and ready for a fight if necessary. "What's going on, Alex?"

"There was... a news broadcast," Alex coughed, his throat tight in fear.

5

GABRIEL

GABRIEL grunted as he came awake. His brow furrowed while he tried to figure out what had awakened him. Alex's voice stating something about a news broadcast brought him upright. "What's going on?" he asked roughly, shoving open the door and stepping out of the SUV.

"There was a story on the news about me and Jason," Alex cried, his body visibly trembling. "They said that we were wanted for questioning in connection with a robbery at a jewelry store."

Swearing, Gabriel slammed his fist into the side of the SUV, leaving a dent that Lizard huffed at him for. "I'll fix it later," he growled. "Let's get moving before someone recognizes them. Alex, get in the car and keep your head down."

Jason poked his head out of the SUV, his eyes bleary from sleep. "What the hell was that?"

Gabriel ignored the other man and strode around to the driver's side. Tank and Bear were close enough to have heard the whole exchange, both quickly getting into the other vehicle. Alex handed off one of the bags of food to Jackal and climbed into the backseat holding the other one. Sirens started wailing in the distance, and Gabriel knew they were headed for the little gas station. The two vehicles tore out of the lot, driving as quickly as possible without attracting attention. They'd have to ditch the SUVs. Bryan wasn't going to be happy.

"Shit!" Gabriel roared, his palm slamming into the steering wheel several times and causing Alex and Jason to jump slightly. "That son of a bitch Vincetti! One of these days I'm going to rip that bastard's head off."

A warm hand came to rest on his left shoulder, surprising him. Alex lightly squeezed his shoulder in a comforting gesture, and Gabriel couldn't fight off a surge of lust for the younger man. Rage at Vincetti and the desire to say fuck it and immerse himself in the green-eyed teenager warred inside him. He had enough experience to know that Alex found him attractive, and the way the Deviant looked at him made his cock harder than steel, but he didn't have anything to offer Alex. Alex deserved more than an emotionally scarred murderer like him.

Taking a deep breath, Gabriel reached over and grabbed the cell phone, hitting the speed dial for Bryan's cell. "'Lo?" came a sleepy inquiry.

"Bryan, it's Gabe. We've got a problem." Gabriel briefly outlined the problem to his boss and heard the man let out a few choice words that made him give a lopsided grin. Bryan acted all refined and elegant, but when the man let go, he let go. The memory of a particularly hot session of sex came to mind. He'd pinned Bryan to the wall of his shower, pounding the hell out of his ass but refusing to let the man come until he begged Gabriel to fuck him. Oh, the sweetness of Bryan's capitulation could still cause his dick to harden. "We're going to have to ditch the vehicles, Bry. Someone saw us."

"Do it. Whatever you have to. Vincetti is going after these

two boys with a vengeance, and I want to know why," Bryan ground out. "What the hell makes them more special than any of the others he's abducted?"

"I don't know, Bry, but whatever happens, we can't let him get his hands on them." Gabriel looked in the rearview mirror, to see both Alex and Jason watching him. "We'll be back in a couple of hours."

"Be safe, Gabe," Bryan murmured.

Gabriel disconnected the call and massaged the back of his neck. "You have no idea why he's got such a hard on for you two?"

Jason snorted. "Maybe because we're so powerful."

He gave a short bark of derision. "Vincetti has control of some of the most powerful Deviants on this planet. Somehow I doubt he'd go to all the trouble just because you're both a level five. Something's different about this. He's trying to flush you out of hiding. I have no doubt by now he knows we have you."

Alex spoke up in a soft voice, "Maybe he needs us?"

"For what?"

"I don't know. Maybe there's something he needs us to do or get for him?"

He pondered the younger man's words. Was Alex right? Did Vincetti need them for something? But what? The twins weren't exactly rich, and they didn't know anyone except each other. So where did they fit into the puzzle? "Let's just ditch the SUVs and get back to the farmhouse. We'll figure it out later."

They stashed the vehicles in a stand of trees outside of the next town and switched over to the two nondescript sedans that Gabriel bought off of an old man with cash for more than they were worth, as long as the man "forgot" him. Most of their gear had to be left behind, since they didn't have a whole hell of a lot of room. Chris would not be happy. "I'll make you a deal. Since Jackal and I were the ones who hoofed it all the way to town to get the cars, you can tell Chris we had to leave behind the gear," Gabriel tossed out at Lizard once they were on the road again.

"Hell no!" Lizard protested vehemently. "I'm not telling him! He's going to be pissed as fuck. At least he won't kill you!"

"Oh, come on, Lizard. He's not going to kill you." Gabriel laughed, his eyes twinkling.

Lizard shook his head. "Who's Chris?" Jason piped up from the backseat.

"Chris is our resident techno geek. He's a super genius. Those neat little gadgets we used to rescue you two are all his inventions," Lizard explained. "And they are his babies. He's going to blow a circuit board when he finds out."

"We didn't leave behind everything," Jason pointed out. "I saw the radios and stuff."

Gabriel shrugged. The kid would find out. Chris freaked when they damaged something, and this was the first time they'd had to leave anything behind. His hands tightened on the steering wheel. If he had to die doing it, he would take Vincetti out. The bastard had been free for too long and was the main reason Normals were still afraid of Deviants. Most Deviants wanted to have a normal life and be able to have a home, family, and live without fear dogging their every footstep. Gabriel had been one of those for the longest time. Until the afternoon his life changed forever. Since then he'd known he wasn't meant to live normally. He wasn't meant to have a partner that he could come home to every night.

The remainder of the trip went smoothly, and Gabriel let out a sigh of relief. At some point in the last five years he'd started thinking of the agency as home. It felt good to be back. He pulled up to the gates and hit the buzzer. "Name?" a voice warbled over the intercom.

"It's Gabe."

There was a click and the gates swung open, allowing the two vehicles into the compound. Teresa stood at the front steps, anxiously waiting for them. She flew down the stairs the second she caught sight of Jackal, throwing herself into his arms and kissing him senseless. "Get a room," Lizard grumbled good-naturedly.

Bryan exited his office as they entered the front doors. A grim expression informed Gabriel that things weren't going as well as his boss had planned. "Gabriel," Bryan greeted.

"Bryan." Gabriel stepped to the right, away from the twins.

His boss offered his hand. "I'm Bryan Sorensen. You must be Alex and Jason. Thank you for trusting my team to protect you. I'd like to show you around the agency and explain how we can help you."

Jason's eyes were wary as he accepted Bryan's handshake, but it was Alex's reaction that captured Gabriel's attention. He watched the way Alex's face seemed to freeze over with hostility and the way it fairly radiated off of him. Frowning, he saw the look Bryan tossed his way, but he could only shrug. "I'm going to handle disposing of the sedans and check on Chris." Gabriel excused himself.

He felt Alex watching him as he headed to the back of the house, toward the security office where Chris spent most of his time. The man in question appeared engrossed in a project, and didn't notice him standing in the doorway immediately. Blue eyes observed him shrewdly the moment Chris glanced up. "Where's the Devs?"

"Bryan's showing them around." Gabriel reached out and picked up the newest gadget Chris had lying on his desk, studying it in his hands. "Is there a way to scan Vincetti's compound for exactly how many Deviants are in there?"

"What are you thinking, Gabe?" Chris asked suspiciously,

typing away madly at his keyboard. "You know we can't rescue all of them in there. Bryan would never agree to it, and you know it."

Gabriel slammed the item back down on the desk, ignoring the wince and glare that Chris drilled into him at the mishandling of his things. "We can't just leave them there, Chris! They were locked up like animals. Like they were in a zoo."

Anger raged through Gabriel, and he knew some of the anguish had to be showing in his eyes. All of his team were aware of his past, the things he'd done, and he was certain Chris understood his urgent desire to release those imprisoned Deviants. "Find out, Chris. Please."

Chris sighed. "All right, Gabriel. Give me some time and I'll get the information you want."

"Thank you." Gabriel reached out and squeezed Chris's shoulder briefly before turning to leave the room.

"Gabe?" Gabriel stopped in the doorway and looked back at Chris. "Where's my gear?"

The deer-in-the-headlights look clearly gave away the situation, and Chris let out an angry shout. "Where the fuck did you leave it?"

Gabriel hightailed it out of the room before Chris could get out of his seat with a flippant, "Lizard did it!"

If the walls could have rattled with Chris's roar for Lizard, they would have. Gabriel could practically picture Lizard's face, and laughed under his breath as he strode out the front door. For the next few hours, Gabriel avoided returning to the farmhouse. He disposed of the sedans before heading to the building they used for physical training. Several Deviants were already using some of the equipment when he entered and walked to the makeshift locker room. He quickly changed into a pair of dark sweatpants and a gray T-shirt. When he returned to the main area, the sound of fists and feet thudding against the hanging punching bags was like a welcomed reprieve from the soft voice haunting him.

He didn't know how he would deal with being around Alex until they trained and relocated the twins. He sat down on a bench near the punching bags and started taping up his fists. The Deviants already using the bags called out a greeting, to which Gabriel nodded in acknowledgement. Using his teeth to tear the tape, he finished his left hand and moved to his right. Once he'd completed the job, he stood and did some minor stretching, raising his arms above his head and working the muscles in his upper back and biceps. Warmed up, he approached one of the unoccupied punching bags and started throwing out simple jabs, quickly increasing to full on punches.

Grunting as he slammed his taped fist into the bag in front of him, Gabriel growled low in his throat at the way his arms tingled at the remembered feeling of Alex wrapped in them. He hadn't even considered the consequences when he'd offered to help ease the telepath's pain. Sweat dripped down his face as memories of another instance assaulted him. Dark amber eyes squinting in pain and tanned flesh paling until almost white screamed through his mind like a train in a dark tunnel. Thud, thud. Gabriel's movements became vicious, almost cruel, in his attempt to outrun the thoughts. His muscles burned in protest as he lost all track of time.

"Yo, Gabe! What did that bag ever do to you, man?" A deep voice came from his left, disrupting the senseless attack.

Turning his head, Gabriel spotted Jackal standing there, arms crossed and eyebrow raised. He scowled at Jackal and went back to throwing punches. "Go away, Jackal."

Jackal snorted and uncrossed his arms, taking on a

fighting stance. "Why not take it out on something that can fight back?"

With the mood he was in, Gabriel knew he could possibly hurt Jackal, but the idea of hitting out at someone who could feel the pain took control of him. Snarling brutally, Gabriel swung around and tossed out a sudden punch at Jackal, except Jackal expected it and sidestepped it smoothly. As they moved adeptly into sparring against each other, the other Deviants in the room gathered around to watch, whispering to each other. They'd never seen Gabriel the way he appeared at that moment: angry, bitter, and full of hate. Perhaps Gabriel *was* full of hate in those minutes. He hated that Alex made him feel more than the detachment he lived by. He hated Alex for stirring the memories he'd long since buried in the back of his mind, and he hated how the mere thought of the younger Deviant made him long for things he'd convinced himself he'd never want or need.

His fist connected with Jackal's shoulder, stunning the other man briefly and giving Gabriel the chance to land a roundhouse kick that sent the man flying into the padded wall. A surprised gasp from the students echoed in the room, bringing Gabriel back to his senses, and he swore violently, rushing over to help Jackal up. "Shit, I'm sorry, Jackal."

Jackal chuckled and rubbed his shoulder. "It's cool, boss. I could tell you needed it."

Guilt struck at Gabriel like a blunt object. He grimaced at the bruise forming on Jackal's shoulder. "Teresa is going to kick my ass."

Chest rumbling deeply, Jackal clapped Gabriel on the back. "I have no doubt she could do it, Gabe."

"I'd let her too," Gabriel muttered, running a tired hand over his face. His head pounded from the overabundance of adrenaline and emotion. "I would certainly deserve it."

"Everyone has their demons, Gabe," Jackal murmured,

giving a fake grin at the Deviants watching them. "You just needed to beat the shit out of yours."

Sighing, Gabriel shook his head. "But those demons aren't yours."

Jackal didn't reply for a moment as they walked toward the locker room to shower and change. When he did speak, it surprised Gabriel. "I hope you know that I'm your friend and that I would never judge you for anything in your past. If you need to talk, I'm here to listen."

Gabriel stopped just inside the door and looked at his teammate. "Thanks, Jackal. I appreciate it."

"No problem, boss. Now, I think dinner should almost be ready by the time we get back to the farmhouse, and I know Bryan is looking for you." Jackal punched Gabriel lightly in the arm and turned to grab a towel along with a bar of soap.

The smell of spaghetti and garlic bread teased Gabriel's nose as he entered the front door of the agency and he breathed deeply, his stomach growling. He hadn't even realized how long it had been since he'd last eaten. Bryan exited his office as Gabriel shut the door behind him and motioned for him to join him. "The twins seem to be very intelligent," Bryan commented the moment his office door closed. "But we might have some trouble with Jason. His attitude is a big concern to me."

"I know what you mean." Gabriel sighed. "Those men found us because of his lack of control, but I think if Hayley works with him she may be able to change that."

Hayley Wright was Bryan's sister and a Normal. She worked with the Deviants who came to the agency, teaching them how to keep their emotions in check. A psychiatrist, she used to work closely with patients at a local mental institution. After Bryan opened the ADA, she came to the farmhouse to help acclimate the Deviants to their situation and prepare them to hide in the real world. Preston, her husband, also worked at the agency as a weapons consultant. Before the outbreak of violence against Deviants, Preston had been a cop on the task force set to gather all Deviants into concentration camps. He'd quit the first night Normals attacked one of them.

"She's going to have her hands full with him, though," Bryan mused, his lips curling up at the corners in fondness. Gabriel felt envious of Bryan in that moment. What would it be like to have a family? "I think you should work with the brother, Gabriel."

Gabriel opened his mouth to protest. Bryan cut him off. "He's taken a liking to you, Gabriel, and you are the only one strong enough to train him on how to protect himself."

"I can't do that, Bryan!" Gabriel stood and started pacing restlessly. "He's…."

"He reminds you of Rafael," Bryan said bluntly. "I know he does, Gabe. I saw it in the way you looked at him earlier. But you're the one person who understands his abilities and how difficult they are to control. The only one who can stop him from burning out his mind."

A sharp sound issued from Gabriel's throat, and he tightened his hands into fists. "Don't do this to me, Bryan."

Sympathy briefly flashed across Bryan's face. "I'm sorry, Gabriel, but I think you need his help just as much as he needs yours."

"Who are you to decide that?" Gabriel snapped.

"Your friend."

"My friend wouldn't force me to relive the worst moments of my life!" he raged angrily.

"It's done, Gabe. You'll start his training tomorrow," Bryan stated flatly.

Gabriel slammed out of Bryan's office, the sound of the door banging against the jamb reverberating through the empty hallway. Alex's laughter reached his ears as he neared the dining room, and his scowl deepened. Bryan had no idea what he asked of him by throwing him together with the green-eyed Deviant. He stopped just outside the door and listened to Alex's animated chatter about the farmhouse and how beautiful it was, how much he loved his room. The lyrical lilt to his voice caused Gabriel's stomach to clench painfully. He took a deep breath and stepped into the room, noticing how Alex's attention immediately centered on him. It took every ounce of control he had not to turn around and walk out when he saw the light entering Alex's eyes. He'd have to be blind not to notice Alex found him attractive.

"Evening," he said as he took the only seat available, next to Alex.

Alex turned slightly in his chair and smiled at Gabriel shyly. "Hi."

Preston set a heaping plate of steaming spaghetti on the table in front of Gabriel and he kept his attention on the food. He barely tasted it, listening to the others talking and joking around. The heat from Alex's body seeped into him, their arms brushing over each other several times as they ate. Intent on reining in his rising lust, Gabriel didn't notice the looks passing between Jackal and Lizard or the concern in Bear's eyes. Bear had been there the day Gabriel's world shattered into a million pieces. It was Bear who'd helped him put the fragments back into a disfigured puzzle. "Gabe?"

He looked up to see Teresa holding out her hand. "What?"

"Can you pass the bread, please?"

A sheepish tilt to his head, he picked up the basket near his elbow and handed it to her. "Sorry," he mumbled.

"So did Bryan tell you who would be training the newest recruits?" Jackal asked curiously.

The sheepish look dissipated in a split intake of breath, and he tensed. "Jason will be training with Hayley about controlling his emotions, and Zack, a level four telekinetic, will be teaching him more about his abilities." Gabriel hesitated before continuing, "I'll be taking over Alex's training."

Silence fell between the other members of his team, but Alex gave a wide grin and said, "That's awesome. You really helped me with my headache the other day, and the way you managed to put up that block to keep me out! Does that mean you'll be teaching me how to fight too?"

Gabriel stifled a groan. He hadn't even thought of that part, and somehow he knew Bryan wouldn't let him get away with having Jackal work with the other Deviant. "Yeah," he supplied gruffly, stuffing another bite of bread in his mouth.

"Outstanding!" Alex exclaimed.

The moment his plate was clear, Gabriel stood, shoving his chair into the table. "Get a good night's sleep, kid. You're going to need it."

Words of advice he later found out he couldn't apply to himself as he lay in his bed, shifting restlessly between the sheets. He sat up with a sigh and ran a hand through his dark hair. "How do I get through this, Rafael? He's so innocent and beautiful, but I can't stop myself from wanting him. If you were here...." He stopped, his throat closing over in agony.

Rafael wasn't there. He'd never be there again. Something Gabriel knew all too well and also knew that it was his fault. His brother was dead because of him, because he'd killed his twin brother to save his own life five years ago. Would Alex still want him if he knew the truth? A bitter laugh welled up inside him at the thought. The way Alex protected his twin so fiercely made it undoubtedly clear that the only way to keep the light in Alex's eyes from fading into disgust was to keep the telepath from finding out. It meant keeping the boy out of his head and his memories. It meant not allowing his body to make his choices for him.

6

ALEX

ALEX grunted as his back hit the ground again. Dazed, he stared up at the vaulted warehouse ceiling overhead, his body throbbing, having been tossed to the mat covered floor more times than he could count. "Get up," Gabriel demanded fiercely.

He'd thought that this would be a way to get to know Gabriel, maybe get closer to him, but the man treated him in such a detached manner that his hopes were slowly losing air and deflating. Not wanting to appear weak in front of Gabriel, Alex forced himself to stand and went back into the slightly crouched position, watching for any signs indicating the other man's next move. A small flicker of muscle in Gabriel's right arm, and Alex dodged to the left, narrowly missing a fist. Satisfaction glimmered in Gabriel's eyes for a split second before the emotion was hidden again behind the wall the man kept in place like a shield.

Gabriel called a halt a half hour later. "Good, but you need to be faster. Process the movements faster. Your opponent in a real life situation isn't going to give you the time you need to watch for his next move."

"I know that," Alex murmured, rubbing his lower back, his bottom lip a bit pouty at Gabriel's backhanded compliment, quickly followed by a slap to his self-confidence.

"Have you been practicing the meditation like I showed you?" Gabriel asked as he unwrapped the tape around his fists.

Exhausted, Alex had fallen into bed the previous night, instantly asleep in seconds. Gabriel woke him up at 5:00 a.m., instructing him to dress comfortably and to meet him at the training building behind the mansion by five thirty. There hadn't been any time to do as he'd instructed. "No," he muttered. "I didn't have time."

"Make time," Gabriel snapped, swiping a towel over the sweat on his face and upper body, neatly drawing Alex's gaze to the rippling muscles under the tan skin and causing him to swallow hard. "As a telepath, your mind is never quiet, never still. Without the meditation you could burn out. Your mind could shatter and leave you nothing but an empty shell. The meditation is to help clear your mind and allow whatever negative thoughts or energy you've absorbed to be released."

The room they were in had slowly begun to fill during the three hours they'd been training. At first, Alex felt embarrassed at the others witnessing his constant failure, but after a while he'd noticed no one even paid attention to the two of them. "I'm sorry, Gabriel. I promise that I'll make the time."

"Go back to the house, take a shower, and meet me by the back door in thirty minutes. I'm going to show you additional techniques to use." Gabriel turned away from him and strode through a door Alex assumed led to the locker room.

Alex stared after him for a long moment, his stomach twisting at the cold way Gabriel treated him. What would it take for a man so beautiful and strong to notice him? "Don't sweat it, Alex." A voice broke into his thoughts, and he glanced over to find Jackal watching him. "He's like that with everyone."

Except Bryan, he thought bitterly. "I know. Lizard already mentioned that."

Beckoning him closer, Jackal leaned in, grinning. "Except I know something he doesn't. Somehow you've gotten under Gabe's skin. He only puts that great big emotionless wall in place when something is really nagging him."

Hope flared anew, and he looked back at the way Gabriel had gone. Was Jackal right? Did he really get the man's attention that much? "Oh, and, just so you know, Gabe prefers men." Jackal winked at him and went back to lifting weights, whistling under his breath.

Shock and elation spread through Alex as he rushed to the house, tearing up the stairs into the bedroom he shared with Jason. Gabriel was gay! Like him. It sent thrills racing down his spine into his lower gut while he started the shower and undressed. Maybe he did have a chance after all. Grinning like an idiot, Alex stepped under the hot spray, almost moaning at the feel of hot water on his aching body. His mind wandered to thoughts of Gabriel joining him, and the idea of Gabriel touching him, kissing him, caressing him with a lover's hand, sent tendrils of heat to his cock. He bit his lower lip as he slumped into the shower wall, his hand squeezing the hard shaft and imagining Gabriel's in its place.

What would the other Deviant's hand feel like touching him? Would his palm be calloused, causing the most delicious friction? Would it be smooth and hot against the sensitive skin? Alex groaned and stroked his cock faster, his eyes closing and head tipped back to the wall. His other hand reached around to lightly probe at the entrance to his hole. He'd never been with a man, but he'd used objects before: a brush handle, a cucumber he'd stolen from his Gram's kitchen, and his own fingers. The tip of his finger pushed inside him, and he groaned, tightening his hold on his straining length. Alex felt his balls tautening, pulling up closer to his body and signaling the release he sought.

Sliding a second finger into his ass, Alex stifled a cry of pleasure, thrusting his fingers as deep as he could reach. The tingling sensation at the base of his spine signaled his imminent climax, and he stroked faster, tugging harder. Unable to keep silent as his orgasm hit, Alex sobbed Gabriel's name. Shudders raced down Alex's body with each hard spurt of come spilling over his fist. He collapsed into the wall, panting heavily, eyes closed.

It took every ounce of energy Alex possessed to push away from the wall, rush through the process of washing himself before wrenching the water off. He breathed a sigh of relief that his brother wasn't in the bedroom when he left the bathroom. If his twin heard the sound of him moaning Gabriel's name as he'd come, he'd never hear the end of it. He quickly dressed in a loose pair of black sweatpants, sneakers, and a light gray T-shirt before darting out of the room and down the stairs. Gabriel stood just outside the back door, waiting for him. His breath caught in his throat at the sight of Gabriel in a black tank top and loose fitting sweats similar to his own. The muscles under the tanned skin of his arms rippled as he motioned for Alex to follow him.

"This way," Gabriel grunted, setting out toward the back of the property into the trees behind the farmhouse. The sun warmed Alex's skin, but he barely noticed, his eyes locked on the broad shoulders in front of him. Sounds of running water reached Alex's ears, and he tore his gaze away from Gabriel to spot a small creek rushing through a clearing ahead of them. Delight rippled along his skin, and he smiled in pleasure, hurrying past Gabriel to reach the stream. He dropped to his knees at the edge, dipping his hand into the creek to feel the cool water on his skin.

Gabriel sank down to the grass a few feet from Alex, crossing his legs Indian-style and setting his hands on his knees. "Do you know what telepathy is, Alex?"

Alex turned to look at the other Deviant, tilting his head in a quizzical gesture. "It's the ability to read someone's mind."

"Sometimes. Telepathy can also be more than that. It gives you the ability to communicate on another level other than verbal. Receiving thoughts as well as sending them. There's also the possibility to transfer physical, emotional, or mental energy without contact. This is usually related to an empath; however, the stronger the telepath, the more likely they will be able to have this ability as well." Gabriel closed his eyes and tipped his face up to the sun. "It can feel like the warmth of the sun on your skin or the cool touch of the water running past you. But it can also feel as painful as the cut of a knife or the sting of a bee. Sometimes it can cause pain beyond the imagination. A pain so deep you'll wish you were dead."

Frowning, Alex shifted, moving to sit closer to Gabriel, mimicking the Indian-style position. "I don't understand."

"Have you ever been in a crowded room and felt the emotions of those surrounding you? Beating at your mind almost like a physical object?" Gabriel's voice held a serene note that spoke to Alex, soothing him.

"I didn't spend much time around others," Alex murmured. "It was only Jason, me, and Grams on the farm. After Grams died and the town discovered what we are, we spent so much time on the move that we didn't really have the chance to be in crowded places."

Gabriel breathed out slowly, bringing his head back down to pin Alex in place with an intense gaze. "First we'll work on meditation, and then we will need to work on your ability to keep others out, emotionally and mentally. You may be a level five, but your inability to protect yourself is your greatest weakness. Without being able to keep others out, you're susceptible to attack."

Alex nodded. "All right. Is the meditation similar to the breathing you showed me back at the safe house?"

"A bit. There are many techniques around the world utilized during meditation. Each soul has three parts: the consciousness, the subconscious, and the intellect. Your thoughts flow from your subconscious to your conscious mind. Feelings and emotions form from the thoughts flowing through your mind. It is those thoughts that determine your current state of being and is why you must control your subconscious as well as your consciousness."

The connection didn't make much sense to Alex. "I don't understand. How does the subconscious control the conscious mind?"

Gabriel tipped his head back once more. "The subconscious is where our previous experiences and thoughts are contained. They control our conscious emotions if we allow them to. The intellect is the controller of both your conscious and subconscious. We use our intellect to discriminate against the lesser or harsher thoughts that may threaten to enter our minds. With meditation, you will be able to strengthen your mind and your intellect."

For the better part of an hour, Gabriel instructed him on deep breathing techniques. The whole process felt strangely intimate to Alex, and made him even more aware of the larger Deviant seated near him. His distraction did not escape the other man's notice, causing Gabriel to reprimand him several times, much to his chagrin. When Alex finally managed to force his mind to the task at hand, a warmth spread through his limbs, his mind clearing and focusing on just being. Alex breathed in and exhaled slowly and evenly. His eyes closed as he drank in the peace he felt pouring through him. A small smile played around his lips. There had never been such calm inside of him. It was unlike anything he'd ever felt before. The thoughts and emotions of others had always been his burden to bear, a heavy weight on his mind and soul.

He felt each breath travel through his nose, through his body. On every inhale and on each exhale another bit of his stress went with it. The breeze lightly tickled the fine hairs along his skin, and he shivered slightly. It felt amazing. Wonderful. Freeing in a way that he'd never experienced in his entire life. "Wow," he murmured once Gabriel called a halt to their meditation.

Gabriel smiled, helping Alex to his feet. "Tomorrow we will add in a few yoga moves as well during the meditation process."

Alex grinned up at Gabriel while they walked back to the house. "I've never felt so calm or at peace. Thank you, Gabriel."

"Gabe," the man mumbled, a light dusting of red highlighting his cheekbones.

"Gabe," Alex repeated softly. His heart flipped over inside his chest, and he had to hold back a pleased smile. "Can I ask you something?" he asked a moment later.

"Go ahead, kid."

"Alex," he said quietly. At Gabriel's questioning look, he explained further, "My name is Alex. Not kid. I'll be twenty next week."

"Sorry," Gabriel murmured, "Alex."

Suppressing a shudder at hearing Gabriel use his name, Alex continued with his question. "How do you know so much about telepathy? About using meditation to fight off the headaches?"

Gabriel stiffened, and Alex wondered if he'd overstepped his boundaries. It surprised him when the taller Deviant actually answered. "Someone I used to know was a strong telepath. A level five who suffered the same kinds of migraines."

"Used to know?" Alex queried gently, itching to learn more about the man's past.

They stopped at the back door of the agency, and Gabriel pinned him in place, his eyes flat and emotionless. "He died."

Alex's lips parted on a small gasp of shock, but Gabriel slammed the back door open and strode into the house, leaving Alex staring after him. Was the telepath Gabriel spoke of the same man named Rafael? He could practically feel the anguish rolling off of Gabriel, and his heart went out to the strong Deviant. Sighing, he stepped into the cool interior of the agency and closed the door behind him.

Sounds of chatter reached him, and he heard his brother's voice. Jason was talking excitedly about something. Alex ambled into the living room to find his twin perched on the arm of the couch and relating some tale about their escapades on the farm with Grams to another young Deviant named Marcus. The look in Marcus's eyes made Alex wonder if Marcus found Jason attractive. He frowned, hoping his brother wasn't leading the other man on. Jason had always checked out the girls on their infrequent visits to town, so he felt fairly confident his brother was straight.

Smiling, Alex sank into the easy chair, pulling his legs underneath him. It was the first time he'd seen Jason acting his usual boisterous self since they'd been on the run. The last year and a half had been hard on both of them. Everything seemed to hit Jason the hardest and most severe. The complete opposites of one another, Alex was reserved and quiet while Jason could be described as outgoing and loud. They'd complemented each other since birth with the differences in their personalities. He'd always been able to keep his brother from getting into too much trouble by being the levelheaded one.

"Sounds like you got into a lot of trouble when you were younger," Marcus commented in a deep voice, dimples appearing as he smiled widely. Tanned skin and dark hair attested to Marcus's Hispanic heritage, yet his voice lacked the accent one would expect. "How did you both end up here at Sorensen's?"

Jason's smile died, and his eyes grew shuttered. Sympathy slipped through Alex. "Grams passed away about two years ago. We went into town to get some supplies one day, and we were accidentally discovered. We've been on the run ever since," Alex explained.

Marcus made a noise of empathy and lightly touched Jason's arm. "My situation has been the same. My mother kept me and my sister hidden after she found we were able to do things outside of normal human abilities. My sister was only eight years old when a neighbor discovered what we were."

Anger rippled across Marcus's features, and his voice dropped several octaves, anguish buried in his tone. "They came for my sister while I was at school. Eight years old and they didn't care. I found her hanging from a tree when I got home. I barely managed to escape. Bryan found me on the streets and gave me a home again.

"To this day, I swear to find the animals who could hang an innocent eight-year-old little girl from a tree. Murdered like a criminal out of fear and misguided justice." Marcus balled his hands into fists. "I couldn't even give her a proper burial."

Alex felt his eyes burn with tears, and he swallowed past the huge lump in his throat. He couldn't imagine what he would do if anything ever happened to his brother. "I'm sorry," Jason murmured, surprising Alex.

Marcus nodded stiffly, the earlier light atmosphere dampened by the somber story. The three of them sat there silently for several long moments, lost in their own thoughts and memories. Alex concentrated on not "hearing" what the other two were thinking. Strong emotions made it hard for him to block out a person's private contemplation. Sadness, anger, the deeper the feeling, the more they beat at Alex. He grimaced and stood, needing to get away from the snatches of self-condemnation he picked up from Marcus. He knew the other Deviant wouldn't welcome the intrusion.

Walking into the kitchen, he found Preston prepping everything for dinner. A pot of water sat on the stove, slowly heating up. "Hi," he said shyly.

"Hey, Alex. How was your first day of training?" Preston asked easily, expertly chopping up carrots and tossing them into a bowl next to the cutting board.

"I think I'm going to be sore in the morning," Alex admitted ruefully, rolling his shoulders. "Do you… can I help you with dinner?"

Preston smiled kindly at him and indicated for him to wash his hands while he set a colander with freshly washed lettuce and a large bowl on the island counter. "Did your grandmother teach you how to cook?"

Alex turned on the water and grabbed the bar of soap from the dish. "She did. She tried to teach Jason, but he could never concentrate long enough to learn even the basics. He'd burn water, as she used to say."

He turned off the water and moved back to the counter, perching on a stool to start shredding lettuce. "How long have you worked for Mr. Sorensen?"

Preston pulled a long cookie sheet from under one of the counters. "About five years now. My wife, Hayley, is Bryan's sister, and after the first concentration camp for Deviants was attacked, I quit the police force and came here. Bryan put me in charge of the armory and cooking." He laughed. "Bastard was waiting for me to give in, because he knows I can cook better than my wife. I think she poisoned at least half the first group of Devs to come through the agency."

A huff came from behind Alex, and he turned his head to see the woman in question. Her arms were crossed over her chest and her eyes burned brightly, indignation shining clearly. "My cooking is not that bad, Preston Wright! You take it back or Alex is going to think you're telling the truth!"

Eyes widening, Alex hid a grin behind a cough. Preston winked at him before giving his wife a bland expression. "Come now, Hayles. You know I love you, but you have to admit there were quite a few complaints of stomachaches back then."

Hayley stepped toward him and smacked him lightly on the arm. Preston laughed and grabbed her, tugging her into an embrace. He whispered something in her ear, causing her face to burn bright red, but her anger faded. Alex politely turned his head while trying to ignore the aching feeling in the pit of his stomach. Would he ever be able to have the same kind of close relationship the two of them had? He wrenched at several leaves of lettuce in depression.

Preston returned to preparing dinner while Hayley wandered closer to Alex. "How are you doing, Alex?"

Alex gave her a wan smile. "I'm doing okay. It's nice not to have to look over my shoulder all the time."

She gave his arm a sympathetic squeeze. "Jason seems to be settling in nicely. He did very well in his session today. Are you and Gabriel getting along?"

The mention of Gabriel's name caused Alex to remember the emotional void in the powerful Deviant's eyes. He wanted to know so much about the other man, to understand what made him so detached. "He's helped me a lot. The meditation he taught me today is really going to help avoid the migraines."

"I'm glad to hear that. Your mind is a fragile thing, Alex. You have to be careful you don't burn yourself out. I have several books on meditation and even yoga, if you'd like to read them. They may be able to offer you additional guidance on practices to help you relax both your body and mind." Hayley slid onto the stool next to him. "My cousin was also a telepath."

"Was?" Alex queried, tossing a handful of lettuce into the bowl.

Sadness dampened the kindness on Hayley's face for a moment. "The concentration camp she was in was attacked one night. Several of the Deviants were killed during the assault. It's why I decided on spending my life doing whatever I can for others like her."

"I'm sorry," he murmured, ashamed at feeling sorry for himself. Things could be so much worse than they were.

She waved his apology away. "It was a long time ago. I learned a lot about telepaths when she started developing the signs of being a Deviant. If you need to talk, I want you to know that you can come to me anytime you need."

"Thanks." Alex smiled softly. The only ones he'd been able to talk to about his ability were his brother and his Grams. They hadn't known anything about it other than what they'd seen in books or movies. "My Grams always used to say my ability was granted to me by God to help others. I think I'd like to learn more about it. Can I come see the books after dinner?"

"Of course! You don't even have to ask. My office is at the back of the house. It's the second to last door on the right. You can borrow them whenever you'd like." Hayley glanced at the clock and frowned. "Which reminds me, I have a session with Marcus in a couple of minutes. Can we talk more later?"

Alex nodded and finished up the last bit of lettuce, adding it to the almost overflowing bowl. He watched her leave the kitchen, wondering if he really could help people with his ability. Preston disturbed him from his thoughts by setting down a cutting board and several tomatoes in front of him. "She has a good heart." Alex looked up at him.

Affection flitted through Preston's eyes. "From the moment I met her, I knew we were meant to be together. I can't imagine my life without her."

Envy swamped Alex again, and he bit his bottom lip as he picked up a nearby knife and began to cut up the tomatoes for the salad. His mind drifted to Gabriel. He knew his attraction to the older man was hopeless, yet he couldn't stop the way he felt inside whenever he saw or thought of him.

"Alex." He turned to find his brother standing at his shoulder.

"What were you thinking so hard about?" Jason teased, leaning against the island counter beside him.

Alex flushed and looked away from his brother. "Nothing."

Jason touched Alex's shoulder lightly. "Alex, you know you can talk to me about anything, right?"

Nodding, Alex tightened his grip on the knife. He'd never told his brother about his attraction to other men, but deep down he felt certain Jason knew he was gay. "It's really nothing. How'd your day go?"

He continued chopping tomatoes while listening to Jason describe his session with Hayley and the physical combat training maneuvers Jackal put him through. "Jackal's pretty cool. Did you know he can run as fast as a cheetah? He could almost outrun a car!"

"Really?" Alex asked in an attempt to pay attention.

Jason pouted at him. "Come on, Alex! That's pretty awesome, don't you think?"

Preston stepped in before Alex could respond. "Hey, Jace, would you do me a favor and set the tables? The plates are in the cupboard there, and the silverware is in the drawer to the left of the sink."

Sighing, Jason nodded and moved to gather up what he needed. He stopped in the doorway to look at Alex but didn't say anything more before continuing into the dining area. The rest of the preparations went by quickly, and the smell of spices and meatloaf with vegetables flooded the first floor of the agency. Alex heard his belly grumble loudly, and Preston laughed, handing him a buttered roll wrapped in a paper towel. "It's almost ready. Why don't you call the masses to the dining room for me?"

Alex took the roll from Preston and hopped off the stool. "Thank you."

"No, thank you. No one ever volunteers to help with dinner. It's nice to have help." Preston winked at him.

Ripping off a piece of the roll, Alex tossed it into his mouth as he walked out of the kitchen. He stopped in each occupied room of the farmhouse in succession to let everyone know dinner was going to be served shortly. The only person Alex wanted to see was nowhere to be found, and he returned to the dining room with his shoulders slumped slightly.

Dinner was its usual noisy affair. Talking, laughing, and the shuffling of dishes echoed through the house. Alex's appetite had fled, and he merely picked at his food. He hadn't meant to upset Gabriel. He'd only wanted to learn more about the other man. Sighing, he set his fork back down on his plate and stood. "I'm going to go to bed, Jace. It's been a long day."

"Are you... okay, Alex?" Jason asked quietly, touching Alex's wrist lightly.

"I'm fine," Alex replied, picking up his plate. "Ending up pinned to a mat multiple times in one day will make anyone tired."

"All right. I'll see you upstairs in a bit."

Alex could feel his brother's gaze on him as he entered the kitchen to deposit his plate next to the kitchen sink. He knew Jason could tell he'd lied, but even if he did want to talk about what was bothering him, he certainly didn't want to do it in a room full of others. The thought of his attraction getting back to Gabriel as gossip made him squirm in embarrassment and discomfort. Gabriel would probably just feel sorry for him.

He trudged up the stairs to the second floor and stopped at the door to the room he shared with his twin. The sound of a gun cocking caught his attention immediately. Silently, he tiptoed in the direction it came from, and a small sliver of light broke up the gloominess of the hallway from a doorway cracked open. Alex peered through the crack into the room, stifling a sound of surprise when he saw Gabriel standing at a dresser, stuffing weapons into a black vest. "You shouldn't spy on people, kid."

Jumping almost a foot, Alex sheepishly pushed open the door. "I wasn't trying to spy. I heard what sounded like a gun cocking," he murmured, his eyes hungrily roaming the bedroom for any hint of Gabriel's life.

"And you came to check it out on your own?" Gabriel turned to look at him, one eyebrow raised at him.

Alex flushed and dropped his gaze to the floor. "I didn't think about it, to be honest."

"Next time, don't go toward the sound. Run away from it," Gabriel commanded sharply.

"Sorry," Alex mumbled. "Are you... going somewhere?"

7

GABRIEL

ABRIEL stormed into the mansion, his chest aching at the reminder of what he tried so hard to forget. Alex's innocent gaze and the curious question forced him to think back to the day he wanted nothing more than to change, to rewind time and make it disappear. Only not even a Deviant had that ability. "Gabe?"

Bryan's voice snagged him midstride, and he halted at the bottom of the steps leading upstairs. Turning, he looked at his boss, unaware of the anguish burning in his eyes. Bryan frowned and beckoned him into his office. Gabriel's lips tightened into a flat line as he strode in. "Is everything okay, Gabe?"

"Assign someone else to the kid, Bryan," Gabriel ground out, pacing the office like a caged animal.

His boss and friend didn't answer for a long stretch of silence before replying, "No."

"Why?" Gabriel demanded in agony, swinging a beseeching gaze toward Bryan. "Why are you doing this to me?"

A sad smile drifted over Bryan's face for a split second.

"Because he's good for you, Gabriel. I haven't seen you look at anyone like that in the years I've known you. Since your brother died, you've been cut off, and even during our time together you never let yourself go enough to feel things."

"I felt things with you!" Gabriel protested.

Shaking his head, Bryan pinned him in place with his stare. "Fucking isn't the same thing as feeling something real. Never once did it go beyond sex for you, Gabe. You always held back your heart."

"That's not true," he murmured, sinking into the chair in front of Bryan's desk. "I may not have shown it, but I did care about you, Bryan. I still do."

"Not enough," Bryan replied gently.

Bitterness swamped Gabriel, and the realization that he'd hurt Bryan came over him. He looked up at his ex-lover, grief stricken. "I'm sorry, Bry. So sorry."

Bryan stood up and moved around his desk to sit in the chair beside Gabriel. He cupped Gabriel's cheek in one hand. "Don't apologize for not being able to love me, Gabe. I just wasn't the person to help you find your way back to who you were meant to be. Don't let the past control your life."

"I can't," he whispered.

"Yes, you can," Bryan insisted, stroking his thumb over Gabriel's cheekbone. "I see that spark in your eyes when you look at him. Give it a chance, and stop fighting so hard to keep everyone away."

Gabriel touched the back of Bryan's hand, leaning his face further into his palm. "I miss you."

"I miss you too," Bryan murmured, carefully extricating himself from Gabriel's grasp. "More than you'll ever know."

Bryan stood up and moved back to his desk. "I have an assignment for you. It'll give you a chance to get away and think. Take Tank, but I doubt you'll need him."

Coughing to hide his emotions, Gabriel nodded and

stood, taking the folder extended to him. "We received a call from one of our contacts a short while ago. Said the boy's been living in an abandoned building for a few weeks on his own. There's not much to go on. Basic details are the kid looks about fifteen or so. Blond, blue-eyed, skinny, roughly six feet. Extremely skittish. Our contact is pretty sure the kid is at least a level four."

Gabriel looked over the brief description and a snapshot of the blond boy looking over his shoulder as he entered what appeared to be an empty warehouse. "How do we know he'll go with us?"

"You don't." Bryan tipped the corner of his lip upward. "But I know you. You can be pretty persuasive when you want to be, Gabe."

He tucked the folder under one arm and turned to head upstairs to begin preparing to leave. "Gabe?"

He stopped in the doorway, turning his head slightly. "Be safe."

"I always am," Gabriel replied softly and walked out of the office. The sounds of dishes clattering in the kitchen and voices rumbling in the living room followed him upstairs. He kicked at the bedroom door to shut it behind him, failing to notice it didn't close all the way. Picking up his cell, he punched in a quick text to Tank and pulled on his weapons vest, sliding his knives in their sleeves. The sound of the 9mm magazine sliding into place covered the footsteps on the hallway floor. Soft breathing and the sweet smell of sandalwood alerted him to the presence at his door.

"You shouldn't spy on people, kid," he said flatly, shoving the gun into his vest.

"I wasn't spying! I heard the sound of a gun cocking," Alex replied as he edged further into the room.

Gabriel turned around to look at the younger Deviant, his

eyebrow raised. "And you came to check it out on your own?"

Alex flushed and dropped his gaze to the floor. "I didn't think about it to be honest."

"Next time, don't go toward the sound. Run away from it."

He went back to making sure he had everything, stuffing an extra change of clothing and the file on the runaway into a small black bag. "Sorry. Are you going somewhere?"

"Had a report of a Deviant living alone in an abandoned warehouse. I'm going to get the boy and bring him back here," he replied stoically, checking his phone to see if Tank was ready.

Alex moved closer to his side. "What do you need all the weapons for if he's just a boy?"

Snorting, Gabriel peered at the younger man. "Haven't you learned anything here yet? Why do you think we're teaching you how to protect yourself? To control your abilities? We're Deviants, and in this world that makes us freaks. If we're caught out on the streets without some kind of protection, active ability or no, it's dangerous. You need to understand that and start doing what you can to protect yourself."

He roughly unsheathed a knife and shoved it into Alex's hand. Alex tried to jerk back from him, but he held on tightly, wrapping Alex's fingers around the handle. "Until you learn to use your psychic ability as a weapon, which will only get you so far, you need to learn how to use this."

Alex protested, "I don't want to hurt anyone!"

"Even if they want to hurt you?" Gabriel challenged. "Or your brother? What then? Are you going to let them injure you or possibly kill you and your brother?"

Fear showed clearly in the younger man's bright green eyes, but Gabriel forced down the guilt, knowing if he didn't make the other Deviant understand, he could end up dead. "This may be the only thing that saves your life or the life of someone you love."

Alex stared at the knife in their hands, the blade shining in the dim lamplight. Gabriel realized he still held Alex's hand and slowly let go, carefully removing his fingers from around Alex's. Neither of them moved for several heavy breaths. Gabriel's eyes locked on Alex's face as emotions flitted over his pale features. He broke the silence. "Sometimes we have to do things we don't want to, kid. It's a part of life. No one knows why we changed, why we have these abilities now, but we do. We have to accept it and do what we can to survive."

Gabriel reached out and gently took the knife from Alex, slipping it into its sheath. His cell vibrated in his pocket, notifying him that Tank sat waiting for him in one of the black SUVs. "Work on it with Jackal while I'm gone, Alex. You can show me what you've learned when I return." He picked up his bag, sliding it over his shoulder, and brushed past the teenager.

"Gabe," Alex called quietly. Stopping in the doorway, Gabriel looked back at the younger Deviant. "Be careful."

"Thanks, Alex," Gabriel murmured before turning and heading out of the agency.

T HE three-hour ride to the city was mostly made in silence. Gabriel's mind wasn't entirely on the mission at hand. All he could seem to think about was the way Alex's hands felt underneath his, the frightened bright green eyes, and the smell of the other Deviant's skin. "Gabe?" Tank's voice disturbed him from his thoughts.

Gabriel grunted in reply, his fingers curled into a fist on his thigh. "You okay?" Tank asked him.

Sighing, he relaxed his fingers and nodded. "I'm fine, Tank. Just a lot of shit on my mind."

"Is it Alex?"

He grimaced. "Is it that obvious?"

Tank shook his head. "No. Not to everyone. But you forget I've known you a long time, boss. I've learned to read under the façade you put in place."

"Bryan thinks the kid is good for me. Only he forgets that I'm not good for him." Snorting, Tank reached out and punched Gabriel in the arm, hard. "Ow! What the fuck did you do that for, asshole?" Gabriel rubbed his arm, scowling at Tank.

"Stop with the maudlin shit, Gabe. Yes, what happened with your brother was fucked up, but you can't deny yourself a life or someone to share that life with just because of it. Alex is a great guy, and I think he's tougher than you give him credit for." Tank flipped the turn signal on, taking the bridge into the heart of the city.

"He doesn't deserve to be saddled with a guy almost ten years older than him and a huge load of baggage. I don't have anything to offer him, Tank. Every day we put our lives on the line, and who knows if we'll even come home. How can I ask him, anyone, to wait around and constantly wonder if I'm coming back?" Gabriel's mouth flattened into a firm line of stubbornness.

Tank smoothly navigated through the well-known streets as he replied. "People do it every day, Gabe. Besides, it doesn't matter if you work in an office building or you're in Afghanistan. September 11 proved that. You could die just by crossing the street. I think you're just scared to let anyone close to you again."

"Fuck you, Tank," Gabriel snapped. "You have no idea what it's like."

"Don't I?" Tank demanded. "The outcome may have been

different, but we both lost someone. You did what you had to in order to survive, Gabe. No one can fault you for that."

"He was my brother! I was supposed to protect him." Gabriel's voice cracked slightly. "We were all we had left."

Tank pulled the SUV over to the curb and turned in his seat. "The family bonds broke the moment he tried to kill you, boss. He chose to let Vincetti control him and manipulate him into trying to hurt you. I know the guilt has been eating you alive since that night, but you have to let it go, Gabe. Let Rafael go."

Swallowing hard, Gabriel breathed deeply, holding back the flood of emotion threatening to overwhelm him. Memories of the fire consuming the compound, the pain as Rafael bombarded his mind over and over, the realization that his brother intended to kill him, and watching his brother engulfed in the flames crashed into his mind, sending the constant, agonizing guilt jolting through him. He gripped his head in his hands tightly, his fingers digging in, causing the muscles in his arms to bulge. "You can't possibly know what it felt like watching him die, Tank. You still have the chance to find your sister again. Rafael is gone. He's dead, and he isn't coming back."

"Which is why you need to move on. You can't spend the rest of your life unhappy and alone." Tank reached out and gripped Gabriel's forearm, gently tugging his hand away from his head. "You've done so much good for our kind, boss. You've helped so many, yet you refuse to let anyone in to help you. I know you think you don't deserve it, but you do. You just need to realize it."

Gabriel's other hand fell into his lap, but he kept his gaze trained on the dashboard. "I think we should get back to the job at hand," he said stoically after a few moments of silence.

Tank sighed and turned back in his seat, pulling onto the street and heading toward a cheap motel not far from the warehouse the Deviant reportedly lived in. They rented a room with two beds, hunkering down for the night. No way would the teenager trust going with them at night. Tank crashed on the bed closest to the door and flicked on the television, flipping through the channels until he found some kind of action film.

Gabriel sank into a chair near the window and watched the cars passing by, not really seeing them. His mind remained locked on the young man back at the farmhouse. Bryan's words rang in his mind over and over again. What could he possibly have to offer the sweet, innocent Deviant? He'd end up hurting him in the long run. Wouldn't he? Look at what he'd done to his own brother just to save his skin. His stomach clenched at the thought of ever hurting Alex, ever using his powers against the green-eyed Deviant.

The memory of Alex's body pressing into his as they'd sparred sent lust rushing straight to his groin. The smooth, supple skin and the scent of fresh soap had tickled his senses, increasing his attraction to the younger male. He'd never wanted anyone the way he wanted Alex, and the more time he spent around the dark-haired Deviant, the harder it got to fight his body. Smart, kind-hearted, ferociously determined, and so, so beautiful, Alex reminded him of Rafael in some respects, but his brother had never stirred these kinds of emotions. A hunger to taste his lips, to feel his skin beneath his palms, grew fiercer the more time he spent in the younger man's presence.

Gabriel snarled under his breath at the restlessness spreading through him. It felt somehow wrong to be away from the agency, away from Alex. He couldn't protect him if he wasn't there. He abruptly stood. "I'm going to take a shower," he said flatly, stalking into the bathroom and closing the door behind him.

Wrenching on the water, he stripped quickly, efficiently

97

folding and setting his clothing on the counter. As the water heated up, he studied the scar left behind by the bullet. It had healed completely within a matter of two days. The scar reminded him of the other Deviants locked up in the compound. Chris hadn't been able to get an accurate count of everyone in the cells. A round about estimate of twenty to thirty had been his best guess. The thought of all those people imprisoned, waiting for death or whatever Vincetti planned for them caused his blood to boil. Bryan refused to let him go after the others. He'd argued with Bryan to let him take his team and go in, rescue as many as they could, but he'd denied Gabriel the chance. He hated when his boss picked and chose certain Deviants to save. In his five years at the agency, it always surprised him how coldhearted Bryan could seem sometimes.

It still didn't make any sense what Vincetti wanted Alex and Jason for. They were level fives, but there were others in his employ just as powerful and even more skilled at using their abilities. Why them? He entered the shower, hissing as the scalding water hit his skin, but he bore it, allowing it to cascade over him. Was it because Alex and Jason were almost exactly like him and his brother? Was Vincetti trying to send him a message? Trying to draw him out and into a fight? He knew Gabriel worked for the ADA. Alex seemed certain Vincetti wanted them to retrieve something, but what?

Gabriel picked up the small bar of soap the motel gave as an amenity and unwrapped it, tossing the wrapper back onto the little shelf. He worked at clearing his mind, breathing deeply and evenly. It didn't work. Alex popped into his mind the second his hand brushed his semierect cock. *Fuck*, he mentally swore, his fingers trailing lightly over the smooth flesh. Maybe if he got off he could stop thinking about the younger Deviant. It'd been a while since he'd gotten laid. Resolved, he wrapped his fist around his dick and stroked himself to a full erection. He leaned his forehead against the wall, concentrating on the sensations trickling through his body and trying to think of anything but Alex.

The scent of soap brought images of Alex rushing forth: Alex on his knees looking up at him, Alex's cheeks bulging as he sucked his long length, Alex on his back as Gabriel buried his cock balls deep in the man's beautiful body. Gabriel stifled a groan, stroking faster and harder. The thought of feeling Alex's hot body wrapped around his hard shaft and watching as the man rode him, cheeks flushed in pleasure, tightened his sac, signaling his impending orgasm. Not even five minutes had gone by when he felt the tingling at the base of his spine. His toes curled as the first spurt erupted from his cock, and he couldn't quite find the strength to muffle his sharp cry or the grunts with each subsequent jet of fluid.

Gabriel collapsed into the wall, his legs shaking, his hand still squeezing his softening flesh. It took until the water began to cool for him to find the energy to push away from the wall and briskly finish his shower. He turned the water off and sighed tiredly, stepping out of the tub to grab a towel. He wrapped the towel around his waist when he'd finished drying off and picked up his clothing. Thankfully, Tank was fast asleep when Gabriel exited the bathroom, and he quietly dressed, pulling on a pair of sweatpants and a tank top he'd brought with him. The sheets were cool against his heated skin, and he sighed tiredly, closing his eyes almost immediately. He needed to keep his mind on the mission at hand, not on the emerald eyes and soft, pale skin of a certain Deviant. Distractions could get you killed.

· · ·

G ABRIEL rose with the sun, beginning his usual morning routine of a hundred push-ups and a protein bar afterward while he dressed. Tank woke as he was brushing his teeth. "I think we should head over there as early as possible. Catch him first thing," he called out to Tank between rinsing out his mouth.

Appearing in the doorway, Tank yawned and scratched his abs. "Sure thing, boss. I need to piss something fierce, though."

The simple act of getting ready for their mission made Gabriel smile. At least this way he knew what was expected of him. The typical routine and preparations calmed him faster than anything else. He perched on the edge of the bed, flipping on the news to look for any further mention of Alex and his brother. It seemed the story about the armed robbery had become old news. There was no reference to the robbery or the twins on any channel.

As soon as Tank finished, they were out the door. Gabriel turned in the key to the desk clerk and climbed back into the SUV. It didn't take more than five minutes to reach their destination from there, and they pulled along the curb across the street from the warehouse. Gabriel discreetly swept the surrounding buildings, noting the broken windows and graffiti on the brick walls. "Keep your eyes open," he instructed Tank as he exited the vehicle.

"The kid's been living here?" Tank grumbled, eyeing the trash littering the sidewalk and the dirty, grimy glass windows not already busted in by some kid looking for a bit of trouble. A painted sign, old and faded, on the side of the building stated Roscoe's Machinery and Parts. The warehouse looked almost ready to fall down, and clearly hadn't been in use for quite a bit of time. A fire escape hung precariously over the main entrance by a single shred of metal, and appeared as if a slight breeze would send it tumbling down. There were other warehouses lining the street, all in some sort of disrepair or another.

"That's what Bryan's contact said." Gabriel surreptitiously slid his gun from its holster, keeping it close to his side to avoid drawing attention. The hairs on his neck tingled, and he could sense someone watching them. "I don't like this. Be careful."

They cautiously entered the front door of the warehouse, instantly assaulted with the smell of musty dankness, rotting trash, and dried up urine. Old machinery, long since abandoned by the previous owners, sat lurking in the dim light, almost giving the place a feel of a suspenseful horror movie. It appeared homeless vagrants used the warehouse frequently. A couple of dirty mattresses lay in the corner; one in particular was currently occupied. Gabriel flicked the tip of his gun toward the lump of rags, indicating to Tank they should check it out.

Treading carefully, both men kept their eyes on the mattress, watching for movement. Tank used his boot to push the soiled, ratty blanket back and immediately crouched down beside the body. It wasn't the Deviant they were sent for. A white male, possibly midforties, with stringy blond hair and bruised flesh lay on his back, his right arm at an odd angle from his body. The man's eyes were opened wide in an expression of fright. His tongue, purpled and swollen, hung out of his cracked lips. Someone had done a number on the poor bastard. No telling if the man had been a Deviant or a Normal, or if the one who'd killed him was a Deviant or Normal.

A pipe hitting the floor toward the back of the building sent them quickly to their feet and stealthily heading in the direction of the sound. Sneakers slapping against the damp concrete signaled someone was aware of their presence.

Gabriel brought his gun up and followed the noise, his eyes scanning every possible exit. Dark red flashed through a door ahead of him, the pipe crashing down in the person's attempt to run. "Stop!" he shouted, cocking his gun as he pursued.

The sight of a scared face a split second before the door slammed shut confirmed it was the boy they'd been sent to find. Gabriel swore and shouldered the door open, Tank following on his heels. "We're not going to hurt you," he called, racing through the alley behind the buildings.

Tank broke off down another alley, attempting to cut the kid off. Gabriel kept his eyes on the slender back of the boy in front of him and pushed himself faster. He brought his arm up and tossed out enough of his power to cause the boy to stumble, giving him the chance to get close enough to snag the boy's arm. "Let go!" the boy cried, struggling to free himself.

"Relax, kid." Gabriel attempted to soothe him. "I'm not going to hurt you."

The teenager didn't stop trying to pull free, his eyes wild and panicked. "I didn't kill him! He was already there when I got here!"

Tank came around the end of the building, panting. "There are a few people on the streets, boss. We need to go before we draw attention to ourselves."

A sound of fright from the Deviant brought Gabriel's attention back to the boy. "We're not going to hurt you. We're from the ADA."

Mentioning the agency seemed to do the trick, and the kid stopped struggling, eyeing Gabriel suspiciously. "How do I know you're telling the truth?"

Gabriel let go of his arm and stepped back, holding his hands up, gun pointed skyward. "Because if I'd wanted to hurt you, I would have done so already. You weren't exactly a hard target. I could have shot you in the back when you ran away. We just want to talk to you."

Tank stood watching carefully in case the teenager chose to run. His stance appeared casual, but Gabriel knew better. Gabriel glanced at the boy's appearance, noting the stained clothing, dirty face and hands. He couldn't be more than fifteen, sixteen max, with greasy blond hair, dark hazel eyes, and a couple of inches taller than Alex. The clothing was too baggy for Gabriel to gauge how skinny the kid actually was. "What's your name?"

"Isaac."

"My name is Gabriel. I work for the ADA. We were sent to help you." Gabriel jerked his thumb over his shoulder, back the way they'd come. "You said you found the body?"

Fear once more entered Isaac's face. "Yes. I've only been staying here a couple of weeks. They kicked me out of the last place when they discovered what I am. I've been staying in an empty office."

"How old are you? How long have you been on the streets?" he asked quietly.

Isaac shifted uneasily from foot to foot, pulling the red hooded sweatshirt he wore tighter around himself. "I'm eighteen. Been living wherever I could for about six months. My dad was killed in one of the camps. I figured it would be safer to be on the streets than in one of them."

Gabriel's lips tightened into a thin line. The government still thought the camps were for their protection, despite the many attempts Normals made to wipe them out. "Do you know what the ADA is?"

Nodding tensely, Isaac nervously chewed his bottom lip. "My dad told me about it. They help Deviants who have nowhere else to go."

"We help Deviants to learn to control their powers, acclimate them to living among Normals, and provide enough financial aid to get you on your feet." Gabriel slipped the gun into its holster, safety lock in place.

"How do I know you're really from the ADA?" Isaac demanded.

Not an uncommon question whenever Gabriel approached one of the Deviants they were sent to help. "I could show you a badge, but how would you know it's real? All I can do is show you. Like I said before, if we'd wanted to hurt you, we could have done so already."

The teenager studied them for a long moment. "Do you really have a badge?"

Gabriel laughed and shook his head. "No. It's not that kind of agency, kid. We tend to avoid advertising who we are. Most people don't even know how to locate our head-quarters."

"If I don't like it, I can leave?" Isaac eyed Gabriel carefully.

"If you still want to leave after seeing the farmhouse and meeting the others that live there, I'll take you anywhere you want to go," Gabriel promised.

With a slightly jerky shrug, Isaac agreed. "Okay. I'll check it out, I guess. Most anything's better than the shit hole I've been living in."

Gabriel couldn't agree more with the boy, but didn't voice his thoughts. "You hungry?" he asked abruptly.

Isaac nodded again, this time almost eagerly. Gabriel's stomach churned at how easily humans could turn on one another and allow a teenage boy to starve just because he wasn't what was considered "normal." "Why don't we go grab something to eat, and we can sit down and talk?"

The three of them headed back toward the SUV. Tank followed behind, still keeping a close eye on the kid in case he decided to bolt again. They found a fast food restaurant and ordered a breakfast of eggs and bacon, finding a place outside to eat. Isaac wolfed down the food so fast it made

Gabriel's throat tight just watching him. "So tell me about this farmhouse?" Isaac asked when he'd finished.

For the next thirty minutes, Gabriel spoke about the ADA, what they did, about the people who lived there and why Bryan had started the agency. By the time he'd finished, Isaac seemed more comfortable around the two of them. "I'll go with you, but if I don't like it, I'm leaving." He repeated his earlier words, his fingers twisting a napkin into little pieces.

"Of course. Like I said, I'll take you anywhere you'd like to go," Gabriel promised again.

"How far is this place?"

Tank still hadn't said much. He'd kept his eyes trained on the other Deviant almost the entire time they'd been sitting there. "Don't worry about it, kid," Tank grunted.

Surprise brought Gabriel's eyebrow arching up at the big muscled wall of a man, but he kept silent. "I need to use the bathroom," Isaac said abruptly, standing.

As soon as Isaac entered the building, Gabriel turned to Tank. "What's going on?"

"I don't like him. Something about him seems wrong. He accepted going with us way too easily for a kid who's been living on the streets for six months."

"Come on, Tank. He's eighteen. What the hell do you think he's going to do?" Gabriel demanded.

"Knowing the world we live in, you have to ask that?" Tank spat, shoving up from his seat. "Remember, even a pup like him could be dangerous. We don't really know what his abilities are."

"What kind of world do we live in if we start becoming suspicious of a kid?" Gabriel stood up, palms flat on the table.

Tank's lip curled at the corner, his muscles bulging in his aggravation. "The kind where we protect ourselves, boss. The kind where we trust our instincts, and my instincts say that kid is dirty."

"We can't just leave him here based on your gut feeling." Gabriel heard the door open behind him. "All we can do is give him a chance to prove it."

Stepping back from the table, he turned toward Isaac. "We should get going if we want to make it back to the agency by lunchtime."

They piled into the SUV, and Isaac promptly fell asleep in the backseat, leaving Gabriel and Tank to their thoughts. The ride was once more made in relative silence. Tension hung between the two men, a thick curtain blocking the urge for conversation. Tank's words rang in Gabriel's mind. Maybe Tank's instincts were right, but how could they just leave the boy on the street because Tank felt the kid spelled trouble? He'd address his team member's concerns with Bryan when they returned to the farmhouse, allow him to decide what they should do.

Anticipation set in the closer they got to the agency, causing Gabriel's blood to rush faster through his veins. His fingers tapped an antsy, noiseless beat against his upper thigh, one he didn't even realize he was making. He stared unseeingly out of the window, watching the trees and other cars fly by.

"Anxious to get back, boss?" Tank asked, his eyes flicking to Gabriel's hand.

Gabriel immediately clenched his hand into a fist. "Always am after a mission," he lied.

Tank grunted but didn't reply, merely smirking at Gabriel's words.

8

ALEX

"**F**IGHTING for your life isn't about being tough or macho," Jackal stated calmly, twisting the large, very sharp double edged knife in his hands expertly. "It's about staying alive. It's about being focused on a goal and achieving that goal by any means necessary."

Alex eyed the shiny blade warily. He still didn't want to do this, but if Gabriel wanted him to learn it, he would.

"You have to let go of who you are and how you think. Holding back isn't going to save your life or anyone else's. It's just going to leave you open for your attacker to hurt you and kill you." Jackal suddenly spun and threw the knife toward the nearby target. The knife hit with a very loud thwack and Alex winced, biting his lip hard.

Striding forward, Jackal yanked the knife out of the target. "I'm going to show you how to disarm your attacker, where to strike to take them out, and the best types of blades to use. This is a double edged blade and is one of the better blades to use since both sides are sharp and you can use either edge to cut your attacker." He turned the blade around and grabbed Alex's wrist, setting the handle in his hand. "The handle should be slightly longer than your palm so that you can strike your opponent with it. Like this one, some knives have a metal pommel on the butt to make striking more effective.

"One of the biggest indicators of an opponent's skill with a knife is the hold they have on the handle. There are four styles of grip: a fencer's grip, the hammer grip, the reverse grip, and the ice pick grip. The fencer's grip, the one I least recommend, as if your hand is struck you may very well drop the knife, is when you hold the handle between your thumb and forefinger, allowing the other fingers to wrap loosely around the rest of the handle." Jackal moved Alex's fingers, showing him the grip. "Ever seen the way a fencer holds their weapon? The point is held out toward your attacker, but despite allowing you maximum reach for the blade, it's the least effective of the four."

Jackal repositioned the knife, turning the blade along Alex's wrist, one edge facing outward. "This is the reverse grip. You'll see the blade is run along the inside of your wrist. The grip hides the knife, but in order to strike your attacker you have to be close to them. Also not a grip I would necessarily recommend, as it puts you in reach of your opponent.

"The ice pick is just what it implies. The handle is held in your fist with the knife pointing downward," Jackal instructed as he once again moved the knife. "It allows you maximum penetration when trying to cut through protective clothing or body armor. Also not one I would recommend, as you leave your chest open for a strike and easily indicate your attack to your opponent."

"There's so much to remember," Alex murmured softly, shivering at the feel of the heavy handle in his palm. "What's the fourth grip?"

"The fourth and most effective is the hammer grip. You hold it like you would a hammer, in a tight fist with the blade pointing up and one edge pointing outward. Keep your wrist flexible as you move. Your attacker is less likely to knock the blade from your hand, and it allows you to use the butt of the knife to strike with if necessary. You can use this grip to slash, chop, or thrust the knife at your opponent."

Jackal moved behind Alex, kicking his feet slightly apart and putting his right hand under Alex's right elbow while gripping his left wrist and pulling it into his lower stomach. "The next important technique is your stance. You also want to hold the knife out in front of your body with your free hand close to your midsection to protect your vital areas. Your free hand is like a shield, yet you can also use it to parry, throw anything you can, distract them, balance yourself, or even grab your attacker's weapon. Just remember, it's better they cut your hand than to lose your life."

Stepping around Alex, Jackal slid another knife from his weapons vest. "The first thing you want to do is look for open targets. They don't always have to be vital areas. Most people skilled in knife fighting will protect those areas instinctively. Drawing first blood is a psychological thing and gives you a huge advantage. Regardless of where you hit, keep striking them. Disabling them by going for the weapon hand is a good course of action as well.

"A simple cut or stab wound will not stop your attacker. Even a direct stab to the heart can still give them the chance to retaliate. There are multiple soft spots and major arteries in the body. The main ones are here"—Jackal touched the cool steel of the blade to the side of Alex's neck—"here"—he lifted Alex's arm and indicated the fleshy underside of Alex's bicep—"and here." Jackal pressed the knife close to his groin.

"Your opponent will bleed out in minutes, maybe even seconds if the cut is deep enough."

Alex's eyes widened, and he stepped back. "I... I don't know if I can do this." The idea of actually taking someone's life caused his stomach to churn. How could he possibly kill someone?

Frowning, Jackal replied, "You may not have a choice, Alex. Whether you like it or not, you are a Deviant. We don't always have the chance to decide if we want to kill someone. If someone is attacking you and intends on killing you, it's either kill them first or be killed. There are several places you can cut muscles or tendons to disable your opponent, but only disabling them still gives them the opportunity to attack you again. It's also not a smart idea, as you really have to get close to them in order to hit the right tendon."

Alex wanted to go back to the farm, to be safe with his Grams again. He didn't ask to be a Deviant. He didn't even have an active ability like his brother did. Why would anyone think he was dangerous? His eyes burned as his chest tightened, and he rubbed at his heart. Despite knowing Jackal spoke the truth, it still caused bile to rise in his throat, and he found himself unable to speak.

Over the course of the next hour, Jackal instructed him on movement, stance, and disarming his opponent. Some of the moves reminded Alex of the martial arts training he'd already received at the ADA. By the time they'd finished, Alex's clothing clung wetly to his skin, soaked in sweat. He wiped at his forehead with the back of one hand, holding out the knife to Jackal. Jackal shook his head and gently pushed his hand back to him. "Keep it, kid, it's yours."

"But I—"

Jackal cut him short. "Just keep it, Alex. You may never know when you'll need it."

He sighed and nodded. Jackal passed him a sheath to carry it in. "You can strap it to your ankle or just carry it in your waistband."

Jackal stopped him as they were leaving the training room. "I thought like you once, Alex. I didn't think I could ever hurt someone, could ever allow myself to do it, but watching other Deviants die the night the concentration camp was attacked changed something in me. I saw the hatred, the cruelty those Normals carried inside of them for our kind, and I knew if I wanted to survive I had no choice." He squeezed Alex's shoulder lightly. "Sometimes we have to do things we don't want, but we never hurt someone just to hurt them. The people I've killed over the years wanted to kill me or one of the people I care about because they fear us, and the fear they carry makes them hate us."

Alex remembered something Grams once told him and Jason. *"People are afraid of what they don't understand, and that fear makes them do things they wouldn't normally do. Things that may seem horrifying to others, but to them makes perfect sense at the time."*

The sheath of the knife dug into his palm as Alex's grip tightened. "I don't want to be like them."

Surprise entered Jackal's face. "You could never be like them, Alex. Defending yourself is not the same as attacking someone for being who they are."

"Isn't it the same thing, Jackal?" Alex demanded. "Where is my killing them for hating me any different from them killing me because they hate me?"

Jackal stared at him for a long moment, unable to come up with a response to Alex's logic. Finally, he sighed and leaned his shoulder against the doorframe. "You are truly a good person, Alex. And I understand what you're saying, but sometimes those people don't leave us a choice, and it's not always the Normals who want to hurt you. Our own kind will also try to do so if they find something to gain from it. Not all of us, but look at Vincetti. The man locks up Deviants, brainwashes them until they agree to join him or they go insane from the constant torture, and doesn't care one ounce when those Deviants are killed for what he considers his cause."

Before Alex could reply to Jackal, his entire body sang out, and he closed his eyes, breathing deeply. "Gabriel's almost here."

Jackal gaped at Alex. "How can you possibly know that?"

He opened his eyes. "I can feel him," he stated simply.

"You've got it bad, kid," Jackal teased, lightly punching Alex in the shoulder.

Alex flushed and looked down at the ground. "It's not about that. I feel a connection to him."

Cackling, Jackal shot him a look, causing Alex to blush even harder. He glared at Jackal. "I'm serious!"

"Whatever you say, Alex."

The SUV pulled into the drive just as they entered the house, and Alex tried to appear casual as he headed into the living area. A couple of the other Deviants staying at the agency were watching television, while Leon, the teenager staying in the room next to Alex and Jason's, sat in the window seat reading a book. Alex wandered over to Leon's side, peering at the book in pretend interest. "What's up, Alex?" Leon asked without looking up.

"Nothing, just wondering what you're reading," he lied.

Leon turned the page. "It's a book Hayley gave me. Some Normal named Jeremy Thorne supposedly wrote the definitive work on understanding a telepath and their abilities. So far it's a bunch of bullshit."

"How can a Normal understand a telepath?"

Shrugging, Leon snorted. "You know Normals think they know everything about us. They've 'studied' us. Apparently, Jeremy's son was a telepath."

The front door clicked open, and Alex's gaze immediately drifted to the hallway, waiting for a glimpse of Gabriel. Tank lumbered past, followed by a boy who looked around Leon's age. The boy stopped in the doorway and looked around the living room. When his gaze landed on Alex, a strange light entered his eyes, sending a nervous jolt through Alex. Gabriel appeared next to the teenager, and the stranger glanced up at him. "Nice place."

"I'll have one of the others show you around and find you a room," Gabriel replied gruffly. He gestured to Alex, causing dismay to flood him. "Alex, can you give Isaac a tour of the house and take him upstairs to the last bedroom on the left?"

Alex bit his bottom lip but nodded and turned to Isaac. "Hi."

Isaac smirked. "Hey, Alex. So you're my tour guide. Lead on, then!"

While showing Isaac where the dining area and kitchen were, Alex did something he never allowed himself to do out of a sense of guilt and respect for others. He reached out to the other boy's mind to try and understand why Isaac inspired a dark foreboding in the pit of his stomach. He was stunned when he hit a wall, a black void it seemed Isaac held as a shield around him. Very little conversation flowed between them until they entered the bedroom Isaac would be using during his stay.

"You shouldn't try to read other people's thoughts without permission." Isaac sounded coldly amused. "It's not very polite and makes me think you don't like me."

Alex struggled to form words to answer him, but even though Isaac rang false to him, he knew listening in on someone's private thoughts was wrong. His Grams had hammered it home for him many times as a child. He did the only thing he could do. He apologized. "You're right. I'm sorry."

Isaac lifted one shoulder in a seemingly careless shrug. "I've been around long enough to know how to block a telepath out. Too many Deviants in the places I've been not to. So, what level are you?"

He almost didn't answer Isaac, but figured telling him wouldn't hurt. "Five."

Whistling, Isaac set the backpack he carried on one of the beds. "Level five, huh? I've heard of level fives but never met one." His eyes raked over Alex briefly in a dismissive manner. "You don't look like a level five, and I certainly didn't think a level five wouldn't be able to get past my weak shield."

The words stung, and Alex clenched his jaw. He may have had to show the kid around the house, but he sure as hell didn't have to stick around once he'd done so. "I have an appointment with Hayley. I'm sure you can find your way back downstairs on your own."

"Sure thing... Alex," Isaac murmured.

Unable to spend another minute in Isaac's presence, Alex strode out of the room as quickly as possible. Something felt off about the newest addition to the misfits living in the farmhouse. He couldn't put his finger on why, but the boy rubbed him the wrong way. Maybe it was the way Isaac looked at him or the fact that he could block Alex out so effectively. Whatever the reason, he didn't trust him. He wondered if he should mention his suspicions to Gabriel, but thought better of it. Grams had always taught him to give people the benefit of the doubt, and Isaac hadn't really done anything to warrant his suspicions. For now, he would keep it to himself.

Eager to see Gabriel, Alex figured a good excuse to strike up a conversation would be to tell him about his knife training with Jackal that morning. He searched through the house, and, unable to locate him inside, he figured Gabriel must be in the building set up for training. The sound of fists hitting a punching bag, the hum of voices from the various Deviants exercising or training, and a body hitting the mat of the small sparring ring set up in the middle of the room met his ears as he stepped into the old converted barn. His eyes instantly located Gabriel, who was currently beating the crap out of an old punching bag.

He'd stripped down to a gray tank top, and his muscles bunched and rippled with each punch. Boxing tape protected his knuckles. Alex barely heard Lizard call out a greeting or noticed the wave another Deviant, Bridgette, tossed his way. He hungrily drank in the sight of the tall, dark male who'd captured his attention from the moment he'd laid eyes on the man. Pure lust swam through his veins. Swallowing hard, he managed to paste a smile on his face. Gabriel didn't notice him at first. His focus was entirely on the bag, like he wanted to take out all of his demons on the inanimate object. When he finally registered Alex standing there, he stopped, grabbing hold of the swinging bag.

"Did Isaac settle in okay?" Gabriel asked, his breathing increased from the exertion.

Alex nodded. "He was claiming the free bed as I left him."

"Good," he grunted. "He's had a hard couple of months. We found him living in an abandoned warehouse."

Guilt instantly assailed Alex at his awful thoughts about the teenager. If Gabriel trusted him enough to bring him back to the agency, then he should trust Gabriel to know what he was doing. "I started training with Jackal like you said," he blurted out, flushing at how his tone made him sound as if he were a little kid dying to please their idol.

Gabriel swabbed his face with a hand towel and studied Alex for a moment. "Show me," he demanded.

"Now?" Alex asked in surprise.

"Yes, now. We can go outside if you'd rather not be around so many of the others." Gabriel offered, slinging the hand towel over his shoulder. "I have a couple of knives in my locker. Let me go grab them and I'll meet you by the back door."

Alex swallowed hard. "Okay."

It never occurred to him that Gabriel actually meant for him to attack him with the knife or that the older Deviant would charge him, expecting him to defend himself. So when Gabriel appeared at the back door holding the two knives, Alex nervously took the knife and turned toward the targets lined up against the back of the barn. "No. Face me," Gabriel instructed.

Shocked, Alex swung around to look at him. "What?"

"You're going to fight me. Now come at me."

He shook his head at Gabriel. "No. I can't!"

Scowling, Gabriel held the knife in his hand and rushed at Alex, who was unprepared for the attack. The knife stopped short of his jugular. Alex could feel the blood leaving his face and rushing to his feet. "There is no can't, Alex," Gabriel snapped, his breath whispering over Alex's cheek. "Training is good, but you have to learn how to let the hesitation go, or you'll end up dead."

He stepped back from Alex and moved a few feet away. "Attack me, Alex."

"What if I… what if I hurt you? Shouldn't I be using a fake blade or something?" Alex asked in horror.

"You won't hurt me," Gabriel replied confidently. "And you won't be using a false knife when you're defending yourself, I see no point in training with one. Now, attack me."

Alex still hesitated. His hands shook, and his breathing grew slightly erratic. "Come on, Alex! What if it were your brother in trouble? What if I were going to hurt Jason? Would you just stand there and let me?" Gabriel questioned harshly.

He sucked in a breath at the thought of his brother hurt. "It's not the same thing, though!"

Gabriel growled and used Alex's ability against him. He pushed out images of Jason being hurt and tortured from his mind straight into Alex's. "Is that what you want? To let them continue to hurt your brother?"

The pictures suddenly flooding his mind made Alex cry out in terror and rage. "No! Stop it!" He gripped his head tightly, the cold steel of the handle pressing into his temple. One particularly brutal image of two men holding Jason down while they repeatedly stabbed his brother sent Alex over the edge, and he raced headlong at Gabriel. "No more!"

Their bodies collided. Gabriel grunted loudly, and then they were falling. They hit the grass with a thud. It took a moment for Alex to catch his breath, and then he immediately sat up, frantically searching Gabriel's body for wounds. "Oh, God!" he cried as he ran his hands over Gabriel's chest. "Where's the knife?"

He heard Gabriel suck in a breath, and then he realized he straddled Gabriel, his bottom pressed firmly into Gabriel's groin. His eyes widened at the feel of the hard cock poking against him. Jackal had been right. Gabriel wanted him. Experimentally, he shifted in Gabriel's lap, relishing the way Gabriel's body seemed to shudder. "Are you hurt?" Alex asked breathlessly, his hands stilling on the bigger man's chest.

"No," Gabriel ground out, his honey-colored eyes glittering up at him, an expression in them that Alex would swear was lust. "It's in my hand."

A few seconds went by before his words sank in. "What is?" he murmured, distracted by the desire racing through his veins.

"The knife." The sun glinted off the blade as Gabriel laid it in the grass next to them.

The world seemed to still. The sounds from the others training faded away, leaving only that of their unsteady breathing. Alex tilted his hips forward, shivering at the feel of his own aching flesh rubbing into Gabriel's belly. "Alex...." Gabriel's chest rumbled with the utterance of his name.

He moved again, his eyes closing on a deep intake of breath at the sheer pleasure coursing through his groin. Gabriel's hands gripped his thighs. "Alex, stop."

Alex opened his eyes once more. He licked his lips, relishing the way Gabriel's gaze followed the pink flesh. "I don't want to stop, Gabe." Leaning down, he lightly brushed his mouth across Gabriel's. "I want you," he whispered.

The older Deviant closed his eyes for a brief moment, seeming to gather himself. When Alex could see the golden orbs once more, Gabriel carefully rolled until he was on top of him. "You may think you want me, kid, but you have no idea what you're asking for."

Gabriel swiftly rose to his feet and held out his hand to Alex. "I'm too old, too tired, and too damaged. Find someone your own age with less baggage," he stated flatly as he helped Alex to stand and stalked away.

Watching Gabriel walk toward the house, Alex hugged himself. Sadness ate at Alex's heart: for Gabriel, for himself, and for the man Gabriel had lost. Whatever had happened years ago left the man believing that he was broken. Grams' voice rang through his mind, *"No matter how deep the scars go, a person's soul can always be healed. They just need someone who doesn't give up when their thorns prick your skin."*

His grandmother had always had faith in people. She'd spent her life helping others, even when they didn't ask for or want it. Alex could never comprehend why she'd refused to give up on the ones who never thanked her or offered a hand in return. Seeing the depth of Gabriel's pain, the refusal to allow anyone close to him, made Alex realize what his Grams meant with her words. It helped him to understand exactly why she'd always break through the thorns despite how badly they cut her. Determination set in. He would make Gabriel see that he was a good man and he wasn't broken. Alex set his jaw, picked up the knife from the grass, and returned it to the training barn before heading up to the farmhouse. If Gabriel thought he'd get off so easily, the man had another thought coming.

At dinner, Alex found himself at a place far down the table from Gabriel. Isaac had taken the open seat to Gabriel's left, while Jackal occupied the seat on his right. Dinner was the usual rowdy affair. The dining room only contained enough seating for half the Deviants in the agency, so they ate in shifts. The first group ate at five, and the second half came in at six. Lizard and Jackal spent most of the hour ribbing each other or cracking jokes. Alex smiled several times, but it didn't quite reach his eyes. Isaac seemed to cling to Gabriel throughout dinner, leaning into his side or touching his arm continuously. The fact that Gabriel didn't brush him off the way he did Alex hurt. He knew Gabriel felt sorry for Isaac, and that concept was the only thing keeping him from walking over and physically shoving the younger Deviant away.

He knew Isaac didn't like him. He could practically feel the dislike rolling off of him. Somehow Isaac seemed to have picked up on his interest in Gabriel and was playing on it to annoy Alex. "Alex?" Jason disrupted his brooding.

"What?" he asked in a surly voice, taking his frustration out on his brother.

Jason lifted an eyebrow at him but didn't comment on his tone. "Can I join you and Jackal for your training tomorrow?"

"Training?"

"Using a knife to fight."

"Oh. Yeah, sure, whatever." Disappointment flared in

Alex's chest. He'd hoped Gabriel would take over the training when he got back.

"Knife fighting?" Isaac asked interestedly. "Can I join you?"

Alex opened his mouth to vehemently refuse, but Gabriel nodded and replied, "That would be a great idea. I'm sure Jackal wouldn't mind another student."

Scowling, Alex dropped his fork on his plate with a loud clang and stood abruptly. "I'm finished."

Jason's eyes bored a hole in his back as he stalked into the kitchen and dropped his plate in the sink. He knew he was acting like a child, yet he couldn't stop. Preston stood at the stove stirring another pot of soup. "Something wrong, Alex?"

"No."

"You sure? You seem a bit upset." Preston tapped the utensil against the side of the pot and set it down on the counter. "You know you can talk to me no matter what."

Alex felt tempted, but thought better of it and shook his head. "Thanks, Preston. I'll be fine."

"All right. Just remember I'm here if you need me."

He thanked Preston again and headed upstairs to his room. Hayley had given him a journal to jot down his thoughts in, and his fingers itched to write. Jason would be tied up for at least another half hour, giving Alex some quiet time. He entered the room he shared with his brother, took the journal from his nightstand, and perched on the window seat overlooking the trees behind the farmhouse. The first few pages were of his feelings for Gabriel, their encounter outside, and the intense emotions he held toward Isaac. Then his words wandered in the direction of his training, what he'd learned since coming to the ADA and his disbelief of ever using those new techniques against someone. How could he intentionally hurt someone? Gabriel said he'd do what he had to, but could he really harm another person just to save himself?

The images Gabriel had forced into his mind flashed through his head, and his fingers tightened on the pen. Would he be able to do it to save his brother? The surge of anger at seeing his brother tortured was not something he'd ever felt before. He'd always believed himself to be peaceful. Grams raised him to use his mind instead of reacting as Jason did. Yet he couldn't allow someone to hurt his twin. Jason would never let anyone do that to him. Was the world really as bad as Gabriel said? Didn't those men who attacked Gabriel prove it was? Or when those people in the diner back home chased after them, forcing him and Jason to run, to leave their home out of fear of worse? Despite all of the facts shown to Alex, he found it hard to consider the whole world to be corrupt. There were still good people in the world. Bryan was a Normal, and he'd started the agency to help Deviants. If he lost the hope he carried inside of him that one day the majority of the population would begin to accept Deviants, then he'd be just as bad as Vincetti.

"Want to tell me what that was all about downstairs?" Jason demanded from the doorway.

Alex shut his journal and hugged it to his chest, staring out the window. "It's nothing."

"It's obviously something, or you wouldn't have thrown a temper tantrum," Jason replied sarcastically. He moved over to the window and sat next to Alex, leaning his head on his twin's shoulder. "I've never seen you like that before, Alex. Growing up you were always the cool one, the calm one, the responsible twin. What's going on?"

Alex knew he wouldn't be able to hide his emotions from his brother. Sighing, he rested his cheek against the top of Jason's head. "It's hard for me here, Jace. They want to train me in all these ways to hurt someone, and I don't even know if I can. And the new kid, Isaac, something isn't right about him. I tried to give him the benefit of the doubt, but I can't ignore the way my instincts are saying something is wrong with him."

"Wouldn't have anything to do with the way he is around Gabriel, would it?" Jason asked softly.

"Jace...."

"I know how you feel about him, Alex. Everyone can see the way you look at him. You know I have always supported you in every way possible, but he's not good for you. He's scarred. Jackal told me something really bad happened to him a few years ago, and he's never recovered from it."

"You think I don't know that?" Alex fidgeted slightly. "Don't you remember how Grams always used to say look past the outside? Look past the thorns? He's not damaged, Jace. I know he's not. He just thinks he is."

Jason sighed, entwining his fingers with Alex's free hand. "I know you want to think the way Grams did, Alex, but you can't save everyone, no matter what she believed."

"I have to try. I need to. I... I love him, Jace."

Silence met his declaration. Alex sensed his brother's concern. "I know he may never love me back, but when you love someone, they matter more than your own desires."

Sitting up, Jason gave him a pained smile and reached up to cup his brother's cheek. "I'll be there for you, Alex, no matter what. Just... just be careful. I need you."

"What do you think is going to happen to me?" Alex gave a strained chuckle.

"You're like Grams, Alex. When you feel something, you feel it so strong that it can consume you. I just don't want to see you get hurt." Jason stared out over the back field behind the farmhouse. "I'll help keep an eye on Isaac. Your instincts about people are usually right, even when you don't listen in on their thoughts."

"Thanks, Jace." Alex stroked his hand over Jason's hair, trailing his fingers through the long, dark strands. Even as kids, they'd been overly touchy feely with each other. He supposed it came from being twins, practically two halves of a whole. They'd grown careful where they expressed their affection for each other after an incident in their home town where rumors started of their relationship being incestuous. Alex loved his brother, but had never thought of anything more than being brothers. "I love you, Jace."

Jace hummed contentedly, snuggling in deeper to his brother's side. "Love you, too, Alex."

9

GABRIEL

ABRIEL watched Alex stalk from the dining room, the hand not holding his fork clenched into a fist in his lap. He fought the urge to follow the younger Deviant. He sensed Alex's dislike of Isaac and the way the teenager clung to him. Admittedly, he allowed Isaac to cling to him, using the boy to push Alex away. Yet it felt wrong. His conscience prickled fiercely. He still felt Alex deserved better, but it didn't stop him from wanting the dark-haired male.

His appetite gone, Gabriel set his fork on the plate and stood from the table. "Are you leaving?" Isaac asked, pouting up at him.

"Can't eat anymore," he answered brusquely, picking up his dishes to bring into the kitchen.

Preston smiled at him when he entered the room. "Hey, Gabe. How's it going?"

"Good, Pres. You?" He set the plate in the sink.

"Excellent! Found out some great news today. Hayley is pregnant!"

"That's outstanding, Preston! I'm happy for you both."

Gabriel clapped Preston on the back. He knew the two of them had been trying for a long time to have a baby. "When is it due?"

"April. I can hardly believe it. We didn't think it was going to happen." Preston's beaming smile dimmed slightly. "I just wish we were going to be bringing him or her into a better world. It disgusts me that there's so much hatred and violence now. I can't imagine what we'll do if the baby is born a Deviant."

Preston seemed to realize what he'd said and gave Gabriel a chagrinned look. "Sorry, Gabe. There's nothing wrong with being a Deviant. In fact, I think it's amazing what some Deviants can do."

"But it's safer to be born a Normal," Gabriel interrupted quietly. "For the baby's sake, I hope they're born a Normal, Pres. In this world, being born anything else leads to a life not easily lived. Always looking over their shoulder, wondering if someone is going to discover what they are, if they're going to walk out of their house tomorrow and end up dead or worse, is not something I would wish on anyone."

Preston grimaced and lightly touched Gabriel's arm. "It will change, Gabriel. You have to know you won't always be feared."

"Do I?" Gabriel asked bitterly. "The three Normals who attacked me would say otherwise."

"Those are only three in a whole world full of people, Gabe."

Gabriel ran his hand through his hair in frustration. "How can you have so much faith, Preston?"

Smiling gently, Preston replied, "Because faith is all we have. If we lose faith and hope, what else is there? What separates us from Deviants like Vincetti?"

"A soul," Gabriel replied darkly.

Preston laughed. "Well there is that too, but I like to think there's more."

Gabriel finally gave in and grinned, clapping Preston on the back. "Let's hope so, Pres."

A few minutes later, Gabriel left the kitchen and headed toward the back of the house. Light shone from beneath Bryan's office door, indicating the man was still working. He knocked and waited for a reply, but when none came, he tried the door handle. Pushing it open, he entered to find Bryan asleep on the leather couch in the room. Gabriel smiled softly and quietly closed the door before treading carefully over to the sofa.

Bryan lay on his side facing the back cushions, one fist propped under his cheek, the other hand lightly gripping the pillow. It always amused Gabriel how mature and graceful Bryan was when awake, yet so childlike when asleep. Reaching down, he gently stroked his boss's cheek, missing the connection they had more than ever. He'd felt as if he were a small sailboat set free from its dock since the day Bryan ended it. With him, Gabriel at least had an anchor holding him in place. But wasn't it wrong to stay with the man if it wasn't love? He knew why Bryan put a stop to their relationship and even agreed, but it didn't stop him from missing the man.

"You shouldn't be touching me like that," Bryan murmured, slowly opening his eyes to look up at Gabriel.

"Why?" Gabriel asked softly. "I miss you."

Pain flashed over Bryan's face for a split second, and Gabriel jerked his hand away as he backed up from the couch. "Bryan," he whispered, his heart aching at the pain he caused his best friend.

Bryan sat up, a sad smile flitting over his lips. "It's not your fault, Gabe. I knew when we went into it, it was nothing more than a physical relationship with you."

Gabriel sank down into one of the leather office chairs and dropped his head into his hands. He'd been hurting Bryan, still was, and didn't even know it. "I'm so sorry, Bry."

Tender hands pulled Gabriel's away from his face. Gray eyes peered into his. "I never blamed you, Gabe. We both knew the stakes, and I let my feelings get involved."

Now he knew why Bryan had ended it so abruptly, why he'd never explained it. Bryan fell in love with him, and he couldn't bear being hurt any longer. "You are the one person in my life, Bryan, that I care about more than anything else. I would never do anything to hurt you." He reached up to cup Bryan's cheek, running his thumb over the man's bottom lip.

Bryan gripped Gabriel's wrist, leaning into the caress for a split second, eyes closed. "I know you wouldn't, Gabe. I'm the one who changed the rules midgame, not you. I knew you loved me, but you weren't *in* love with me." He pulled away from Gabriel's touch and stood from his crouch to walk over to the desk. "It wasn't meant to be."

Gabriel watched sadly as Bryan distanced himself once more. He opened his mouth to speak, but Bryan cut him off. "Chris informed me of a new concentration camp set up outside of Atlantic City, NJ. The papers were full of information pertaining to the location and how many Deviants reside there. I don't think they could advertise any further on the whereabouts." The last bit was stated in a sarcastic tone.

Chris created a program that searched through thousands of Internet websites, combing for any information about Deviants, concentration camps, or Vincetti. "Are we going to do anything?"

Shaking his head, Bryan sank down into his office chair and sighed. "There's nothing we can do. We don't have the space here, and the more Deviants we have on the property the further we risk exposure. There's been talk of Normals trying to locate the agency. Who knows what they'll do if they find us."

Preston's words of faith echoed in Gabriel's mind. How could he possibly have faith when every day a new danger threatened their safety? "We'll beef up security. Tighten patrols and make sure no one is alone on their shift."

"We have to be careful, Gabe. The others can't know or they may become frightened. If the ADA isn't safe, where else can they go?"

Gabriel's mouth tightened, and he balled his hands into fists. He'd fought these last five years to never feel helpless again, but knowing that the people he cared about most could be hurt just for being who they were meant to be brought that feeling slamming back into his chest like a sledge hammer. "We'll protect them, Bryan. I won't let anything happen to them."

The clock flashed over to midnight when Gabriel finally stood to leave. He told Bryan good-night and headed upstairs to his room. Several of the others were still awake. He could hear them moving around their rooms or talking to one another. Bryan was right. The ADA meant protection and home to the Deviants living there. Gabriel remembered each rescue: the living conditions he found them in, the fear they wore as if it were a cloak, even some who were injured during an attempt on their life at the concentration camps. The government did nothing to protect the Deviants. They allowed them to live in squalor, to be attacked by Normals, and murdered in their beds.

The Deviants staying at the farmhouse were taught the necessary survival skills: defense, disguise, and awareness. They were given lessons in hand-to-hand combat as well as training in how to manage their powers more effectively. Once the Deviant felt confident enough in their training and abilities, they were relocated and given a new identity with the ADA's assistance. The organization had saved many lives in the past five years. More than Gabriel could count or remember. Only a few remained etched in his memory. Alex would be one of them.

He stripped off his clothing, tossing it into the hamper in his closet before pulling on a pair of sweatpants. Yanking the sheets back, he sat on the edge of the bed and slipped beneath the covers. The same question he asked himself every night whispered through his mind. What would tomorrow bring?

S URPRISINGLY, the next few days were uneventful. Chris kept them updated on the concentration camp while Gabriel continued teaching Alex meditation techniques and started him on basic martial arts. He postponed Jackal's continuing education of knife fighting to concentrate on Alex in case the agency was attacked. For the better part of the morning several days after Bryan's confession, the two of them were seated out by the small creek running through the trees behind the house. Alex would need a clear head to keep others out of his mind.

"Very good, Alex," Gabriel praised, slowly standing. "We're going to work on basic martial arts movements again. The more you know how to defend yourself the better, because if you come across that one person who knows how to use your gifts against you or block out your gifts they become useless to protect yourself."

Alex nodded, concentrating hard. He wanted to make Gabriel proud of him and to show the older Deviant he wouldn't be more baggage on his shoulders. He stood, waiting for instructions from Gabriel.

"Martial arts aren't like you see in the movies. It takes years to perfect, and even a black belt can't take out multiple attackers with one flying leap through the air. Those types of moves are cool to watch, but aren't the most effective way to defend yourself in real life. The basic techniques involve blocks, footwork, stances, submissions, takedowns, strikes, and throws.

"As I'm sure Jackal explained, blocking is the act of stopping an opponent's strike. Usually the arm is used in martial arts, but other appendages may be also be used. Footwork, though it may not sound impressive, is an absolute must have skill. Stances are also as important."

Gabriel paused, eyeing Alex's clothing. "We'll have to see if we have a karate *gi* to fit you. I'll check in storage when we're finished here. Submissions are basically joint locks or choke holds. If you've ever watched wrestling, although to me that's all a farce, you'll see those are generally done on the ground, but there are some which can be executed while standing. These are used to attempt to force your opponent to give up or submit. You'll want to be careful with these, because if they refuse to give up then you could cause serious damage. That's only in training. If you ever need to use it, don't give your opponent the chance to retaliate."

Alex grimaced and shook his head. "I still don't see myself being able to hurt someone on purpose."

"You will if your life or your brother's life depends on it," Gabriel stated flatly. "Don't let this place lull you into a false sense of security. You can't hide here forever. Once you're back in the real world, you'll need all the skills you're learning here to survive."

"But I like it here!" Alex protested.

Gabriel didn't comment, instead he continued with his training. "Takedowns can be extremely effective. I'm sure you can guess it means taking your enemy to the ground. You can do this either with wresting moves, like single and double leg takedowns, or throws. Throws are more defensive than a mere takedown. You rely more on the opponent's strength than your own to take them to the ground."

Alex nodded at him. "The final piece is strikes. They are basically offensive rather than defensive. These can be punches, kicks, head butts, knees, elbows, and can even be used in ground fighting. You want to keep these to when the opponent leaves himself open for a strike. Stay on the defensive until you see a chance to take a shot at him."

Gabriel crouched down slightly, spreading his legs a bit wider than shoulder width, and bent his knees. He held his back straight and pushed his chest out, keeping his hips forward. He pulled his arms in, his elbows jutting out behind him with his fists close to his sides. "The most common stance, used in kung fu and karate, is called the Horse Stance. It is used during exercises and forms. It strengthens your legs and also can be used in actual combat.

"It's called the Horse Stance due to the similarity of riding a horse. Position your legs a bit wider than your shoulders, bend your knees, and keep your back as straight as possible. Push your chest out while keeping your hips forward."

Alex attempted it several times, falling to his bottom over and over until finally he managed a shaky replica of Gabriel's position. "This is harder than it looks," Alex grunted.

He merely nodded in response. "Your legs will ache for some time after as well, but you'll get used to it. This is the most basic of stances, and you should practice holding this position as often as you can for as long as you can."

When Gabriel noticed Alex tiring, he stood straight and beckoned Alex to do the same. "Today we'll work on a couple of stances you can practice on your own. It's not something you can learn overnight. Another stance commonly used is the forward stance. Face me with your shoulders squared and your feet shoulder width apart. Bend your front leg while keeping the back leg straight. Keep both of your feet facing forward and most of your weight on the front foot. Throw your left fist forward while pulling your right fist back, close to your side. This stance allows you to put a great deal of power into a strike or block. However, it does not allow much flexibility or agility."

After several moments, Gabriel switched to another called the Monkey Stance. "This is referred to as the dodging stance and allows you to dodge left to right or front to back. Place your hands on your hips and keep your feet together. Take your right toe and place it next to your left instep. Let your knee point forward and your heel point straight up. Bend your left knee and squat down. Hold it there. With enough practice, you'll eventually be able to sink down far enough to where you're able to allow your thigh to be parallel with the floor."

He called a halt to the workout when he saw Alex's exhaustion. They'd been practicing for about four hours now. Guilt set in when Alex sank to the ground and started rubbing at the muscles in his legs. Gabriel grimaced and knelt down beside him. "I'm sorry, Alex. I tend to be single-minded when I'm training."

"I'm fine, Gabriel. I want to learn everything you can teach me," Alex replied, smiling shakily.

"Come up to the house. Take a hot shower, throw on a pair of shorts, and meet me in my room. I have an ointment that will help," Gabriel offered without thinking. He could have bitten his tongue off a few seconds later when the reality of what he'd said sank in. The thought of his hands on Alex's legs and thighs made him stifle a groan.

Surprise flashed over Alex's face, but the teenager didn't say anything and merely stood, walking slowly toward the house. Gabriel watched him go for a moment before getting to his own feet and heading in through the back door. Most of the house was empty, since training took place throughout the day. He could pick up the sounds of Chris's computer keys clacking away, and he smiled. He gradually took the stairs to the second floor, snagging a towel from the closet on his way to his room. Alex would be a few moments, and he wanted to grab a cold shower in the hopes it would help control his body, being so close to the younger man.

Not all of the rooms had their own private bathroom. There were only two, his and Bryan's. Once inside, he snapped the cold water on and set out the ointment on his nightstand. Stripping his clothes off, he gritted his teeth as he stepped beneath the stinging water and allowed it to rinse away the dirt and sweat. He tipped his head back, soaking his hair, and picked up the shampoo bottle. An image of his hands gliding over Alex's silky locks went straight to his groin, despite the icy water running down his body. He growled under his breath and forced the thought away. The more time he spent around Alex, the worse it got. The idea of saying to hell with it and letting his body control him rose to the forefront of his mind more than once, but how could he possibly do that to Alex? Alex deserved better than that. Gabriel was the responsible person here. He had to be the one to keep a cool head, and not just from taking a freezing shower.

"Gabriel?" Alex's voice through the wood of his bathroom door startled him. He dropped the shampoo and swore.

"I'll be out in a minute. Just have a seat on the bed."

He hurriedly picked up the bottle and washed his hair. The realization didn't hit him until he turned off the water, stepped from the shower, and grabbed his towel. He'd forgotten to bring clothing with him into the bathroom. It had never been a problem before, but the knowledge of walking almost naked into the bedroom while Alex sat on his bed made him groan aloud this time. "Gabriel, are you okay?" Alex called out.

"I'm fine," he bit out. Steeling himself, he tied the suddenly all too small towel around his waist and opened the door. Alex sat cross-legged on the bed, his eyes closed in meditation. Gabriel's prayers that the dark-haired beauty would keep his eyes shut weren't answered.

Those green eyes opened, pinning him in place, and a small intake of air gave away Alex's interest in his still damp bronze chest. Gabriel could see the hunger in the depths of Alex's gaze but attempted to ignore it, striding over to the dresser to grab a pair of sweats and a tank top. "Sorry," he mumbled on his way back to the bathroom. "Not used to someone else being in the room."

"It's okay," Alex replied huskily.

Gabriel could feel Alex's eyes on him as he walked the entire length of the room. It wasn't until he shut the bathroom door behind him that Gabriel released a sigh of relief. His cock had instantly filled at the interest Alex displayed, begging for him to sample the delights of the other Deviant's body. He squeezed his cock hard, trying to force the erection away. The touch merely left him sucking in a deep breath, and he stroked himself, sliding his palm along the stiff shaft. He fantasized about ignoring his conscience, saying fuck it and going back out to the bedroom, shoving Alex down onto the sheets and roughly burying himself in the firm, no doubt virgin, backside. The thought of Alex's tight heat engulfing his aching prick brought him straight to the edge. He grunted as he came, pure liquid flame racing through his body and splattering the floor, spilling over his grasping fingers. His knees shook at the intense orgasm, and it took several breaths before he found the strength to return to standing upright. He mopped up the floor with his towel and wiped his hand clean of the salty fluids.

He couldn't quite meet Alex's eyes when he exited the bathroom. It felt as though what he'd done could be seen all over his face, despite how ludicrous that sounded. "Lie down on your stomach," he muttered.

Alex turned from his seated position and lay down on his belly, his shorts riding up enough to almost show off the lower curves of his firm rear end. Gabriel wanted to smack himself for suggesting this. At the time all he'd thought of had been Alex's discomfort at holding the stance positions for so long. Not only was Alex's delectable body splayed out on his bed, but the scent of his skin would cling to his sheets, and the shampoo he used would permeate his pillow.

When he hesitated for longer than a few breaths, Alex lifted his head from Gabriel's pillow and turned a questioning gaze on the older Deviant. "Something wrong?"

God, if you only knew, he growled to himself. "No."

He walked over to the bed and sank down on the side. Not only would he be touching Alex, but to effectively massage his legs, he'd be forced to straddle him. Biting back a groan, he snatched up the bottle of massage oil and moved until he sat astride Alex's lower legs. He snapped open the cap and poured a liberal amount in his palm before closing it again and tossing it aside. Rubbing his hands together, he felt the smooth oil slicking up his palms. His hands glistened in the faint light from the nearby lamp as he brought them down to Alex's left leg. "Just relax," he managed to choke out.

Warm skin met his hands, sending lust striking through him once again. He slid his palms along the tight muscles under Alex's skin, clenching his jaw while trying to remind himself why he was no good for the younger man. Alex let out a groan when he hit a particularly tense area. "I'm sorry I pushed you so hard today," Gabriel murmured, pressing his fingers into Alex's thigh and kneading gently.

"It's okay," Alex replied sleepily.

"I just want to make sure you're prepared in case something happens." He switched to the other leg, working up along the calf.

Alex grunted, but didn't respond. Gabriel had the sense Alex was well on his way to falling asleep. Once he'd reached his upper thigh, he instructed Alex to turn over onto his back and slid over to the side, waiting for Alex to move. His eyes immediately strayed to the obvious bulge in the shorts he wore. He could feel his own body responding, despite the release he'd found less than a half hour ago in the bathroom. A lazy heat burned up at him from the intense green of Alex's eyes, a heat he tried to disregard. Without thinking, he leaned over Alex to grab the massage oil from the side table and ended up face to face with him.

Surprise held him still as Alex lightly touched his face, trailing the tips of his fingers over Gabriel's cheekbone and along his nose to his lips. No words were exchanged, just whispers of breath drifting across skin, warmth radiating from where flesh met flesh. Alex brought his other hand up to cup his cheek, and he slowly guided Gabriel's mouth down to his, stopping a mere flick of a tongue away to give him the chance to stop him. But the resolve Gabriel held so tightly to his chest melted away, and he groaned, capturing Alex's lips in a deep kiss, his tongue plundering Alex's mouth wholly and completely. The restraint of holding back brought more passion into the kiss as Gabriel let go, savoring the sweet taste of the younger man beneath him.

Alex hooked his hand around Gabriel's nape, pulling him further into him. He responded eagerly and innocently, his tongue tentatively rubbing over Gabriel's. Gabriel allowed himself free rein to explore Alex's chest, sliding his hand beneath the hem of the T-shirt to touch bare skin. "Gabriel," Alex mewled into his mouth.

The slender yet muscled chest felt exquisite under his palm: warm, supple, firm. Gabriel could feel the outlines of

Alex's ribs and sternum on his way to the hard, pointed nipples. A whimper flooded his mouth the moment the roughened flesh of his palm brushed over one of the stiff nubs begging to be sucked. The innocent sound awakened the protective urge inside Gabriel even more, and reminded him of why he could never be with the other Deviant. He broke the kiss on a gasp, ignoring the sound of dismay Alex gave.

Rolling away from Alex, Gabriel sat up and scowled. "That never should have happened."

"Why not?" Alex demanded, sitting up.

Gabriel tried to push away the tenderness seeping into his belly at the site of Alex's disheveled hair and swollen lips. "Because I don't want this."

Alex lifted an eyebrow at the ludicrous lie. "Then why did you kiss me? Touch me? Why are you hard?"

"You don't know much about men, kid," Gabriel snarled. "I haven't fucked in a while. You're a warm, willing body."

Guilt pricked him at the flash of hurt that danced over Alex's features for a moment. He stood from the bed and walked to the window, his back to Alex. "Now get out."

There was silence behind him for a few breaths before he heard the sheets rustle and bare feet pad along the wooden floor to the bedroom door. It seemed almost forever until the soft snick of the door closing reached his ears. Gabriel sank tiredly down to the window seat, dropping his face into his palms. He never should have suggested the massage, never should have touched Alex like that. The more his life came into contact with Alex's, the more darkness he brought into the boy's life. He couldn't drag Alex down into the hell he lived and breathed every day.

"God, Rafe. I wish you were here. I wish it had been me instead of you." Gabriel's voice hitched at the thought of his brother. "How could I have killed my own brother?"

10

ALEX

LEX stared at Gabriel's broad back, his heart aching so hard it felt as if it could burst at any moment. He allowed Gabriel's words to keep him silent, to force his body to stand and walk toward the door. His hand hovered over the knob for a brief second before wrapping around it and turning. The soft snick of the door closing behind him seemed so loud in the quietness of the hallway. He leaned against the wood and breathed slowly, evenly. His body had never felt so alive. The touch of Gabriel's hand on him, the spicy taste of his kiss, the slickness of Gabriel's tongue over his, all of it caused every nerve ending in his body to sing, to dance as if electricity zipped through him. Did Gabriel not feel the connection between them?

The memory of Gabriel's hard length pressing him into the bed, the bulge digging into his thigh, sent a shiver racing down his spine. No, Gabriel hadn't been unaffected by him. A soft smile drifted over Alex's lips. Gabriel wanted him. Alex reminded himself of Gabriel's words outside the training barn yesterday. He just didn't believe he deserved to have him. His hurt over Gabriel's rejection faded, and he pushed away from the door to saunter to his bedroom, an even bigger grin now forming. He'd find a way to break Gabriel's resolve.

Alex spent the rest of the afternoon and evening talking to Jason and relaxing in the common room. Gabriel avoided him for the remainder of the day, and it wasn't until the following morning at breakfast that Alex saw him again. "Good morning, Gabriel," Isaac piped up, smiling.

Looking up from his plate, Alex found Gabriel standing in the doorway with a slight scowl on his face. Alex grinned and winked at Gabriel, stifling a laugh at the frustration that passed over Gabriel's features. "Good morning, Gabe."

Gabriel practically stomped to the seat beside Isaac. Alex didn't even let it faze him this time. The man was using Isaac to hide from Alex, and it amused him greatly. Throughout the entire breakfast, Gabriel steadfastly ignored him, but Alex continued to attempt to bring Gabriel into the conversation by asking his opinion of whatever topic the group discussed. The older Deviant had no choice but to respond. He could practically feel Gabriel gnashing his teeth at being forced to join in on the conversation.

Jason came in about halfway through the meal and plopped down next to Alex. "Hey, bro."

"Hey, Jace," Alex said, smiling happily.

"Happy birthday." Jason nudged him slightly and dropped a small gift onto the table next to Alex's plate.

"It's your birthday, Alex?" Jackal asked loudly, causing everyone at the table to start throwing out birthday greetings.

Laughingly, Alex replied, "It's our birthday."

Jackal gave a chagrined look at Jason. "Sorry. I forgot. You're both so opposite of one another that it's almost easy to forget you're twins."

Alex shrugged. "Jason's never liked getting older, so he

doesn't enjoy celebrating his own birthday, but he does like making a big deal over mine. Although neither of us really enjoys a big fuss being made. Grams usually just made us a cake and let us pick out something in town."

Jason leaned into Alex's side at the mention of Grams, and Alex could feel the melancholy drifting from his brother. He reached down and grasped his twin's hand, squeezing lightly. Even though Jason didn't really talk about his feelings, Alex usually picked up on his brother's emotions. Aside from his telepathic ability, he supposed it came from being twins and them being closer than the average family after everything they'd been through. Other than Grams, they'd never really had anyone but each other.

"Open it," Jason urged, extracting his hand from Alex's and reaching out to fill his plate from the platters of food.

In his pursuit to train and the emotional upheaval in the time since their abduction, Alex had forgotten about their birthday. "I didn't get you anything," he murmured quietly.

His brother waved his hand in a careless gesture. "I don't need anything, bro. You know that."

Alex gave him an exasperated look. "It's not about needing something, Jace. It's about being shown how happy I am you're in the world. I don't know what I'd do without you."

"Let's hope you never have to find out," Jason cackled jokingly.

Sighing at his twin's joke, Alex picked up the small object next to his plate. He could tell it was a book by the shape and weight. He pried up the tape carefully while Jason huffed in exasperation and tapped impatiently on the table. "You always did piss me off with how slow you are to open gifts. Just rip the paper! It's going in the trash anyway."

"Just let me do it my way, Jace!" Alex scowled and

continued to gently open the package. Grams taught him not to waste as they grew up on the farm, so he tended to be cautious on how he unwrapped gifts in case they could reuse the paper. Even though he knew it wouldn't be likely, he still couldn't tear into it. A small gasp slipped free when the paper fell away. "Where did you get this?"

Somehow in the middle of nowhere on a hundred acres Jason managed to find the one book Alex loved more than anything. The same book his grandmother used to read to him as a child and Alex read to her the day she died. Tears stung his eyes, and he blinked them back quickly, the words *The Call of the Wild* blurring into one long string.

"I promised Hayley I'd work it off." Jason flipped the cover over and pointed at the copyright page.

Alex shook his head and tried to push the book toward Jason. "I can't accept this! It's a first edition!"

"Yes, you can and you will." Jason paused, looking down at his hands. "I owe you so much more than the book, Alex. It's my fault we were discovered and haven't had anywhere to call home for over a year. I want to make up for everything."

"What a lovely thought, Jason," Hayley interjected, smiling.

He didn't want to argue in front of the others, so Alex settled for a nod and a murmured, "Thank you."

"You're welcome." Jason ruffled his hair and started stuffing his face.

When Alex finished breakfast, he had a session to attend with Hayley, and wandered to the back of the house after dropping the book off in his room. Her office door stood ajar, and he could see her sitting at her desk, typing something into the computer. They'd had a computer at the farm, but it was so ancient the thing took forever to start up and even longer to load up the Internet. Grams bought it second-hand for them when they started high school level work.

"You coming in, Alex?" Hayley prodded him from his thoughts.

Alex entered her office and shut the door. He sat down in one of the chairs facing her desk. "Sorry, just thinking about Grams."

Hayley gave him a sympathetic look. "We never really talked about how you came to live with your grandmother. Were your parents deceased?"

"No, they weren't." Alex shifted uncomfortably. He didn't really like talking about his parents. He knew his father cared about them. Up until they'd had to leave the farm, he'd sent money to Grams for their care. It was how they'd managed to stay living on the farm without having a job. "Our father sent us to live with Grams when our abilities manifested."

"Why is that? Was he afraid you'd be discovered?" Hayley pried gently.

Alex shrugged. "I'm sure that was part of it as well, but the real reason came down to being because our mother tried to drown us when she realized what we could do."

Hayley made a small sound in her throat. "I'm so sorry, Alex."

"It was a long time ago. I don't even remember them, to be honest. Our father sent money every month to Grams to take care of us. I'm guessing they're still alive, since the money kept coming even after Grams died. They never came to her funeral." Bitterness coated Alex's tone. Even after all this time, they still hadn't found it in them to accept him and Jason enough to at least attend Grams' service. "I guess even then they were afraid of what we could do."

"Do you think it was fear or guilt which kept them away?"

Alex paused to think for a moment. Could they feel

guilty? "If they felt guilty, why not try to see us in the fourteen years we'd been on the farm?"

"Guilt and shame are not easy emotions to deal with. Apologies are never easy either. In my years as a psychiatrist, I've seen more relationships torn apart by shame than any other reason. I wouldn't necessarily say that's why they kept away all this time, but perhaps you could give them the benefit of the doubt." Hayley made a notation on her notebook and glanced back up at Alex. "How's the training going?"

"Pretty good, I guess. I still don't see myself hurting someone like they want me to."

"Why do you think they want you to hurt someone?"

"Isn't that the whole point of learning knife and martial arts fighting? To hurt someone?"

Hayley set her pen down and leaned back in her chair. "Do you really think that is why Gabriel and the others are training you?"

"Isn't it?" Alex challenged. "I'm supposed to use these skills to defend myself, but in the end, it's still hurting someone."

"And you feel it's wrong to hurt someone when they're trying to hurt you?"

"Yes, I do. Isn't there the saying that violence promotes violence? If I hurt someone in the name of defending myself, doesn't that make me the same as them?" Alex traced the arm of the chair, feeling the grooves carved into the wood. "Gabriel showed me images of someone hurting my brother, and I grew angry. I almost hurt him because of that anger, my need to defend my brother. I had a knife in my hand. If we'd have landed wrong when we hit the ground, or if he'd been a fraction of a second too slow, I could have seriously hurt him."

Hayley stood and came around to sit beside him. She

rested her hand on his forearm. "Gabriel knew what he was doing, Alex. He wouldn't have done it if he hadn't. You have to trust him."

"I do trust him!" Alex blurted out, flushing afterward.

She smiled knowingly but didn't comment. "The ADA is here to help Deviants learn to defend themselves if necessary. They aren't training you to hurt people so you can go out and fight. They're showing you skills to use in order to get away if you're discovered. Only you can choose how to use them and when.

"Have you been working on your meditation?" Hayley inquired.

"As much as I am able to. It's kind of hard to meditate and clear your mind when there's people talking in the other rooms or their emotions run high and their thoughts invade my mind," he muttered.

"Perhaps I can have one of the others accompany you to a quieter environment in the early evening hours? If you'd like to, that is."

The thought of getting to spend more time in Gabriel's presence made him perk up slightly. "I'd like that."

"Great. I think Lizard is available." Hayley looked at the clock on the wall over her desk. "We can make it a regular appointment at six each night. At least until you get control of it and are able to tune out the others."

"I thought… isn't Gabriel supposed to be helping me?" he asked while trying to hide his disappointment.

Hayley laughed and nudged Alex lightly. "You have it bad, don't you?"

He tried to deny it, but she stopped him. "It's okay if you like him, Alex. Just be careful. Make sure you don't confuse gratitude or your first crush as love. Gabriel has been through a lot since his abilities manifested, and he's scared to let anyone close to him again, but I've seen the way he looks at you. He cares about you already, no matter how hard he tries to fight it."

"You think so?" Alex murmured.

"Oh, he may try to push you away and act all tough, but it's only a front, a way to protect himself. It's why I'm asking you, as a friend, to be careful with him. Make sure your feelings are really there before you push him into a corner."

He nodded and looked at her somberly. "I don't know if I know what love feels like, but I do know I feel more than just a crush with him."

She patted his hand and stood, going back to her office chair. "Good. Now then, tell me more about the relationship between you and your brother."

They spent the next half hour discussing Jason, Alex's unsettled feelings about Isaac, and it ended back up at the subject of meditation. "I'll talk to Bryan about Isaac, and let's go see if Lizard is around. We'll get you set up with an hour every evening for him to escort you to a quieter place on the property."

"Why do I need someone with me?" Alex asked curiously as they left Hayley's office.

"Unfortunately, even here at the ADA, there's potential for danger. We never allow anyone to go anywhere on the property alone. Everyone goes in pairs." Hayley guided him out of the farmhouse toward the training barn. "The agency's location is kept secret, but there is always the possibility one of our enemies could locate us."

Alex made a small noise in the back of his throat. She squeezed his shoulder gently. "We're prepared if they do, Alex. There's underground tunnels Bryan had built in when he bought the place and other avenues to escape, such as vehicles and the chopper Bear went to pick up the other day."

He'd wondered why he hadn't seen Bear around the

farmhouse for the last couple of days. "Did he go on his own?"

"No, he took Bridgette with him. She drove the SUV back while Bear flew back in the helicopter." They entered the training area, and Hayley called out to Lizard, "Vinnie!"

Lizard scowled at her as he approached. "You know I hate when you use my name."

She waved his protest off. "It is your name, you know. I need you to do me a favor."

"Yeah, yeah. What do you want?"

"For a couple of weeks, I need you to escort Alex in the evening, maybe after dinner, to a more solitary place on the grounds so he can work on his meditation."

Lizard lifted an eyebrow at Hayley. "Isn't Gabriel supposed to be helping the kid?"

Alex glared at Lizard for calling him kid and for acting like he wasn't even there. "I am standing right here, you know!"

"Sorry, Alex. No offense," Lizard apologized. "But Bryan did want him working with you."

Bryan? Why would Bryan want Gabriel to be the one to train him? Alex would have asked, but Hayley stopped him. "Gabriel is still handling his normal duties as well, and I'm requesting you to help Alex. You know no one is supposed to be going anywhere alone, and Alex really needs some quiet space."

"I got it. After dinner okay, Alex?' Lizard looked at him in question.

"Whenever you have time, Lizard. I don't want to be a bother."

"You aren't a bother, Alex," he protested. "Besides, Hayley's right. No one should wander the grounds by themselves."

They set a time for after dinner, and Alex accompanied

Hayley back into the farmhouse. He trudged upstairs to his bedroom, deciding to take a nap for a little while. He thought back over Lizard's claim of Bryan assigning Gabriel to train him. Why would the man push Gabriel to spend time with him? Sighing, he shoved open the door to his room and entered, closing it behind him. His eyes downcast, he didn't notice the small package resting on his pillow until he flopped down on top of the bedspread and it poked him in his cheek.

He sat up and picked up the little white box. No wrapping, no bows, and no name to indicate who left it there. Alex frowned as he tugged the top of the box off, his eyes widening and his breath catching at the gorgeous silver cross on a sterling silver chain inside. He immediately lifted it out, fingering the simple charm. Who'd left such a beautiful gift for him? The cross measured probably about two inches long and an inch wide. He turned the box over, looking for a name, but didn't see anything to give him a clue where it came from.

Alex stood and walked to his mirror, slipping the chain over his head, and studied himself. The chain seemed almost delicate against the tanned skin, the cross glinting as it shifted with each breath he took. Smiling softly, he went back to his bed and lay on his back, enjoying the tinkling sound of the cross sliding on the chain. His Grams would have loved the simple cross. Memories of his grandmother reading to them from her Bible every Sunday flitted through his mind as he began to drift off to sleep. The good memories gradually changed, becoming vicious and unbelievably horrifying.

In the dream he woke to find his twin lying in a pool of blood on the floor of their room. Jason's bright green eyes stared unseeingly up at the ceiling above them, his face twisted in fear. His heart had been wrenched from his chest and dropped carelessly on the carpet beside him. Alex tried to scream for help, but no sound came out. He stood, stumbling over his brother's body while rushing to the door. Pulling it open, he found the hallway littered with the bodies of the other inhabitants of the ADA. Jackal lay in such a grotesque way, his limbs seemingly pulled from their sockets, his jaw broken, leaving his mouth gaping wide. Alex gagged, tears streaming down his cheeks.

"Alex," a voice called from the end of the hallway.

He looked up to see Gabriel standing there, his hands covered in blood, his face twisted and cruel. *"I killed them, Alex."*

"No," Alex whispered, his hand coming up to cover his mouth while shaking his head furiously.

"I did. I killed them, Alex, just like I killed my brother." Gabriel stepped closer, his hand rising up toward Alex.

Alex flinched backward, his breathing coming fast and furious. *"Stop, Gabriel. I know this isn't you."*

Gabriel's power slammed into Alex's chest, nearly caving in his ribcage and causing him to scream out in pain as he flew backward. His lower back cracked into the nightstand, sending the lamp crashing to the floor. He tumbled to the floor after it, glass from the broken light cutting into his palms and forearms. *"You're so pathetic,"* Gabriel spat at him, advancing into the room to tower over him. *"Do you really think someone as powerful as me could be interested in a weak, sniveling little kid? Your feeble attempts to seduce me actually disgust me."*

Pain lanced through Alex's heart, and he struggled to stand, to get away. Gabriel merely laughed maniacally and flicked his fingers at Alex, power surging from the tips to force him back down into the glass. *"Did you truly believe I wanted you? As if you were anything but a plaything. A toy to amuse me until something better came along."*

A noise behind Gabriel alerted Alex they were no longer alone. Isaac appeared in the doorway, a sinister gleam shining in his eyes. He smirked and leaned his shoulder on the doorjamb, crossing his arms over his chest. Alex glared at Isaac. *"You. What did you do to him?"*

Isaac cocked an eyebrow at him, pushing away from the door to stride to where he lay, and crouched near him. He stroked one finger down Alex's cheek. *"Me? What makes you think I did anything to him, Alex? He speaks the truth. You know it deep inside. Why would a man with Gabriel's power and sexuality want a gnat such as you? Did you know his cock tastes as spicy as his lips? And when he comes, mmm, the lusty growl he lets out makes me spunk just from hearing it."*

"No!" Alex shouted, denying what he heard, yet unable to cover his ears or block out the images of Isaac touching Gabriel, of Gabriel fucking the other Deviant.

Isaac looked up at Gabriel, grinning wickedly, and reached out to open the man's jeans. Alex sobbed as Isaac lifted Gabriel's hard shaft free of his clothing, his hand sliding down the length while he leaned forward to swipe his tongue over the weeping tip. Shutting his eyes, Alex tried to block out the sounds. But the reprieve of not having to watch was short lived. *"Open your eyes,"* Gabriel demanded.

"No," Alex pleaded.

Lightning danced along his skin, and he screamed, trying in vain to fight the inevitable. More electricity crackled through him, this time causing his eyes to fly open wide to the sight of Isaac's mouth engulfing Gabriel's prick. Gabriel groaned, his gaze holding Alex's malevolently. His fingers buried in Isaac's hair, he guided the other Deviant's movements. Pleasure built on Gabriel's features, his mouth parting and his breath coming faster. Alex would have given anything in that moment to be able to look away, to stop the awful scene in front of him. A final guttural groan issued from Gabriel, signaling his release and shattering Alex's heart into a thousand pieces.

Isaac drank greedily. He gasped for air when he pulled off, but turned to look into Alex's eyes. *"What should we do with him, Gabe?"*

Alex brought his gaze up to Gabriel, praying in his heart the man he loved would wake up and realize what he was doing. The next words Gabriel spoke froze the blood in his veins. *"Kill him."*

He screamed in terror, willing his muscles to move. "Alex. Alex!" His brother's voice came from far away, shouting over and over. A sharp, stinging pain exploded across one cheek, and Alex sat up, still crying out. "Alex, please wake up!"

Tears poured from Alex's eyes. Jason shook him, hard. "Alex, it's a dream. It's only a dream. Wake up."

Blinking furiously, Alex focused on his brother's face, a look of fear etched into it like in the dream. "Jace?"

"Oh, thank God," Jason breathed, gathering him into a tight hug.

Alex clung to his brother, his face buried in the crook of his neck. He felt Jason smooth his hands up and down his back, and realized he was shaking so bad his teeth practically rattled in his head. He'd never experienced such terror or helplessness before. Not even when they were on the run. There'd always been a way to survive. "Jesus, Alex. When I heard your screams downstairs, my heart nearly stopped. I thought… we all thought you were in danger."

Alex registered the sound of others in the room and pulled away from Jason to see several Deviants standing in the doorway. He flushed and glanced away. Surprise jolted him when he saw Gabriel staring intently at him from near the window. "Everyone out," Gabriel rumbled fiercely.

The door closed behind the others, leaving Jason and Gabriel in the room. Jason ran a shaky hand through Alex's hair while peering into the identical green eyes. "What happened, Alex?"

"It... I...." Alex stuttered to a halt, shuddering at the memory of what he'd seen in his dream. It had felt so real. Had it only been a dream? He'd felt the pain from Gabriel's power brutally slamming into his body. The cuts on his palms stung like bees. He looked down into his hands, his breath hitching at the sight of dried blood.

"Alex!" Jason exclaimed, gripping his hands in his. His thumb brushed over several of the cuts, causing Alex to wince. "What the hell is going on?" Jason glared at Gabriel.

Gabriel strode to the side of the bed and sank down onto the edge. Alex couldn't stop himself from flinching away from Gabriel, fear and panic streaming through him. Gabriel halted his hand in midair before he let it fall to the bed. "I would never hurt you," he ground out.

Alex instantly felt guilty. "I know. I'm sorry," he apologized in a whisper, reaching out to touch the back of Gabriel's hand.

Gabriel lightly gripped Alex's wrist and rolled Alex's palm upward. He studied the dried blood and the thin cuts for several moments. "What were you dreaming about?"

Alex's throat clenched, forcing him to swallow repeatedly. He didn't want to relive those horrible images. Sweat beaded along his upper lip as he fought against himself. His skin still felt abraded, roughly exposed by the feeling of Gabriel's power. He knew it was irrational to be afraid of the other man from just a dream, but if it had been only a dream, why were there cuts on his palms? "I...." His voice cracked, and he strained to keep going, "I woke up here, in my bed, and everyone was dead.

"Jason... Jason lay on the floor, blood everywhere. When... when I went into the hallway, all of the others were dead too. There were bodies everywhere. Blood. And

Jackal... oh God, Jackal...." His voice cut off this time on a sob.

Jason moved to hug him, but Gabriel beat him to it, gathering Alex into his arms and holding him in a warm embrace. "You don't have to tell us any more," he murmured in a soothing voice.

Alex burrowed deeper into Gabriel, his silent tears soaking the shoulder of the man's T-shirt. He barely noticed Jason moving off the bed or leaving the room. Every time he closed his eyes, all he could see was blood and the look of contempt on Gabriel's face. When Gabriel shifted, he made a sound of protest. "Shhh. I'm just making us more comfortable."

His distress kept him from feeling embarrassed at being so needy. Gabriel eased them into a prone position, their legs tangling naturally together. "What time is it?" Alex whispered, seeing the edges of darkness easing in through the window.

"Just after six."

He'd slept for over three hours! Breathing in deeply, he allowed the scent of Gabriel's skin to soothe him. "I'm sorry."

"For what?"

"Being so much trouble."

Gabriel gave a small, humorless laugh. "If only bad dreams were our biggest problem." His chest rose and fell in a sigh. "You have nothing to be sorry for, Alex. You've been through a lot in the last few weeks, and nightmares are naturally a part of that."

Alex tipped his head back to look up into Gabriel's eyes. "In the dream, you... you hated me. Called me weak. I don't want you to think of me as weak. I want—"

Gabriel's finger pressing over his lips stopped him. "You are not weak, Alex. I would never think that, and I would never hate you. The strength you have inside of you astonishes me. After everything you've been through, you still haven't given up or looked for the easy way out. There are a lot of people in this world who would never have been capable of handling it all and coming out as unscathed."

Warmth invaded Alex's heart, and his lips tilted into a soft smile when Gabriel's hand fell away. "Thank you."

11

GABRIEL

Gabriel listened to the soft, even breathing in the darkness. Alex had eventually fallen asleep again. The nightmare concerned Gabriel, but the cuts on Alex's hands even more so. How could something in a dream cause injury outside of it? When the first scream came, he'd been in his bedroom putting away some of his laundry. His heart nearly stopped inside his chest. Adrenaline sent him racing from his room, almost running into Jason as they frantically rushed to help Alex. Bursting into the room to find no one but Alex inside, they'd held onto their confusion long enough to wake the younger man from what appeared to be a horrible nightmare.

Now Alex lay curled in his arms, sleeping peacefully. He knew he should leave, but the idea of letting go left an acrid taste in his mouth. He felt drained. He'd been fighting so hard not to let Alex in, and yet somehow the other Deviant still found a way around the walls he'd built to protect his heart. The thought of Alex being hurt or worse sent a chill racing down his spine. Would he be able to protect him if something happened? Or would Alex end up like Rafael?

That question once more reminded him of why he'd tried to keep Alex out in the first place. He couldn't take the chance of losing him.

Carefully, he extricated himself from Alex's grasp and slid from the bed. He secured the covers over Alex and brushed the back of his index finger down Alex's cheek, noticing the younger Deviant wore his silver cross. Hearing it was Alex's birthday, his mind had instantly started looking for something to give Alex. While in the shower after working out, his fingers had touched the sterling silver chain, and he immediately knew Alex would appreciate the cross. He'd never even hesitated to give it to him, and now to see it gracing the soft, lightly tanned throat, his desire blazed even higher for the dark-haired Deviant digging his way under his skin.

He needed to talk to Bryan, figure out what happened and how. The door shut quietly behind him. Jason sat slumped down against the wall right outside. Memories of his concern for his own brother struck through him. They'd always had each other's backs. Up until that fateful night five years ago. He spent night after night agonizing over the choice he'd made and what he could have done differently. It took two years before he could sleep a full night without waking up in a cold sweat.

He reached down and lightly shook Jason. "Hey."

Jason mumbled and would have slid down to his side on the floor, but Gabriel caught him. "Hey, kid, wake up." He shook Jason a bit harder.

"Wha?" Jason blinked owlishly. "Oh. Is Alex asleep?"

"Yeah. You should get to bed." Gabriel helped Jason to stand and nudged him toward the bedroom door. "Jason?"

The identical image of Alex turned back to look at him. "Keep an eye on him, okay?"

"Sure thing, Gabe." Jason yawned tiredly, stumbling into the room and shutting the door.

Gabriel headed down the stairs and straight to Bryan's office. Bryan held out a glass of bourbon the moment he stepped through the door. He gratefully accepted and tossed back a huge mouthful before sitting in one of the chairs. "I'm guessing you've heard about Alex's nightmare?"

Bryan nodded, leaning against the front of his desk. "Jason and I talked for a while. He seemed pretty upset about his brother's nightmare, especially the cuts on his hands."

"How is that possible, Bry?" Gabriel demanded. "How could he be injured in the dream and the injury manifest itself outside of it?"

Sighing, Bryan reached for a file on the desk behind him. "It's a rare ability, one I have only heard of a handful of times before, but there are some Deviants who are able to project themselves into someone's dreams. They can manipulate the dream and make the person see the best or worst things in their life. The Deviant can make them feel real pain and even carry the bruises or cuts back to the real world. I'm guessing one of these people invaded Alex's dream."

Gabriel took the file and began thumbing through it. There were only six names inside, which meant it really was a very rare ability. "You think it could be one of them?"

"I don't know. It's possible there could be someone whom the agency hasn't identified yet, but we have no way of knowing how far that person is away from the farmhouse. Depending on their control and the level of their ability, they could be thousands of miles away or right in our own backyard, for all we know." Bryan expelled a tired breath. "Which means the agency may be compromised."

Gabriel swore vehemently, his fingers tightening around the glass he held until it cracked. Bryan plucked the glass from his hand. "We don't know for sure, but starting tonight each team will patrol the property in four hour blocks. I've already informed all of the others. Alpha squad is already on patrol. No one is to be unarmed. Abilities or not."

"What is so special about Alex?" Gabriel snarled furiously. "Why is Vincetti after him?"

"You don't think it's both of them anymore?" Bryan asked curiously.

"It could be, but they targeted Alex, not Jason."

"But it could be possible they only targeted Alex because he was the easiest to reach," Bryan pointed out. "We have no guarantee what or who they want, Gabe."

Frustration ate at Gabriel's belly. "I am going to kill that son of a bitch. I swear to God. He won't get the chance to hurt anyone else ever again once I get my hands on him."

"Let's hope we flush him out soon. Before he finds us."

Handing the folder back to Bryan, Gabriel told his boss and friend good-night and went to find Jackal and Lizard. The two of them were sitting in the dining room, suited up and ready to go. "When is Alpha squad off duty?" Gabriel asked.

"About an hour, boss," Lizard replied, tossing a card in his hand into the discard pile. "Preston put a plate of food in the microwave for you since you couldn't make it down for dinner." He gave Gabriel a knowing look.

Gabriel glared at him but didn't reply, instead choosing to walk into the kitchen to nuke the food set aside for him. When it finished heating, he brought it out to the dining table to join the other two men while they played cards to pass the time. He'd joined many games before and knew how cutthroat they could become, yet tonight they seemed almost careless in their choices. He saw Jackal glance at the clock more than once, and knew the men were anxious to begin their patrol. The farmhouse was quiet, all of the inhabitants on edge. Gabriel could only imagine what the younger Deviants were thinking or feeling, especially the ones who'd come from a concentration camp. The agency had always felt like home, but now fear and apprehension wiped away the sense of security everyone knew at the ADA.

Lost in his thoughts, he failed to notice the other two men cleaning up and checking their weapons. "Earth to Gabe." A hand waved back and forth in front of his face.

He grunted and stood, taking his plate to the sink, and headed upstairs to his room to grab his knives and the two guns he normally carried. Lizard, Tank, Bear, and Jackal were waiting outside the back door of the house when he came back. "Good of you to join us, boss," Jackal taunted cheerfully.

"Bear, Tank, take the east perimeter of the property. Jackal and Lizard take the west and the rear. I'll take the front and the farmhouse." Gabriel didn't want to stray too far from the house if something were to happen.

"No one is supposed to patrol alone," Jackal protested.

"I'll be fine," Gabriel replied flatly. "I'm right near the house, and one of the other teams will hear if I need them."

Jackal nodded and fidgeted in agitation, but he didn't argue. "Sure thing, boss."

"Keep your radios open at all times," Gabriel commanded shortly. "If you see anything out of the ordinary, do not check it out without notifying me immediately. Understood?"

The members of his team agreed, and they broke up, going in their respective directions. Gabriel glanced up at the moon, no more than a smudge in the blackened sky. No lights from the city reached this far out, so the stars stood out starkly against the inky darkness. A sharp sense of foreboding trickled along his spine, causing his stomach to tighten almost painfully.

His footsteps were silent in the already dew-dampened grass as he walked around to the front of the agency. *You're just being paranoid,* he snapped at himself. No one could possibly know where the ADA was, not this far out from the city. Bryan made sure to have his contacts give out false rumors of their possible location every few months, most of them nowhere even close to their actual vicinity. Yet he couldn't shake the awful feeling in the pit of his gut that something or someone was close and just waiting for them to look away, for them to drop their guard and pounce.

The windows of the farmhouse started to darken, each room's occupants turning out the lights and going to bed, though who knew how many would actually sleep. Gabriel followed the driveway, eyes scanning the surrounding trees and the fence which ran the length of the property. When he reached the main gate, he paused and glanced in either direction down the main road. No headlights, and nothing looked out of the ordinary, so he turned back toward the house. The pattern repeated itself, uneventful and boring, until the last thirty minutes before his team were due to return to the house for the next squad to pick up the patrol.

"Gabriel," Lizard's voice came over the radio, startling him slightly. "Found a breach in the fence. We're going to check it out."

"Keep me posted and be careful," he demanded sharply. He drew his gun and double checked the clip as he stealthily made his way around to the rear of the house. Opening the door, he flipped on a switch and flooded the yard with light. The glow reached all the way to the training structure, giving him a clear view of the area surrounding the agency. He saw no movement and clicked on his radio.

"Lizard, check in." Silence met his demand, and he hit the button again. "Lizard, what's your position?"

Gunshots rang out over the compound, and Gabriel swore, rushing inside the agency to slap the alarm. The blaring sound rang through the house, alerting the others to the threat heading their way. Bear and Tank met him at the back door. "What's going on?" Tank shouted over the alarm.

"Breach at the south perimeter. I heard gunshots. Bear, make sure everyone makes it into the tunnel. Tank and I will back up Lizard and Jackal." When Bryan set up the farmhouse for the purpose of a safe haven for Deviants with nowhere else to go, he'd had a tunnel made beneath the house which led to just inside the fence at the south end of the property. They'd hidden the entrance beneath a set of bushes. "I'll radio you the moment it's safe to bring everyone out."

Bear tipped his chin in a sign of understanding and raced into the house. Gabriel could just barely hear his booming voice. "Everyone into the tunnel!"

As they turned to rush to help Jackal and Lizard, a scream came from inside the agency. Gabriel swore and dashed back in to find a team of unknown assailants streaming out of the door leading to the tunnel. "Get everyone out, Tank!" he shouted over the alarm, bringing his gun up and aiming for one of the larger men.

Shock stunned him for a split second when the gun flew out of his hands. They were Deviants! Vincetti's people had found them. Rage set in quickly. He flung out a bit of his power, tossing the guy through the kitchen wall and into the living room. Gabriel spun back to stop the next one, shattering the bones in one leg instantly. The man shrieked, dropping to the floor in agony. One of the attackers rushed him, his shoulder barreling into Gabriel's solar plexus, putting him through the same wall Gabriel had thrown the other one through. He grunted as his back hit the ground, knocking the wind from him.

The stranger loomed over him, about to crush his skull in with his boot, when a loud cry of "No!" stopped him. "That kill belongs to *him*."

The man scowled, but relented and backed off, allowing Gabriel to stand. Gabriel tried to find the source of the voice, but there were too many people fighting and running through the farmhouse. He faced off against the mountain in front of him, sliding one of his knives from his vest, having lost his gun in the shuffle. "Who the fuck are you? What do you want?" he snarled.

Smirking cruelly, the Deviant replied, "You really don't think that little blade is going to hurt me, do you?"

"I won't ask again. Who the hell are you?" Gabriel gripped the knife tighter, waiting for a chance to strike.

Instead of replying, the mountain of a man charged, bending a bit at the waist in an attempt to repeat tossing Gabriel through the wall. Gabriel expected it this time and sidestepped, tossing his hand holding the knife toward the man's ribcage. He growled triumphantly when it sank deep between two ribs and the bastard let out a howl of pain. But his celebration was cut short when the other Deviant suddenly twisted back and his fist struck the side of Gabriel's face, sending him careening backward into the couch. He hit the arm and struggled to remain upright. "Gabriel!"

Distracted by Alex's voice calling his name, he glanced toward the doorway to see Alex standing there, wearing nothing but a pair of dark shorts, a dark T-shirt, and a terrified expression. "Alex, get out of here! Now!"

"Gabe, look out!" Alex cried and started to him.

Gabriel darted to the side, putting himself between the mountain and Alex. The other Deviant's fist slammed into the arm of the couch with enough force to go through the fabric and the wood inside, sending chunks raining to the floor. If he hadn't moved, that may well have been his kidney. He wobbled, his head pounding from the blow moments ago, and he shook it to clear it. "Just the kid I was looking for," the mountain rumbled, grinning maliciously.

"Stay away from him," Gabriel ground out, his hands balling into fists.

The mountain laughed and eyed Gabriel. "You going to stop me, boss man? 'Cause to me it looks like you can barely stand."

"You lay one finger on him, you hulking heap of garbage, I'll tear you limb from limb," he challenged.

Lifting an eyebrow, the man gave him a look of disdain. "No one can hurt me. Not even you. Now, kid, why don't you make this easier on everyone and get over here?" The last was directed at Alex.

"Stay where you are, Alex."

"And here I thought this would be easy," the man sighed. "At least I'll get to maim you, even if I can't kill you."

At those words, he again attempted to charge Gabriel. Gabriel knew if he sidestepped the bastard would hit Alex, but a complete hit could possibly knock him unconscious and then he wouldn't be of any help to the others. Drawing in as much of his power as he could in his current state, he pushed it out at full force, stopping the other Deviant in his tracks. A look of bewilderment flashed over his features for a breath of a moment before he dropped to his knees and fell face down to the ground. Gabriel felt a light touch on his forearm and swung around to glare at Alex. "I told you to get the fuck out of here. What the hell were you thinking?"

Chaos all around them and still Alex dominated his mind, distracting him from the danger waiting in the shadows. "I couldn't leave you," Alex shouted over the noise. "What did you do to him?"

Gabriel shook his head and gripped Alex's upper arm tightly. "Don't worry about it. Let's just get you out of here."

Alex furiously shook his head. "Not without Jason. We were separated, and now I can't find him."

"I'll find him. Go to the main gate, hide, and wait for me!"

Gabriel instructed harshly, pushing Alex toward the front door. "Go, now!"

"But—" Alex was cut off by a loud explosion at the back of the agency, which shook the very house on its foundation. Gabriel shoved Alex against the wall, shielding his body with his as things fell down around them. Glass shattering, thuds of heavy items hitting the floor, and screams filled his ears, increasing his fear for Alex's safety.

Lizard suddenly appeared in the doorway, bruised and bleeding. "Boss, we gotta go. There's too many of them. Bear and Tank have started getting the SUVs ready. Three headed out already."

"Take Alex," Gabriel shouted, pushing the younger man into Lizard's arms. "I have to find Bryan."

"They've got him, Gabe."

"What? What do you mean they got him?" Gabriel demanded.

"He's alive, but we can't help him if we aren't. Now let's get out of here. The only ones left in the farmhouse are us and the other teams."

The alarm cut off abruptly, leaving only the sound of fighting. Gabriel knew Lizard was right, but the idea of leaving Bryan in the hands of the Deviants controlled by the one man he hated more than anyone else on the planet left a foul taste in the back of his throat. "Fine," he replied tersely.

Shielding Alex's body with his own, he followed closely on Lizard's heels, throwing out more than one burst of energy at assailants trying to stop them. He felt Alex's fear, but couldn't do anything until they were away from the house and safe. A bullet whipped by him, slamming into one of the porch railings. Gabriel snarled and spun around to retaliate. Only his intentions were too late. Several bullets thudded into Lizard's back, sending his longtime friend and squad member to the ground. "No!" he heard Alex cry out, and rage crashed over him, blinding him to anything but his friend and the son of a bitch who'd shot him.

Gabriel brought his hands up and pulled all of his power into the blast he sent toward the Deviant holding the gun. The shooter screamed in pure agony, his bones liquefying inside his skin, and he crumpled to the floor. Gabriel barely noticed the blood seeping from the dead Deviant's orifices. He moved quickly, picking up Lizard as carefully as he could manage, and barked at Alex, "Run to the garage. Keep as low as you can."

"What about you?" Alex argued.

"I'll be right behind you. Just go."

Alex obeyed, racing to the open door of the building Bryan had built to house the vehicles. Gabriel could sense Lizard's heartbeat fading fast, warm blood soaking his clothes and staining his skin. "Don't you die on me. Don't you dare die, Lizard."

He breathed a small sigh of relief when he saw Alex dart inside the building. There were only two SUVs left when he reached it, and one of them was just leaving. The last one only had enough room for Lizard. Gabriel made a quick decision. He handed Lizard off to Bear. "Take him. Get him to a hospital. Alex and I will take one of the bikes."

Bear nodded and lifted Lizard from Gabriel's arms. "Take care, boss."

"As soon as I'm sure we're safe, I'll call you with a rendezvous point." Gabriel shut the door and looked at Alex, who stood next to him, his face as pale as snow. "Come on. We'll be right behind them."

"Where's Jason?" Alex asked anxiously, trying to peer inside the vehicle as it pulled away. "I can't leave without my brother."

"He's probably in one of the other cars. Let's go. Once we're safe, I'll contact the others to find out where he is."

Gabriel gripped Alex's elbow and led him over to one of two black motorcycles in the far corner. They'd been a gift to him and Lizard from Bryan for their fifth anniversary at the ADA. His jaw clenched at the thought of Bryan in the hands of his mortal enemy, and Lizard's life currently hung in the balance because of the same bastard. "Put this on," he said, handing one of the helmets to Alex.

Alex hesitantly took it and slipped it over his head. Gabriel slid onto the bike and started the engine. "Get on," he instructed, revving the motor. "Put your arms around my waist and hold on tight. Once they catch sight of us, they aren't going to let us go easy."

Gabriel felt the warmth from Alex's body as the younger Deviant threw his leg over the motorcycle and pressed close to his back. Any other time he would have savored it, drank it in for the cold nights when Alex left the ADA, but there was no time for him to enjoy it. The longer they remained in the garage, the more likely they would be discovered. "No matter what, don't let go," he shouted over the motor and gunned the engine again.

The back tire squealed as he slammed on the gas, forcing the speedometer needle to spike to a high number and rocketing them out of the garage. Gabriel heard shouts and a couple of guns go off, but they were going too fast for it to matter. In seconds they reached the main gate and were on their way into the city.

In a matter of minutes, the ADA was gone, compromised and leaving everyone scattered. Gabriel's hands tightened on the handlebars. He could hardly believe how it all fell apart so easily, as if a dream stomped into the ground. The only thing keeping him sane these last five years was the agency. Without it, he knew he would've ended up dead in his pursuit for revenge on Vincetti. This time... this time he would kill the bastard, no matter what it took.

He didn't stop inside the city. Instead he headed straight through, wanting to put as much distance between them and the farmhouse as possible. Alex hadn't said a word since they'd left the agency. Gabriel could feel Alex's arms squeeze reflexively on each curve and turn of the road which reassured him the younger man was at least aware of their surroundings. Considering Alex's aversion to violence, he figured Alex had to be in shock or at the very least upset. When he felt safe enough to stop, he pulled the bike over into a deserted rest stop station and parked.

Alex didn't let go immediately, his cheek pressed into Gabriel's shoulder. "Alex?" Gabriel prodded gently.

A shudder ran through Alex's body, and he slid off the bike, holding onto the seat to keep from falling over. Gabriel dismounted the motorcycle and turned to Alex. He reached up to carefully remove the helmet. Alex's eyes were red-rimmed, and he wouldn't look Gabriel in the eye. "Hey," Gabriel said softly. "Everything's okay. We're safe."

Alex shook his head and covered his face with his hands. Unable to fight it, Gabriel pulled Alex into his arms, holding him fiercely. "It's okay. Shh."

"It's not okay," Alex sobbed. "People died tonight. Bryan's been kidnapped, and I don't know what happened to my brother."

Gabriel ran his fingers through Alex's dark hair, his other hand rubbing soothingly up and down the slender back. "We're alive, Alex. We're safe and we're going to find your brother and rescue Bryan. I promise you."

"What if…." Alex stopped, his voice catching.

"No. We will find them and everything will be fine." Gabriel refused to have it any other way. If Vincetti laid one finger on Bryan, he'd torture the prick before killing him.

He continued to comfort Alex, wanting more than anything to take his pain away. They couldn't remain there long though. It was too exposed being out in the open. "Why don't you go inside and wash your face? I'm going to call Tank to check on Lizard and set up a rendezvous point."

Alex nodded and started to pull away, but Gabriel stopped him. He tilted Alex's face up, forcing him to meet his gaze. "I won't let anything happen to you or your brother, Alex. I will do everything I can to keep you safe."

He gave Gabriel a wobbly smile and lightly touched Gabriel's cheek. "Thank you."

Gabriel watched the lean form until Alex disappeared into the restroom. He pulled out his cell phone and hit the speed dial for Tank's number. The instant Tank answered the phone, he knew. "Boss…." Tank started, his voice flat.

"He's gone."

"He didn't make it, Gabe. He died before we even made it to the city."

Acid stung the back of Gabriel's throat. His fingers clenched on the phone to an almost shattering pressure. Lizard was one of his men. He should have protected him. Instead he'd let him die. Swallowing several times, he finally managed to ask, "Is Jason with you?"

"No. Bear said he saw one of Vincetti's Devs grab him."

"Fuck!" Gabriel snarled. How could everything have gotten so messed up so fast? "Fuck…." What did he tell Alex?

"We're heading to the safe house in Kansas. I already contacted the other squad leaders, and they're heading for safe houses all over the country. Alpha Squad lost three of their team. I had reports of at least five of the resident Devs being killed and six more injured, but not enough to warrant a hospital."

"Jackal? Chris?"

"Both are okay. Chris managed to grab some of his equipment and is attempting to locate Bryan and Jason as we speak."

Gabriel tiredly ran his palm over his face. "I'll meet up with you all at the safe house in Kansas. Have Chris and Jackal head there as soon as they can. We need to regroup and set a plan for going after Bryan and Jason."

"What?" he heard croaked behind him, and Gabriel grimaced. He'd been so involved in the conversation with Tank he hadn't noticed Alex's return.

"Keep me posted, Tank," he instructed and disconnected the call. He faced Alex and saw the little bit of color leave Alex's cheeks. "Vincetti has Jason."

Alex's eyes filled again. Tears trickled over, silently sliding down his cheeks. Gabriel reached out to touch him, and Alex jerked back. Hurt speared Gabriel, but he roughly shoved it aside and let his arm fall back down at his side. If Alex hated him, so be it. It would make it easier in the end, anyway. "We're going to get him back, Alex. Vincetti won't hurt him. He wants him for something."

"What? What could he possibly want from him? From us?" Alex shouted.

"I don't know. I just don't know, but we're going to find out. For now, we're heading to a safe house in Kansas to meet up with the rest of my team and then figure out how to get them both back." Gabriel paused and looked at the blood on his skin. His shirt, black, didn't show the red liquid, but he needed to get it washed off his skin. "I need to clean up some of this blood to prevent drawing attention. Stay here. If anyone comes, I want you to run for the building. Got it?"

Alex nodded, but didn't say anything, his arms tight across his chest.

Knowing he couldn't leave Alex for long, Gabriel rushed into the rest stop bathroom and scrubbed off as much of Lizard's blood as possible. He tried to ignore the ache in the pit of his stomach at knowing his teammate was gone, dead, in the blink of an eye, and he hadn't been able to save him.

The red-stained water swirled down the drain as he turned off the faucet and grabbed some paper towels, drying his arms and hands. He walked back out to see Alex hadn't moved from the dejected posture, staring at the ground and seemingly trying to keep from falling apart.

Approaching from the back, Gabriel picked up and handed the helmet to Alex and swung his leg over the bike. Looking at Alex, he held out his hand and waited. The hesitation in Alex's acceptance bit deep. "Once we get to the safe house, you won't have to be around me, but until then, you'll have to put up with me. Get on the bike, Alex."

12

ALEX

ALEX knew he'd hurt Gabriel by his rejection. He didn't blame Gabriel for Jason being abducted. He blamed himself. His pulling away from the other man wasn't because of rejection of Gabriel, but rather of the comfort he provided. He didn't deserve it. Not when Alex should have refused to leave the farmhouse until they'd found Jason. He'd abandoned his brother, the one person who would do anything for him. How could he possibly accept comfort when God knew what Jason was going through?

The wind whipped past them as Gabriel sped toward Kansas. Alex hadn't been on a motorcycle before, but he knew if things were different he'd have loved it, with the added bonus of being pressed so close to Gabriel. When they'd left the agency, he'd been too distraught and frightened to enjoy the freedom of touching the bigger, muscular Dev. Now guilt kept his pleasure in check. Why should he be safe and happy while his brother could possibly be hurt or dead? His throat grew tight, tears threatening again. He prayed Jason was okay. He couldn't bear losing his twin too.

Fingers of light were just beginning to spread across the sky when Gabriel pulled the bike into a shabby highway motel. When Alex looked at him in question, Gabriel explained flatly, "It's safer to travel at night. Less exposure. We'll stay here for the day, rest and eat, then head out when it gets dark. Stay here. I'll go get us a room."

Alex watched the broad back disappear into the main office. Despite the situation, his stomach flip-flopped at the idea of being alone with Gabriel in a motel room for the entire day. Then he berated himself for his stupidity. Gabriel had more on his mind than seducing him. He sighed and slid off the bike, pulling the helmet off and running a hand through his hair to straighten it.

"Here's the key," Gabriel said behind him, and he turned to see him holding out the room key. "Go inside, lock the door. I'm going to get us something to eat."

"I'd rather go with you," Alex protested.

"No. We're more conspicuous with two of us. I'll be back in ten minutes. Clerk said there's a McDonald's a couple miles down the road. Go." Gabriel set the key in Alex's palm and took the helmet from him.

Alex walked to the room, aware of Gabriel's gaze on him until he shut the door. He heard the engine roar and then listened to it slowly fade away. He looked around the shabby motel room, his brain barely comprehending the ugly green carpeting and salmon pink walls, and sank down to the floor, his back against the door. Wrapping his arms around his upraised knees, he rested his chin on them. While growing up he'd never thought his life would turn out this way. Even knowing his mother tried to murder him and his brother, he'd always hoped somehow things would be okay. How could everything have gone so wrong? From the moment Jason lost control of his powers, the two of them had been set on a path leading to here, this moment in time, and Alex had no idea what to do.

Was Jason okay? Were they hurting him? Would he trade having known Gabriel for his brother's safety? Was it wrong that he didn't want to give up Gabriel but still wanted his brother back? Questions whirled around inside his head, making him feel nauseous. Bile rose in the back of his throat, and he struggled to stand, rushing to the bathroom to retch into the toilet. It had been since dinner the night before that he'd eaten, so nothing but a clear fluid came up. Alex heard the bike returning and managed to stand upright and rinse his mouth at the sink. The door opened and shut. "Dammit, Alex," Gabriel swore. "You didn't lock the door!"

He suddenly felt angry. Angrier than he'd ever felt in his life. In the back of his mind he knew it was wrong and Gabriel really wasn't to blame, but it didn't stop his reaction. Practically flying out of the bathroom, Alex launched himself at Gabriel, his fist connecting with the other man's stomach muscles. Gabriel grunted and tried to restrain him, but Alex dodged his hands. "Alex, stop!"

"Why did you leave him?" Alex cried, slamming his palms against Gabriel's chest over and over. "Why did you rescue me and not him? I should have been the one they took. Not Jason."

Gabriel closed his arms around Alex, pulling him tight into his body. He resisted a bit longer before finally giving up, exhausted and weak. Alex found himself being guided to the bed and pushed into a sitting position. Gabriel crouched down in front of him, peering up at him. "Alex... whatever else you may feel, please believe me when I say that I will do everything I can to get your brother back. I will not let you go through the same thing I did."

Ashamed at taking his anger and sense of helplessness out

on Gabriel, Alex didn't know what to say other than, "I'm sorry."

"Don't. You don't have anything to apologize for. I should have done more. I knew Vincetti wanted you and Jason for something, and I should have tried to find him. To keep both of you safe and away from him. You're right to blame me. I let my fear for your safety prevent me from doing my full job." Gabriel abruptly stood up, pacing back and forth. "I never let anything impair my judgment, but ever since I met you it seems like I can't think of anything else."

Alex's breath quickened, and he slowly lifted his head up to look at Gabriel. The older Deviant seemed to realize what he'd said and cut off his words, halting with his back to Alex. "You think about me?"

When Gabriel didn't answer his question, Alex hesitantly approached him, touching the center of his back. A visible shudder went through Gabriel, and Alex walked around in front of him. "Gabe?" Alex queried.

Gabriel's eyes were shadowed, his head tilted down a fraction, and not until he looked up did Alex see the pain shimmering in Gabriel's golden honey gaze. His heart skipped a beat, causing an ache to build in his chest. He'd never seen such agony before. "Why?" Alex asked gently, reaching up to trace the well-defined cheekbones. "Why do you carry so much pain alone?"

Grams would have seen the burden Gabriel carried from the very beginning. Alex knew the man's past kept him from believing in a future, but he'd neglected to see the weight on his soul. "You have so many people around you who care for you very much. Why won't you let anyone help you bear the weight of it?"

"Because it's mine to carry," Gabriel choked out.

Alex slid his arms around Gabriel's waist and leaned into

the more muscular form. "It doesn't have to be. Let me help you, Gabriel."

For several breaths it seemed as if Gabriel would reject him again, but when the other Deviant hesitantly brought his arms around Alex, he couldn't quite stifle his smile of pleasure. Gabriel held onto him tightly, his face burrowed into Alex's neck. Their abrupt role reversal should have left him reeling. Instead it left him feeling accomplished at having broken through some of the wall Gabriel kept up as a shield. He snuggled closer, stroking his hands along Gabriel's back and savoring being in the older man's arms. He could feel Gabriel's chest moving with each breath he took. At some point Gabriel had removed his weapons vest. It lay on the bed near the bathroom.

"I shouldn't... we shouldn't be doing this," Gabriel murmured.

Alex pulled back to look into Gabriel's eyes. "Why not?"

"Because...." Gabriel paused, seemingly searching for the right words.

When he would have spoken again, Alex covered Gabriel's mouth with his hand. He could see the surprise in Gabriel's gaze and grinned. "Sometimes speaking is overrated."

Having said that, Alex promptly removed his hand and recovered Gabriel's lips, but this time using his own instead. Gabriel didn't respond right away, and Alex coaxed him, trailing his tongue along his bottom lip. Despite having never truly had a boyfriend, Alex had watched more than his fair share of movies and read a large amount of books. There hadn't been anything else to do on Grams's farm so he'd done a lot of both. He'd seen the way Leonardo DiCaprio and Kate Winslet kissed in *Titanic* and the way Brad Pitt and Angelina Jolie almost killed one another, leading to a round of hot sex in *Mr. and Mrs. Smith*. The sheer description of kisses in some of the stories he'd read had made him ache for someone to share those same sensations with.

He also had a near photographic memory, and he put those images to good use, almost dying in satisfaction when Gabriel let go. His blood pumped faster at the groan that rattled in Gabriel's chest and the way he suddenly found himself grasped in a hard, passionate embrace. He ran his hands up Gabriel's body to wrap behind his neck. Gabriel's slick tongue swept inside his mouth, eliciting a sigh from Alex, who responded in kind.

A squeak echoed in his throat when Gabriel abruptly cupped his rear end and lifted him up, Alex's legs instinctively wrapping around Gabriel's waist. Gabriel set him on the nearby dresser without breaking the lustful kiss. Alex could feel the evidence of Gabriel's desire for him grinding into his own and gasped in pleasure when Gabriel broke the kiss to trail wet kisses along his jawline to his ear. The heat between his thighs encompassed his entire body at the feel of Gabriel's tongue tracing the shell of his ear. "Oh God," he panted, his head falling back against the wall with a small thud.

Never before had he felt something so exquisitely sexual, so electric that it sent chills throughout his lean frame. Alex could barely tell which way was up. The only thing he knew was Gabriel. The touch of him, the musky scent of his skin, the taste of his kiss, all of it bombarded his senses and blocked out everything else. "Gabriel!" he cried out when the Deviant's teeth scraped the lobe of his ear.

But the power of it didn't compare to the hand unexpectedly cupping his hard length over the shorts he wore or the way Gabriel's fingers massaged him through the fabric. The dim sounds of whimpering reached his ears, and he realized it was him, but the desire for Gabriel to continue caressing him outweighed the embarrassment he may have felt over the wanton noise. Alex arched into Gabriel's hungry mouth sucking hotly at his throat. Running his hands through Gabriel's short fade, he savored the tingles racing through his palms and gripped Gabriel more snugly between his thighs, grinding instinctively into Gabriel's palm.

The next sensation almost sent him flying over the edge. For the first time in his life, Alex felt the intimate touch of another. Gabriel's hand wrapping around him, squeezing the hot shaft, was unlike anything he'd experienced. "Oh...." he mewed, gasping.

"Okay?" Gabriel purred softly.

"More than okay," Alex managed to breathe out.

A low chuckle rumbled in Gabriel's chest, sending vibrations through Alex's. Gabriel slowly began stroking his cock, twisting his hand on each downward stroke. Alex barely noticed Gabriel fumbling for the front of his jeans or registered the sound of the zipper teeth separating. The cool air suddenly drifting over his hot flesh and the slick heat of Gabriel's cock against his tore a moan from his throat. Overwhelming emotions, feelings, crashed through him. He lost himself in it, gave himself to the passion and desire winding tighter and tighter inside. Heat built in his lower belly, signaling his impending orgasm. Alex bit down on Gabriel's shoulder, his fingers digging into the muscles on his broad back, his hips thrusting unconsciously upward into the firm grasp.

He thought he heard Gabriel whisper his name, but each new awareness strumming along his nerves, his skin, dampened the sound and muffled it beneath the roar of lust swelling inside him. Seconds later, Alex cried out, his body stiffening as he came. White hot spurts of fluid sprayed across Gabriel's hand, both their bellies, and wetted their T-shirts. Breaths later, Gabriel followed him over the edge, soaking them further in the sticky liquid. Gabriel slumped into Alex, resting against him. Alex could hear his deep breaths as he struggled to regain control himself. Trying to fight back a grin of triumph, Alex pressed a kiss to the side of Gabriel's neck, enjoying the fine tremble of the man's skin, and did it again. "We should eat," Gabriel murmured into Alex's throat, yet he still didn't move.

Alex hummed contentedly. "Don't want to move."

"We need to at least get cleaned up."

Gabriel's voice made Alex realized the other man regretted what they'd done. His heart ached inside his chest as, bit by bit, Alex could feel Gabriel withdrawing from him, locking his feelings behind the wall he'd built around his heart. "No," he murmured, clutching at Gabriel. "Don't pull away from me, not this time."

"That never—"

Alex cut him off, clamping his hand down over Gabriel's mouth, and pulled back to glare into the honey orbs he loved. "If you say it never should have happened, I'm going to hit you. Why shouldn't it have happened? And don't give me that shit about you being broken or needing a warm body. You wanted it just as much as I did, and I refuse to accept that as an answer or to let you toss away what we just shared as nothing more than a way to get off."

Gabriel's eyebrow went up, and he waited for Alex to remove his hand before speaking. "I think it's up to me what I choose to do with what we did. But I was going to say that never should have happened here. Not while we're still in danger."

"Oh."

A tender smile crossed Gabriel's lips, surprising Alex. In the few weeks since Gabriel rescued him and Jason, he'd only seen the man smile once. He reached up to lightly touch the edge of Gabriel's mouth. "You should smile more often."

"Not much to smile about before," Gabriel replied, finally

stepping back and holding out his hand to help Alex down from the dresser.

Alex noted the word he chose to use and coughed to hide a grin while accepting Gabriel's offered hand. He wrinkled his nose as his shirt clung to his skin, cold and wet. They were both a mess. "We should take off our clothes."

Gabriel gave him an exasperated look. Alex held up his hand and shook his head, smirking at the obvious misinterpretation. "I meant so I can wash them in the sink and let them dry. It's not like we have other clothes with us."

He wanted to laugh out loud at the look on Gabriel's face, but stifled it and reached for the hem of his T-shirt, pulling it over his head. His shirt had received the brunt of their passions, his shorts only spotted in certain places. He could see Gabriel's jeans had dark splotches. Holding out his hand, he looked at Gabriel expectantly. The man hesitated for a moment before toeing off his boots and pushing his pants to his ankles to step out of. Alex eyed the strong, muscular legs appreciatively while accepting the article of clothing. But it was the tanned chest and six-pack which caused his breath to catch. He didn't think he'd ever get enough of looking at Gabriel. Taking the shirt from him, Alex headed into the bathroom to wash the clothing in the somewhat dingy bathtub.

Half a bottle of harsh complimentary shampoo later, he wrung out the excess water and hung the shirts and jeans to dry. When he entered the room again, Gabriel sat at the small table, eating some kind of processed egg and cheese biscuit. Several more of the same were scattered on the surface. Alex grimaced but walked over to the table, sitting in the chair opposite Gabriel. He picked one up and peeled the wrapping back. Sniffing at it, he wrinkled his nose. "People actually eat these things?"

"You've never had McDonald's?" Gabriel mumbled around a mouthful of food.

Alex shook his head, biting off a small piece. "Grams always cooked, and when we did eat out, it was at the only diner in town."

The food tasted pretty good despite the congealed mass of cheese on it. They polished off the five remaining biscuits and hash browns. Alex sighed in contentment when he finished, sipping from the can of Coke Gabriel bought from the vending machine down at the end of the building. He hadn't realized how hungry he actually had been. "So what's the plan?" he asked, yawning unexpectedly.

Gabriel glanced at the nearby clock. "Get some sleep, and then after sunset we'll be back on the road again. We'll stop somewhere and get you some shoes and a change of clothing."

Another yawn broke free, and Alex nodded, pushing away from the table to stand. He wobbled over to one of the beds and collapsed on it. It'd been a long night. Probably the longest night he'd ever had. Life had been so structured on the farm. Chores, home school, helping Grams in the kitchen, all of it seemed so far away, as if from another lifetime. After being on the run for over a year, Alex wondered if they'd ever have a normal life again.

He felt Gabriel tap him lightly on his hip. "Hmm?" he breathed.

"Get under the covers, kid. "

Alex grabbed the edge of the comforter and yanked half of it over him. He heard Gabriel chuckle quietly, and then his world shifted. He found himself airborne and deposited in the other bed, the quilt tugged back. Gabriel pulled the duvet over him, moving to stand. Alex snatched at his wrist, preventing Gabriel from moving away. "Stay."

"I really don't think that's a good idea," Gabriel replied gruffly.

"You think too much," Alex rebutted groggily. "It's only sleeping."

At first he thought Gabriel would refuse, but then the man let out a sigh and said, "Move over, kid."

Happy to have gotten his way, Alex shifted over to the side of the bed closest to the bathroom and waited for Gabriel to join him, snuggling into the older Deviant instantly. In less than a minute he'd fallen into a deep sleep, exhaustion overwhelming him. The events of the previous night haunted his dreams, bringing his worry and fear for his twin once more to the surface. Memories of Lizard being shot, his brother's hand slipping free of his own, the sight of Gabriel fighting the huge Deviant in the common room, and the terrifying ride away from the agency streamed through his mind as if he were watching a film. Except all of it was real. It'd happened.

The dream changed suddenly. The agency faded into a place Alex had never seen before. Looking left and right, he saw nothing but a long white hallway. Which way should he go? He hesitated, glancing both ways several times. Figuring he could check both ways, he chose to go right first, walking carefully to hide his footsteps. No matter how softly he trod, they echoed off the walls. He started going faster, eyes trained on the end of the hallway. What felt like hours later, he reached the end, turning the corner only to find another vacant corridor. Alex turned around and ran to the other end, praying to find something, anything. His hopes were dashed when he found the hallway empty yet again. Panic sizzled along his spine, and he tried to push it away, telling himself it wouldn't solve the problem, but he couldn't stop it from consuming him.

Beginning to run, Alex found each one the same. They

became a blur as he raced through the endless, empty corridors, calling Jason's name. There were no doors, just hallway after hallway, every turn leading to another one. Alex cried out again, hearing his voice echo but receiving no answer. Minutes, hours, an unknown amount of time passed, yet he never stopped, never gave up his faith in finding his brother.

Turning another corner, he expected to find it empty once more, but he came to an abrupt halt when he saw Gabriel standing at the far end, holding Jason by the throat. Frowning, he tried to call out, but his voice refused to come forth. Why did it seem as though Gabriel intended to hurt his brother? Gabriel promised he'd help save him. Something was wrong. He started running toward the two men, never taking his eyes from them. The closer he got, the more certain he became that Gabriel wasn't himself. A black iron mask covered the right half of Gabriel's face. A cruel smile quirked the visible side of Gabriel's mouth. Alex could see tears rolling down Jason's cheeks, and his bright green gaze met Alex's, a hopelessness in their depths. Gabriel wrenched Jason's head to the right, effortlessly snapping his neck, the crack bouncing along the walls to ring in Alex's ears.

Alex watched in utter horror as Jason crumpled to the ground, all of his life drained from his body, snuffed out like a candle's flame. *"No,"* he whispered, sliding to his knees beside his brother's prone form once he'd reached him. *"Jason!"*

Gabriel laughed evilly and glared down at Alex. *"So you're the one. The weakest of the two. Surprised me, but I guess it shouldn't."*

Alex looked up at Gabriel, his eyes streaming. *"Why? Why did you kill him?"*

Laughing again, Gabriel crouched down beside him, trailing the backs of his fingers over Alex's cheek and causing him to flinch. *"Because if you suffer, he suffers."*

"I don't understand," Alex cried out, slapping Gabriel's hand away. *"What are you talking about?"*

"You'll learn soon enough, Alex. But for now...." Gabriel trailed off, standing.

Suddenly, pain exploded in Alex's head. He screamed, clutching at his temples and falling to his side to curl into a fetal position. Pure agony wracked his body. He'd suffered through more than one serious migraine in his life, but the sheer volume of pain stabbing at his skull was unlike anything he'd ever felt. He begged Gabriel to make it stop, sobbing and shaking. Gabriel just smirked and leaned casually against the wall, his arms crossed over his chest. *"Give Gabriel a message for me, will you? Tell him let the games begin."*

Alex didn't understand any of it. Why would Gabriel tell him to give himself a message? The nausea rising in his stomach prevented him from answering, fear of vomiting kept his words locked inside. "Alex! Alex, wake up!" penetrated the fog of anguish, and he struggled to lift his head.

"Alex!" Hands gripped his shoulders, shaking him briskly. "Wake up, dammit!"

The face of the masked Gabriel faded away, replaced by the normal, rugged features peering down at him. Alex gasped, staring up at Gabriel. "Why?" he croaked out.

Gabriel frowned and slid his thumb over the tear tracks on Alex's cheek. "Why what?"

"Why are you so cruel in my dreams?" Alex whispered softly, turning his head away from Gabriel. He knew they were dreams, but the pain, the fear, it all felt so real.

Alex jerked when Gabriel suddenly gripped his chin, forcing him to look up at him. "Alex, no matter what you see in your dreams, you have to remember none of it is real. There are Deviants out there who can manipulate a person's dreams. They can make them see anything they want them to, and they can make it feel so real that it manifests itself outside of the dream."

Breathing deeply, Alex's lips trembled as he nodded. "Okay."

"Will you tell me about your dream?" Gabriel asked, sliding down beside Alex and gathering him close to his side.

"I... I want to, but it was... so horrible." Alex shuddered in memory. He knew he needed to tell Gabriel, if only to let him know about dream Gabriel's message. Haltingly, he began to relay the details of his nightmare. When he reached the point of Gabriel murdering Jason, his voice hitched, and he felt his eyes sting with fresh tears. "He looked just like you, except... he had a mask covering part of his face. He said... he said to give you a message."

Alex felt Gabriel tense, waiting to hear it. "The other you said to tell you let the games begin."

Gabriel stiffened and sucked in a deep breath, as if punched in the solar plexus. He bolted upright, moving to sit on the side of the bed. Surprised, Alex just stared at Gabriel's tense back for long moments. He carefully sat up, reaching out to touch the center of Gabriel's back, and asked softly, "You understand what he meant, Gabe?"

13

GABRIEL

THE words Alex stuttered out roared through Gabriel, stabbing him straight in the chest. Rafael, competitive by nature, always used to say that whenever he'd gone up against someone in a competition. It had been his way to try and psych out his opponents. He could picture the arrogant smirk on Rafael's face, the confidence and almost malicious glint in his eyes. His fingers dug into the side of the mattress, his jaw clenched so hard it could have fractured. Vincetti had hit an all-time low. To use another Deviant and manipulate Alex's dreams was one thing, but to use his brother to hurt Gabriel pissed him off. This time, he'd make sure he'd killed the son of a bitch.

Alex's hand rubbed up and down along his spine, reminding him he wasn't alone, and he forced himself to regain control. "It's something my brother used to say."

He heard Alex make a low noise behind him and then felt the bed dip as Alex wrapped his arms around his chest, resting his chin on his shoulder. Gabriel could feel his soft breath along his neck. "Tell me about him?" Alex murmured.

Gabriel hadn't really told anyone the complete story of

his twin brother. Not even Bryan knew everything they'd gone through in Vincetti's hands. He almost denied Alex's request until a whispered, "Please," brushed over his ear.

That small word did something to him. His heart fluttered, and his head dipped down, his lips twisting wryly. Despite how hard he'd tried to prevent it from happening, he'd lost the battle anyway. He'd fallen in love with Alex, wholly and completely. The realization crashed over him, and he closed his eyes, knowing once they'd taken out Vincetti he'd have to let Alex go. But wouldn't it be selfish to accept what Alex offered just to say good-bye later? Could he do that to him? And what if he found out the truth about what really happened to Rafe? Would he be able to bear it if Alex hated him for killing his own brother just to save his skin? Perhaps it would be best if Alex learned the true details of his brother's death. It would be easier if he hated him now rather than later.

Keeping a tight rein on his emotions, he started to talk. "Rafe and I were twins, just like you and Jason. Our personalities were completely opposite of each other. I guess that's what happens with twins. He was the hotheaded one, fast tempered and impulsive, rash. While I was calm, coolheaded, and always thought things through before acting. From the day we were born, we became inseparable. Wherever he went, I went, and vice versa.

"Our abilities didn't manifest themselves until we were in our early twenties. About a year after the fear of Deviants had grown to an insurmountable height, I was on my way home with a friend from college. Paul. His ability... apparently someone saw him use his ability at the college and reported him to one of the more known groups of Normals attacking the Deviants. He could control electricity and turn lamps on and off at will, power anything requiring electricity without it being plugged in.

"We were almost to the house when two trucks pulled up next to us. Several men jumped out of both, grabbed Paul and restrained me. They beat him, accused him of being a freak, and threatened to kill us both, but the leader stopped them and instructed them to tie Paul to the bumper of one of the trucks." Gabriel heard Alex gasp and felt him tighten his arms around him. "They drove around and around the block, dragging him behind them. All I can remember is feeling so helpless, unable to do anything to save my friend. By the time they'd stopped, he'd been torn to shreds. He was dead, and they wouldn't even let me go to him. They'd been laughing and backslapping each other. My anger caused my abilities to come forward. I did things that day I never thought I would."

He paused, swallowing hard at the memory of their screams and their bones shattering to tiny splinters inside their bodies. Just like he'd done back at the agency to the hulking Deviant threatening Alex. "It wasn't your fault, Gabriel," Alex said fiercely. "You were only protecting yourself."

Gabriel grunted and shook his head. "I didn't need to kill them."

Alex moved until he could lean forward to gaze into Gabriel's face. "They killed your friend, intended to do only God knows what with you, and I'm pretty sure they murdered dozens of Deviants before Paul. Do not feel guilty about doing what you needed to save yourself."

He wondered if Alex would say the same when he found out about Rafe. "I went straight to Rafe. Told him what happened. I guess as twins we were connected somehow, because his powers came out at the exact same moment in time. He was a telepath, like you. He told me how he'd been in the middle of class when he'd felt as if his head would explode. Thoughts from every direction bombarded him. We figured out pretty quickly that we couldn't stay there and, after getting some things together, left. Somehow we made it a year before we were caught."

"What about your parents?" Alex asked, leaning into Gabriel's side.

"We called them about a week after we left, told them what happened. When they found out we were Deviants, they told us that we were dead to them and hung up on us. I came across a newspaper article a couple years ago with the story of where a rogue Deviant group were randomly bombing the homes of Normals. Our house was one of them." Gabriel remembered feeling detached, unaffected by the thought of his parents' death. "When I heard it, I didn't care. They died the day they cut us out of their lives."

"What happened when they caught you?"

"We were brought to a facility, similar to the one you and your brother were in, and put into separate cells. For almost a week, we were kept there. Someone would bring us food, but otherwise they left us alone. Rafe started practicing using his abilities. It didn't take long for us to be able to communicate through our minds. I didn't know the extent of my own power, and after what I had done to those men who killed Paul, I was too scared to try. Even to protect myself."

Gabriel gave a sardonic smile. "Vincetti somehow knew what we were capable of. They finally brought us to see him, to find out what they wanted. He outright told us that he intended for us to join his ranks and help him kill Normals who attempted to harm Deviants. Both of us refused. For the next two years, he put us through relentless torture. He targeted Rafe's mind and my anger to force our abilities to expand, pushing the level of power we possessed higher and higher. They would whip, beat, and put Rafe through unimaginable pain to make me use my ability. It wouldn't stop until I used my power to hurt the person hurting him."

"Jesus," Alex breathed out, the hand resting on Gabriel's forearm gripping tighter. "How could they be so cruel?"

"The only thing keeping us sane was each other, but they found a way to take that away from us. Remember when I told you there are Deviants and even Normals who have found a way to keep us from using our abilities or to use them against us?"

Alex nodded.

"I still feel the empty void where Rafe used to be. We were no longer able to communicate unless together in the same room. But they saw to it that we couldn't, and after three months, Rafe changed. I could see it in the way he'd calmly accept the beatings they'd put him through while attempting to 'train' me."

The muscles in Gabriel's arms tensed as he thought back to the moment he knew his brother's mind had snapped, when the bridge between them collapsed and he lost his brother forever. "The night Bryan and a team from the ADA raided Vincetti's compound, I did something I never thought I could. Bryan found me first. Vincetti had started allowing Rafael the run of the compound. He knew Rafe wouldn't try to escape. At first I didn't believe Bryan, but when I saw his team releasing others from their cells, I knew I had to take the chance to get out. Except I wouldn't leave without Rafe. What I didn't expect was my brother not wanting to leave or that he would try to stop us from leaving."

He broke off, concentrating on breathing and forcing the empty ache in his chest away. Alex didn't say anything, just waited for him to continue. The heavy warmth pressing into his side and the quiet acceptance he felt from Alex gave him the strength to finish. "Rafe bombarded my mind. I thought my head would explode from the pressure, the intense pain, and the knowledge that my brother caused it. Something distracted him long enough for me to push out a blast of my power, knocking him into a nearby wall. The next thing I knew there were shouts, and people began streaming out of the building. A fire had been started, and it didn't take long to consume the building. I tried to go to my brother, but I could barely see through the smoke."

Something betrayed his emotions despite his attempt to remain strong. Alex grabbed his hand and squeezed. "Stop, Gabe. I didn't mean to bring up bad memories."

A snort rattled in Gabriel's nostrils. "You don't have to worry about bringing them up, Alex. They're always there, haunting me."

"But it's obvious it hurts you to talk about them," Alex protested.

Shaking his head, he replied, "You need to know this. You need to understand why we can't be together."

Alex let out a sound of frustration. "No matter what you did, it won't change the way I feel about you. I—I—"

"I killed my own brother, Alex," Gabriel snarled, shoving Alex away. "How can that not change how you feel about me? To save myself, I killed him. His blood is on my hands!"

Several seconds of silence met his declaration. Then Alex wrapped his arms around Gabriel's shoulders, hugging him fiercely. "He didn't leave you a choice."

"How can you possibly know that?" Gabriel murmured, shocked at how easily Alex had accepted the admission of the worst moment in his life.

"Because I know you, Gabe. You're an honorable man. Kind, strong, and fiercely loyal. You would never do anything you didn't have to do." Alex pressed a kiss to Gabriel's temple. "If you weren't a good man, you would have taken advantage of me the moment you knew I wanted you."

"Alex...." Gabriel's eyes burned, and he blinked furiously.

"Vincetti is the reason for your brother's death. Not you. Rafe's blood is on his hands."

"He came at me out of the smoke. I reacted without thought, using my ability to throw him back into the fire. I can still hear his screams. In my dreams, awake, it's always the screams I remember most," Gabriel murmured. "I lost sight of him in the fire. If Bryan hadn't remained with me, I would have died in the fire too. Some nights, when the memories drive me from sleep, I wish I had died that night. It would only be what I deserve."

Alex tightened his embrace. "Don't say that."

"Why? It's the truth."

"No, it isn't. You've done so much good since then, Gabriel. Because of you, Jason and I didn't suffer the same fate. If you hadn't rescued us, we'd still be Vincetti's prisoners. And there are many Deviants at the agency who would say the same thing."

"The only reason Vincetti targeted you and your brother is because of me. He was going to use you both to get to me."

"Would you listen to yourself?" Alex demanded. "You're letting him win by allowing those memories to haunt you. I'm sorry Rafe died, but, Gabriel, you're still alive. You need to let go and move on. If your brother were still here and the person he was before Vincetti, would he want you to feel guilty for the rest of your life? Or would he want you to be happy? To live a full life and find a way to forgive yourself?"

Gabriel knew Alex's words made sense. Rafael would never have tried to harm him if Vincetti hadn't brainwashed him. Yet he couldn't let it go. Maybe once he'd found revenge for everything Vincetti put them through he could try to go back to living a normal life. But he knew it would be selfish to allow Alex to stay with him even then. "I think we should see about getting you some shoes and a change of clothing," he said flatly, standing from the bed.

The shadows of evening crept in around the edges of the cheap motel curtains, and Gabriel wanted to get on the move. The longer they stayed in one spot, the more likely Vincetti would find them. Especially after Alex's nightmare. "It's getting late, and I want to get moving. They may still be looking for us."

Alex didn't say anything, but Gabriel could feel the hurt and disappointment flowing off of the younger Deviant. The bedsheets rustled as Alex got off the bed. "I'd like to take a shower," Alex said quietly.

"Go ahead. I'm going to call Bear and the others to check in for news."

When the bathroom door clicked shut, Gabriel picked up his cell and dialed Bear. It took several rings for his second in command to answer. "Hey, boss."

"Any word on Bryan or Jason?" he asked immediately.

"Sorry, Gabe, no there isn't. Chris is working with the little bit of equipment he could salvage and the few pieces stored in the vehicles in case the agency ever went down. He's hoping to pinpoint where Vincetti took them. It'll take longer than usual since, and I quote, 'this is absolute caveman shit'. How's the kid?"

"To be expected. Upset, angry, and worried. He's in the shower." Gabriel glanced at the bathroom door. "We'll be stopping to grab some clothing for him and then heading on the road again to the safe house."

"I think there's something you should know, boss." Bear hesitated for a minute. "One of the others saw Isaac talking to the Deviants who attacked the agency."

Ice trickled down Gabriel's spine. "Where is he now?"

"I'm guessing he took off during the attack. None of the other teams have seen him."

Clenching his jaw, he bit out, "If he shows up, detain him. Don't let him leave."

"Sure thing, boss"

They said their good-byes, and Gabriel almost threw the

phone. At least one other death rested on his shoulders. Who knew how many others had died in the attack? Tank had been right all along about Isaac. If he'd listened to his friend, they would never have found the agency and Lizard would still be alive. "Goddamn it!" he roared, punching the wall and leaving a huge hole in the plaster.

"Gabriel?" Alex queried softly behind him.

Gabriel closed his eyes, his fist dropping to his side. Blood oozed from the cuts on his knuckles. "Give me five minutes to dress, and then we're out of here."

"What happened?" Alex tried to ask again, but Gabriel just brushed past Alex on his way to the bathroom, ignoring the question.

Slamming the door, he snatched up his pants, yanking them on and fastening them quickly. They were still damp, but they'd dry during the drive. He pulled his shirt on over his head, rinsed his mouth out with some water, washed his hands, and went back into the motel room to put on his boots and weapons vest. Alex stood at the window, watching out the curtain. "You shouldn't be standing there," Gabriel muttered darkly, sitting on the edge of the bed.

Alex didn't reply and kept his back to Gabriel, still staring out the window. At some point, he'd turned on the light, casting a soft glow through the dingy motel room. "Will you tell me what happened to make you so mad?" Alex finally asked.

Gabriel slipped the weapons vest over his chest, snicking the closures together one by one. "I didn't listen to the instincts of a friend, and everyone else paid the price."

"What do you mean?" Alex turned and frowned at him.

"Isaac was a plant. He's working with Vincetti. He infiltrated the agency for information, and that's how they found us."

Alex protested. "But that's not your fault!"

"Tank insisted the kid's dirty, and I refused to listen. I chose to ignore his instincts and bring Isaac back to the agency anyway. Lizard paid the price with his life!" Gabriel ignored Alex's gasp of shock and walked to the dresser to pick up the keys to his bike.

The touch of Alex's fingers on his bicep caused him to freeze, his hand curled around the keys. "You can't blame yourself for something someone else chooses to do, Gabriel. Isaac chose to deceive everyone. Tank's instincts aside, you followed your heart because you wanted to help him, didn't you?"

Alex moved in front of him, forcing Gabriel to look at him. "You think by saving every Deviant you can, you'll make up for not being able to save your brother, don't you?"

Gabriel stiffened, his mouth flattening into a thin line. "You shouldn't talk about things you know nothing of. Just because I told you about my past does not mean you can say whatever you want and pry into things that don't concern you."

Flinching, Alex stepped away, his shoulders high and tight. "I'm sorry. It won't happen again."

He ignored the guilt pricking at him for hurting Alex and glanced around the room to make sure they hadn't left anything behind. "Let's go. We've got a long drive ahead of us."

Alex followed him out of the room without a word. "Wait by the bike," Gabriel instructed.

Gabriel turned in the key to the front desk, and they were on the road within a few minutes. They turned into a small shopping center with a Target and several small businesses. He pulled into a space, shut off the engine, and waited for Alex to get off the bike. There were little to no words exchanged as they entered the store, going straight for the shoes and clothing section. Gabriel merely trailed Alex, allowing him to choose what he wanted while keeping an eye out around them for anything suspicious. When Alex had a pair of jeans, black shirt, and sneakers, they paid, and Gabriel directed him into the men's room to change.

The fact Alex wasn't talking to him didn't escape his notice, but he couldn't do anything to change it. It would be better if Alex hated him sooner rather than later. Then it would be easier when they parted. He leaned against the wall just inside the door, listening to the sounds of Alex digging through the plastic bag, ripping the price tags off, and getting dressed. Right as Alex opened the stall door, the one to the bathroom swung open. Gabriel tensed, eyeing the big male who'd entered and stepped up to a urinal.

He saw Alex pause hesitantly, and he held out his hand to Alex, never taking his eyes off the other occupant. Alex's palm slid over his, and he closed his fingers around Alex's wrist, pulling him closer. He reached for the door, but before he made contact the man turned to face them, an evil grin quirking a corner of his mouth. "I've heard so much about the legendary Gabriel Romero, yet it was almost too easy to find you," the stranger rumbled. "I figured you'd be more of a challenge than that."

Gabriel studied his newest opponent, taking in the large muscles, bald head, and thick neck. "How do you know I didn't want you to find me?" he taunted, edging Alex closer to the door while shielding him with his body.

The man snorted derisively. "Because if you're anything like he says you are, then you're smart enough to know when to hide. Especially since you're protecting the boy."

"Boy!" Alex exclaimed behind him.

Gabriel squeezed Alex's hand to quiet him. "Why does Vincetti want Alex?"

"You really aren't as bright as I thought you were. Just hand over the boy and I'll let you walk out of here in one piece. He said I can't kill you, but I can hurt you. Now give him to me."

Alex's hand trembled in his, and he stroked his thumb over Alex's wrist in a soothing gesture. No way in hell he'd let the bastard take him. "Not going to happen."

"I was hoping you'd say that." The stranger cracked his knuckles, and when he pulled his hands apart, a blue streak of electricity zipped from palm to palm, surprising Gabriel.

He'd never seen such an ability before or known one like it existed. Paul's had been limited to having to physically touch something for it to have any effect. Where had Vincetti found the Deviant? "Alex. Run."

"No, I'm not leaving you!" Alex protested.

"I said get out of here," Gabriel gritted out between clenched teeth, his eyes carefully watching the power building between the man's hands.

"Yes, run, little bunny. It'll be fun to chase you once I'm done with him."

In the blink of an eye, the bigger Deviant tossed out a blue ball of electricity, and Gabriel shoved Alex into the corner between a sink and the wall, covering him protectively. The energy crashed into the door, blowing it outward and off its hinges. Gabriel could hear screams and shouts coming from outside of the restroom, but kept his concentration on the other male. "Not long until the cops get here," the man taunted, casually flicking another bright light in their direction.

Gabriel pushed Alex down to the floor and sidestepped, plaster raining to the floor around his feet. Anger built inside of him, but he tried to rein it in. Staring at the Deviant's hands, he flung a bit of his power out, satisfaction singing through him when the man screamed at the bones shattering in his hand. "You son of a bitch!" he roared.

"You have no idea who you're messing with," Gabriel said

flatly. "You have thirty seconds to walk out of here and let us go."

"Or what?" the man spat, cradling his hand to his chest.

Gabriel focused on the other Deviant's uninjured hand. Pushing out a bit more power than before, he knew the bones splintered into tiny pieces, rendering the hand useless and quite possibly leaving it unable to be repaired. "Or I will shatter each and every bone in your body until you're nothing but a bag of skin."

"Fuck you," he snapped, bringing the less injured hand up and firing out multiple balls of electricity at Gabriel. All but one slammed uselessly into the tiles of the bathroom walls, causing craters in the plaster. The last one grazed Gabriel's arm, leaving a huge burn mark and the scent of singed skin permeating the air.

Ignoring the pain, Gabriel allowed his power to gather, building into a crescendo of anger and pure hatred. The ground shook when he released it. A look of shock crossed the Deviant's face a split second before he crumpled to the tiled floor, blood seeping from his eyes, ears, and nose. Gabriel knew they couldn't stay and reached out for Alex, pulling him to his feet and rushing out of the bathroom. He saw people gathered around as they exited, and they instantly backed off in fear. Starting to run, he never let go of Alex's hand, tugging him along behind him.

The sound of sirens echoed in the distance when they entered the cool night air, and Gabriel swore under his breath, racing toward the bike. They were almost to it when gunshots rang out from the front of the store. Bullets whizzed by them. Snarling, Gabriel turned and knocked the shooters off their feet, sending them crashing through the glass door. He jumped on the bike, started it up, and shouted, "Get on!"

Alex hurriedly slid onto the motorcycle, gripping

Gabriel's waist tightly. The engine roared as Gabriel gunned it and took off, narrowly missing one of the cop cars speeding into the parking lot. He prayed they wouldn't give chase, but the prayer went unanswered when the car spun around and started coming after them. Gabriel urged the bike faster, the speedometer needle creeping toward a hundred, then one twenty. The lights on top of the police vehicle flashed brightly in the small mirrors, letting him know they still hadn't shaken their tail. "Hold on," he commanded over the roar of the wind flying past them and the sirens trailing them.

He felt Alex squeeze his waist harder and press further into his back. He pushed the speedometer higher. It wasn't until they reached one fifty that the cop cars started to lose ground. The lights dimmed the further away they got, and finally they were nothing but pinpricks of blue in the distance. Gabriel didn't slow the bike back to a normal speed until the lights had disappeared completely and been gone for several minutes.

For the next couple of hours, they rode in silence. Gabriel could only imagine what was running through Alex's mind after seeing what he'd done. The hulking Deviant at the agency had suffered the same fate. Most of the men who'd tortured and killed Paul had died the same way too. Would Alex be afraid of him now? The idea of Alex being scared of him sat in his belly like a rock. He couldn't deny it or brush it off this time. When they stopped, Alex would surely ask what he'd done, and there would be no way to avoid telling him the extent of his power.

Gabriel stopped at one of the rest stop stations along the freeway for gas and to give them the chance to get a bite to eat. Pulling up next to a pump, he waited for Alex to step off and swung his leg over to stand. He groaned as he stretched the kinks in his back and then gave the singe on his arm a cursory glance. When they reached the safe house, he'd need to put ointment and a bandage on it. "I'm going to fill up. Why don't you go on inside and see what they have to eat? As soon as I'm done here, I'll head in."

Alex nodded, set the helmet on the seat, and turned without a word, walking toward the building. Gabriel watched him leave, pensive at how silent the younger man was being. He took out his wallet, swiped one of the credit cards registered in the false identity Bryan created for all Deviants at the agency, and began fueling up.

When he entered the building after the pump stopped and he'd moved the bike to a regular space, he saw Alex sitting in a booth and staring out the window. He approached slowly, never taking his eyes off of him. "Alex?"

Green eyes cut away from the window to look up at him. Still no words were said. "Did you decide what you'd like to eat?"

"I'm not hungry," Alex replied listlessly, going back to looking out the window.

Gabriel stifled a sigh and went to grab something for them both. He came back to the table with a couple of sandwiches, chips, and sodas. Setting one of each in front of Alex, he slid into the booth across from him. "You want to talk about what's bothering you?"

Alex shook his head. "No."

He lowered his voice to keep the other people around them from hearing. "Look, I know what I did to that man back there scared you, but I would never hurt you."

"That's not what's wrong!" Alex exclaimed, his eyes darting to Gabriel's. "I could never be afraid of you, Gabe. Ever."

"Then what has you so upset?"

Alex toyed with his can of still unopened soda. "Everything's such a mess. Since Grams died, my entire world has changed. Now I'm being chased, shot at, and tormented by a man I never even met. I don't even know if I'll ever see my brother again."

Gabriel set his sandwich down on the plastic wrapping and reached out to grab Alex's hand. "We will get Jason back, and you will go back to having a normal life, Alex. I will personally see to it that you can do whatever you want with your life. I know it's a lot to handle right now, but things will get better."

Alex smiled grimly. "Grams always used to say that no matter how cruel someone seemed, they had a good soul. I'm starting to doubt it after everything I've seen. The man back there. He wanted to hurt you. Why? What could possibly be his reason when he's never even met you before?"

"Sometimes people are born with a darkness in their souls. Sometimes they go through things in life which they allow to change them, twist who they are until they're no longer the person they were." Gabriel looked down at their hands, his on top of Alex's. He didn't want to admit out loud how scared he'd been for Alex's safety, especially when the bystander had started shooting a gun at them. "Don't let these events change you, Alex. You have one of the most beautiful, purest souls I've seen in a long time."

Turning his hand over, Alex entwined his fingers with Gabriel's. "I'm sorry if it seemed as if I was afraid of you, Gabriel. I didn't mean for it to appear that way."

"I wouldn't blame you if you were. There have been other Deviants and Normals over the years who've seen the power I hold and been terrified of me. Few have seen the true depth of it and lived, though. I never use it against anyone innocent and try to avoid using it at all."

Silence fell over them until Gabriel gently extracted his hand from Alex's. "Eat. We've still got a long way to go."

Ten minutes later, they got back on the road. Gabriel

hoped they could make it to Kansas without further incident. This time he found his prayer granted, and they were almost to the Kansas safe house when the light of day began to cut through the shadows. Pinks, purples, and oranges dusted the horizon. Gabriel didn't figure stopping would make much difference now. The faster they got to the safe house, the better.

1 4

ALEX

Jackal sat lounging on the porch steps of the safe house when they arrived. Standing, he approached the motorcycle as soon as Gabriel stopped. "Glad to see you're all right, boss."

Alex slipped from the bike, stretching and letting out a groan after so many hours on it. He took off the helmet and waited for Gabriel to dismount before setting it on the back. "We need to talk. Gather Bear, Tank, and Chris," Gabriel instructed.

"Sure thing, Gabe." Jackal headed back into the house to get the rest of Gabriel's team.

"You should go inside, grab something to eat, and get some rest, Alex."

"No. I'm staying. I want to hear what we're going to do to rescue my brother." Alex crossed his arms over his chest, giving him a stare that dared Gabriel to stop him.

Gabriel sighed. "You aren't going on the rescue mission, Alex. That'll put you right where Vincetti wants you. Within reach. I also don't think it's a good idea for you to know our plan since they've invaded your mind more than once in your sleep. If they wanted to, they could extract it from you without you even realizing it."

Hurt shafted through Alex. Gabriel thought him weak. "Jason is my brother, Gabe. I have the right to be there. I am not going to stay here and sit around, waiting to see if he's alive or dead and wondering what's happening to you."

Glaring at him, Gabriel snapped, "You aren't going. End of story, Alex. You'd be more of a liability than an asset."

Alex flinched, and his arms dropped to his sides. It felt like his dream all over again. "You said I wasn't weak," he accused.

Anger flitted over Gabriel's features, and then he grabbed hold of Alex by the upper arms, shaking him slightly. "Don't you understand, Alex? If you're there, I won't be able to do my job because I'm only going to be worried about keeping you safe!"

Alex made a small sound of surprise and stared at Gabriel. "You care about me that much?"

Gabriel growled, and suddenly Alex couldn't breathe. He found himself under assault by Gabriel's hungry kiss. Moaning, he leaned into the other Deviant, his arms twining around Gabriel's neck. Just as abruptly, it was over, and Alex panted, resting his forehead on Gabriel's shoulder. "You have to stay here, Alex," Gabriel's voice rumbled near his ear. "I can't worry about your safety and concentrate on getting Jason and Bryan out of there at the same time."

Pulling back, Alex locked Gabriel's gaze in his. "I'll stay here, but promise me that you're coming back."

"I'm coming back, Alex. We're all coming back."

He knew Gabriel referred to the team, Jason, and Bryan, but he held real fear in his heart that Gabriel would sacrifice himself to ensure everyone else got out all right and to make sure Vincetti died. The sound of a throat clearing interrupted whatever else Alex might have said. They both turned to see

Jackal, Bear, Tank, and Chris standing there, all of them smirking ear to ear. Gabriel scowled at them. "Any progress, Chris?" he barked out while releasing Alex.

Alex hid a grin when Jackal winked at him and listened as Chris detailed what he'd found. "It took me a while since I didn't have much in the way of equipment to work with, but I was able to ascertain Jason and Bryan are being held in the same compound we rescued Alex and Jason from previously. There is one thing, though. There are a lot more heat signatures than before. I was unable to hack into their CCTV system to get further information regarding the type of Deviants we'll be up against. It would take a lot more sophisticated equipment to get in undetected, and I didn't want to tip them off to our location."

"Keep working on gathering whatever intel you can, Chris. Have you been in touch with the other teams?" Gabriel asked.

"They're gathering whatever weapons and equipment they can and waiting on instructions from you, boss," Jackal replied.

"Chris, how long will it take to find out what we're up against at Vincetti's compound?"

"Few hours, maybe a day. I need to run into town to grab some more supplies."

Gabriel nodded and looked at his watch. "Go. Get what you need. I want to head out in forty-eight hours. Vincetti's had them too long as it is. Jackal, call the Alpha squad leader and explain the situation, tell him to sit tight until we make a full-on plan of attack."

Chris agreed and headed back into the house to prepare for his trip to town. Jackal moved away from the group to make the call on a pay-as-you-go cell phone. "Alex, why don't you go inside, get something to eat, and find a room to rest,"

Gabriel suggested, nudging Alex in the direction of the house.

"I'm not tired," Alex protested, resisting Gabriel's light push.

"Come on, Alex," Theresa called from the front porch. "There's breakfast in the kitchen. You too, Gabe."

Alex grabbed hold of Gabriel's hand and tugged him toward the safe house. It looked a bit like the one he'd been taken to when Gabriel's squad rescued him and Jason the last time. Run down, paint peeling, and most of the screens were torn off the windows. The fresh scent of cut grass clung to the air, and Alex grinned, figuring Tank must have been busy. The steps creaked beneath his feet, and the screen door screeched as they opened it. He could hear a television playing somewhere and the sound of voices coming from the kitchen. Gabriel tried to extricate his hand, but Alex held on tight, refusing to let go. "Alex," Gabriel said in exasperation.

He gave Gabriel an innocent look. "What?"

If the older Deviant really wanted him to let go, he could have forced Alex, but he just sighed in resignation and stopped trying to pull away. Preston and Hayley stood at the kitchen sink, washing and drying dishes. "Hey, Alex! Gabe!" Preston boomed, dropping the hand towel and giving them both backslapping hugs, causing Alex to drop Gabriel's hand. "Glad to see you made it. Though not without injury," he added when he spied the burn on Gabriel's bicep.

Hayley greeted them, her gaze zeroed in on the way their hands were linked. She studied Alex a moment before turning back to the sink. Alex moved to grab a plate of eggs and some toast, sitting down at the table with two of the other Deviants who'd been living at the agency, including Marcus. Gabriel remained by the stove with Preston and Hayley, discussing the events of the other night and Bryan's situation. "Hey, Marcus," Alex greeted quietly.

Marcus had a sympathetic look on his face. "I heard about Jason. Are you okay?"

He shrugged and picked at his food. "I'm dealing."

"Any word on what's happening?"

Alex shook his head. "No. Gabriel believes he's alive, but we don't know for sure."

"Are they planning a rescue?" Marcus asked curiously.

Suspicion rose in Alex, and he eyed Marcus, but he didn't see anything other than concern and curiosity in the other Deviant's features. "I don't know. He won't tell me anything," Alex lied. "Did you hear anything otherwise?"

"Nah, they won't let us get involved. I want to help, though." Marcus frowned, toying with his fork. "At least then I wouldn't be sitting around here being useless."

Marcus practically echoed Alex's sentiments from earlier. "I know what you mean," he stated flatly. "I want to go, but—"

"Alex," Gabriel interrupted him, his hand coming down on Alex's shoulder and squeezing for a moment.

Biting his lip, Alex couldn't believe what he'd almost done. No wonder Gabriel didn't want to tell him anything. When Gabriel sat down across from him, Alex gave him an apologetic look. He didn't speak after that, just listened to Marcus talking to one of the others who'd joined them at the table. A huge yawn broke out when he finished eating, and a sheepish grin crossed his lips when the others laughed. "Sorry."

"You should go get some rest," Gabriel told him when the others took their plates to the kitchen sink. "It's been a long couple of days."

The thought of having someone invade his dreams again made Alex drop his gaze to the table, anxiety rushing in. "What if... what if he comes back?"

"Who?" Gabriel asked, confusion evident in his tone.

"Him. The other you."

Gabriel touched the back of his hand lightly. "Whoever is pushing these dreams into your head, Alex, is trying to mess with your mind. You have to fight to keep them out."

He stared at the long, blunt fingers resting on his hand. "I don't know if I can."

"This is what we've been training for, Alex. If he comes to you again, use your gift to push back. They can only enter if you let them. You don't understand the full capacity of your abilities yet, Alex, but you're a level five. Someone must have mentioned how level fives are rare. The most common are threes, fours are slightly less common, but fives are few and far between."

"I'll try. Everything in the dreams feels so real. It's as if I'm really there, and when I see you, or rather the other you, it's hard to imagine trying to hurt you," Alex murmured.

"That's just it, Alex. It's not me. You need to remember that. The Deviant uses my face because he knows you'll hesitate in fighting back, but you have to get past seeing me. Look into the person, find their weakness, and use it against them. I know you can do it."

Alex flushed at the confidence Gabriel had in him, but he didn't feel it in himself. He picked at a small groove in the wood table unconsciously. "How can you be so certain?"

Gabriel smiled in a way Alex had never seen, and he turned Alex's hand over to lightly trace the lines on his palm. "Because in the last few weeks, if I've learned anything at all about you, it's that you're a very strong, very stubborn," he said teasingly, "person who doesn't give up when they want something. All you have to do is want it bad enough."

Alex's heart swelled at the affection on Gabriel's face and in his voice. He knew, no matter what happened in the coming days, that he needed to tell Gabriel how he felt about him. Taking a deep breath, he opened his mouth to tell the older Deviant he loved him, but he didn't get the chance. "Gabriel, Preston would like to speak with you. He's in the living room. I can show Alex to one of the unoccupied rooms so he can rest," Hayley interjected from the doorway.

The loss of Gabriel's touch left him bereft when Gabriel pulled away at Hayley's voice. He watched as Gabriel stood, but stopped him before he could leave. "Will you come to see me before I sleep?"

"I will," Gabriel promised and walked out of the dining area to find Preston.

Hayley waited at the kitchen door for him to follow, and he didn't say anything as they climbed the stairs. He knew Hayley believed his love was nothing more than a crush or gratitude for Gabriel saving him, but he knew in his heart it was much, much deeper than the surface. Had she interrupted them on purpose? Did she know he'd intended to tell Gabriel he loved him? "The bed is already made up. If you want to take a shower or clean up before sleeping, the bathroom is just down the hall and there are clean towels under the sink," Hayley said as she opened the door to the last room on the right.

"Thank you, Hayley," he replied.

She entered the bedroom behind him and closed the door. "I wanted to see how you were doing, Alex. Jackal informed me of what happened to you two last night, and I know you must be worried for Jason."

Alex shrugged. "I'm okay. I'm just hoping they aren't hurting Jace. I can't say I wasn't scared, but Gabriel handled the guy who came after us."

"I see things have developed further between you and Gabriel." She hinted at wanting to know more.

"I know you said you wanted me to be careful with him, Hayley, but I care about him. It isn't a crush or hero worship." He wandered to the window to look out at the yard below. He could see Bear and Tank talking while Jackal and Theresa sat under a nearby tree holding one another. Their love for each other shone so clearly from their faces. It almost made him jealous. Would Gabriel ever free himself from the burden he carried enough to let him in? "I love him," he murmured quietly.

She approached him and touched his shoulder. "I wasn't going to say you didn't, Alex. I wanted to thank you."

Surprise brought Alex's head around to look at her. "Thank me?"

Smiling, she squeezed his shoulder and explained, "I've known Gabriel since he came to the ADA. In five years, I've never seen him smile the way he did today. You've changed something in him, Alex. There's a light in his eyes I didn't think I'd ever see. Don't let him push you away. Fight for him, because even if he hasn't told you, he's in love with you."

"You think so?" he asked.

"I know so. You're wearing his cross, something he never takes off."

Alex touched the chain around his throat and looked at her in astonishment. The cross was Gabriel's? He'd been the one to leave it on his bed? "I didn't know."

"You didn't? How did you end up with it, then?"

"I found it on my bed the day of my birthday," Alex replied softly. "No card or name of who it was from."

"It means a lot to him." She hugged him abruptly. "Tomorrow let's talk about what happened at the agency and the last few days. I think it will help."

Alex nodded and hugged her back. "Thanks, Hayley. I'm glad I met you. You remind me of Grams. She used to always see the light in everyone. I almost forgot about that after everything. And… I'm sorry about Bryan. I hope he's okay too."

"Bryan is one of the strongest men I know, Alex. I have

faith in my heart that he'll be fine. Now get some rest." Hayley stepped away and left him alone, closing the door behind her.

He perched on the edge of the bed, toeing his sneakers off. The room didn't have much: a queen bed, a small nightstand, and a three-drawer dresser. He could detect the faint scent of Pine-Sol and furniture polish. The walls were a dingy beige and seemed somehow depressing on top of the situation they found themselves in.

Lying down, he brought his knees to his chest, wrapping his arms around them. He figured he probably should have taken his clothing off, but didn't really have the energy to move again. His thoughts returned to his brother. Were they hurting him? Did the dream yesterday mean Jason was dead? His heart ached at the thought of being without his brother. Ever since their mother tried to drown them as children, they'd been inseparable, and no matter what happened they were there for each other. Grams instilled family in both of them, never letting either of them dwell on the hatred and fear their mother had toward them.

He began to drift between awake and asleep, struggling to stay conscious until Gabriel came to see him. The stress of the last few days won the battle, and he fell into the dark abyss of sleep. He couldn't be sure how long it was before he began to dream, but the dream started out differently than the last. When he sat up this time, he found himself in the clearing by the creek that ran through the ADA property. The sun shone brightly through the trees overhead, and Gabriel sat across from him, legs crossed and eyes closed. Alex realized it was one of their meditating sessions.

"You're not focusing, Alex," Gabriel admonished, his eyes opening to look at him. *"You need to clear your mind and just let everything around you go. Close your eyes and breathe."*

Alex obeyed and allowed his eyes to close, breathing

deeply and evenly. Peace spread through him, warming his limbs. *"Good, Alex. Very good,"* Gabriel praised.

Silence fell around them. The only sounds Alex could hear were the trees rustling in the light breeze and the soft trickle of water nearby. Even the sound of Gabriel's breathing faded away, a fact Alex didn't fail to notice. Opening his eyes again, he found himself looking into a mirror, except it wasn't a mirror. Jason smirked at him and stretched his arms above his head, moaning at the pull of his muscles. *"Hello, little brother."*

"Jace?" Alex asked in surprise while looking around for Gabriel.

Jason leaned back on his hands, tilting his head back to enjoy the warm sunlight sifting down through the leaves. *"Missed me?"*

"Of course!" Alex exclaimed, moving to his brother's side. *"But how are you here?"*

His twin tipped his head until he could pout at Alex. *"You sound like you don't want me here."*

Alex shook his head. *"That's not it. I just don't understand how you can be here. You were... taken."*

"You're right, but when you sleep there's an open doorway. They told me I could talk to you if we are both asleep. I... needed to see you."

Staring at Jason, Alex noticed a bruise along his brother's jawline, another on his throat, and several along his arms. *"What are they doing to you, Jace?"*

The smirk on Jason's face faded, and his eyes dimmed. *"They want me to tell them about the ADA, their resources, everything, but I refused. I couldn't risk them finding you. I had to keep you safe."*

Alex knew his brother hid his fear and pain behind anger or an overly cocky façade. When Grams died, Jason buried his grief so deep he'd never allowed himself to cry or release the pain. There seemed to be such hopelessness in Jason's voice, a resignation that he would die and this was his last chance to see Alex before he did. Desperate to reassure Jason he would be okay, Alex revealed everything to his twin. *"They won't find me. I'm at a safe house in Kansas, but we're coming for you, Jason. You and Bryan. Gabriel said they'd be on the move in two days. His team knows where you're being held captive."*

"Alex, no!" Jason cried out, his eyes widening and his hands suddenly gripping Alex's shoulders. *"Why, Alex? Why did you tell me that? Now... now they know where you are!"*

Jason's form began to dissolve, becoming translucent, see through. *"Alex, you have to warn Gabriel. Warn the others they know. Don't come here. Don't let* him *win! Please, Alex!"*

Alex watched in terror as his twin faded away in front of him, the grip on his shoulders lessening until it was gone. *"Jace!"*

A scarred Gabriel stepped out of the shadows of the trees nearby, a satisfied grin on his face. The mask had hidden the scars on Gabriel's face, and Alex swallowed hard, fighting back his fear at the disfigured mirror image of the one man he trusted as much as he did his brother. *"Thank you, Alex. I knew you'd slip up if you could see your brother's pain. You're so weak. Hard to believe you're a level five."*

Horrified, Alex struggled to stand, to run, but a weight unlike anything he'd ever felt pressed down on him. *"This is my world, Alex. I control it. I show you what I want you to see, what I want you to hear. Of course, it won't do if you remember this enough to warn him, now would it?"* Gabriel said tauntingly and gestured behind him.

"Make sure you get the exact location of this 'safe' house, Connor," he demanded of the tall, dark-haired man who came forward.

Alex tried to move, to back away as the man approached him, but he couldn't move, couldn't even lift a hand to fight him off. Connor knelt next to him and placed his palms on either side of Alex's face. *"I'm not going to hurt you,"* Connor murmured, looking into Alex's eyes.

He could see true regret in the man's ocean blue eyes as he did something to Alex's mind. *"When you wake up, you'll remember nothing, say nothing, about this dream."*

Tears welled in Alex's eyes as he realized the very thing Gabriel feared had happened. Gabriel's reluctance to tell him their plans had been justified, and now he'd betrayed the very man he loved. *"Please don't,"* he begged of the stranger, pleading for him not to remove the memory of the nightmare or reveal the location of the safe house.

"I'm sorry. I don't have a choice," Connor whispered and closed his eyes, his fingers spanning Alex's temples.

Alex felt an odd warmth spread along his skull and invade his brain, almost as if Connor's fingers were actually touching him inside. A shudder twisted through him at the violation of his mind and body. His eyelids drifted down, shuttering the images in front of him, and when he next opened them, he found himself alone in the clearing near the stream. Alex smiled in happiness, the moments with Jason and scarred Gabriel wiped from his mind. He lay down among the blades of grass to savor the happiness of being in one of the places he found to be the most peaceful. Whenever he thought of it, it reminded him of Gabriel.

The dream remained uneventful for once, and when Alex woke, the room was darkened by twilight, and he felt more rested than he could ever remember being in the last two years. He sat up, stretching almost like a cat and moaning softly as his muscles elongated and expanded. When he brought his arms back down to the bed, he saw that he wasn't alone. Breath catching in his throat, he realized Gabriel had stayed with him while he slept.

Gabriel sat in a chair near the bed, slumped down slightly,

his lips parted in easy breathing as he slumbered. Alex smiled affectionately, quietly moving until he sat on the edge nearest to Gabriel. He took those unguarded moments to lovingly study each feature he could see in the waning light from the window: the strong chin and high cheekbones, the slight scruff on his face, and the firm lips that brought him such pleasure. Unable to stop himself, he leaned forward to press a warm, soft kiss to them. Gabriel started a bit, waking up at the tender touch of lips on his, but didn't attempt to push him away or utter a word to end it.

Alex didn't deepen the kiss. He kept it light and gentle, just a brushing of lips over lips. A small, wanton noise escaped him when Gabriel's hand came to rest on the side of his neck, his thumb caressing along his jawline. He leaned into the touch, bringing one hand up to press over Gabriel's heart, feeling the steady beat beneath his palm. He tentatively flicked his tongue against Gabriel's lower lip, tasting him. It pleased Alex when Gabriel responded by teasingly darting his tongue into Alex's mouth.

Gabriel pulled Alex from the bed into his lap, the movement seemingly effortless, their bodies melting together as though two pieces of a puzzle, sliding into one another. Alex eagerly leaned into the embrace, craving the affection Gabriel offered. No words passed between them. Their movements, their breathing, the only sounds in the darkness. Alex took the chance to explore Gabriel's body, his hand sliding beneath the hem of Gabriel's T-shirt to trail his fingers over the defined muscles of Gabriel's stomach. The skin fluttered beneath his touch, fascinating him immensely, and he did it again, smiling into the kiss.

"You find that funny, do you?" Gabriel said huskily, moving his lips up Alex's jaw to the sensitive earlobe, huffing sexily when Alex shuddered.

"Gabe," Alex whimpered, pushing his hand higher under

Gabriel's shirt to rub his palm over the hardened point of Gabriel's nipple. Satisfaction speared him when Gabriel growled into his ear and nipped the delicate flesh of his lobe.

"Keep that up and you may find yourself in trouble," Gabriel rasped, dipping his tongue into the shell of Alex's ear.

Pure lust slammed into Alex's groin, and he moaned. He managed to gasp out, "Promise?" between wheezes.

Gabriel suddenly stood up, bringing Alex with him, and moved the two paces to the bed to lay them down among the covers. Alex immediately wrapped his legs around Gabriel's hips, his arms encircling the broad chest to pull him harder against him. His head tilted back and to the side as Gabriel ravaged the side of his throat, the other Deviant's mouth sucking wetly, his teeth scraping over the pale flesh. Alex could barely keep from drowning in the sensations, so many bombarded him at once. The scent of Gabriel's skin, the feel of his lips, the warmth of his body pressing his into the bed, everything crashed over him, sending him under the waves of passion and desire in a way he'd never experienced. He felt as though he was drowning, yet he prayed he'd never surface.

15

GABRIEL

"WHAT the hell is this?" Gabriel demanded, staring down at the two little foil packages in his hand before glaring at Preston.

Preston lifted an eyebrow at him. "If you don't know what they're for, then maybe we need to have the 'talk'." He made air quotes on the last word.

Gabriel scowled at him. "You know what I mean, smartass!"

Preston laughed for a moment and then grew serious. "Well, it is pretty obvious something changed between you and Alex these last couple of days. Hayley and I just wanted to make sure you were being safe."

Gabriel almost choked at Preston's words. "We didn't... Alex and I haven't...."

"Then they're just in case." Preston shrugged.

"I am not going to have sex with Alex," Gabriel snapped, clenching his hand around the condoms.

"Why not?" Preston asked.

"Several reasons, Pres! He's too young, I'm too old, and

we're all running for our lives right now. Do I need to go on?" Gabriel folded his arms over his chest, shaking his head.

"Bullshit," Preston replied lazily.

Gabriel's mouth dropped open in surprise. "What?"

"Bullshit," Preston repeated. "You're only a few years older than him. He's over eighteen, obviously knows what he wants, and you don't have to hit anyone with a frying pan to see that you want him. We're in a safe house, Gabe. No one knows where we are."

He moved up to Gabriel and gripped his shoulder with one hand. "You've been running since the day Bryan brought you to the agency. Even Bryan could see it, which is why he ended your relationship. Stop running, Gabe. It's been five years. No one blames you for what happened. It was self-defense."

Preston's words nearly echoed Alex's from the motel. "He deserves better."

"Better than someone who loves him? Someone who would die to protect him?" Preston asked quietly.

Gabriel's eyes widened, and he stared at Preston in astonishment. Preston smiled and squeezed his shoulder lightly. "Don't be so surprised, Gabe. It's not hard to tell when you care about someone. You focus your whole being on protecting the people you love. Plus you look at him the way I've looked at Hayley since the day I met her."

The fight left Gabriel, and he ran a tired hand over his face. "I can't."

"Again I ask, why not?" Preston pressed.

"Because I love him."

Preston smiled. "Then there's never been a better reason why you should."

Gabriel opened and shut his mouth several times before giving up. He shoved the condoms in his pocket and shook his head. "Tell Hayley thanks, and Bryan will be home soon."

Winking, Preston responded, "Sure thing, Gabe."

Gabriel walked up the stairs, very aware of the foil packets pressing into his upper thigh. Preston's words weighed heavily on him. His mind screamed at him to throw them away, to let Alex go and ignore his heart, but his heart shouted even louder, demanding he grab hold of Alex and never let go. Would he be able to give Alex all that he deserved? It wouldn't be fair to hold the younger Deviant to him if he couldn't give his heart freely.

Stopping in the restroom, he found the basic first aid kit in the cabinet under the sink and set it on the counter top. He applied a small amount of the ointment inside the kit to the burn on his arm, placed a gauze pad over the singed area, and managed to wrap more gauze around his arm and tie it off. Replacing everything, he continued down to the room Hayley had escorted Alex to earlier.

Gabriel knocked lightly on the bedroom door, waiting for an answer from Alex. When nothing came, he twisted the knob and pushed the door open to spot Alex lying on the bed fast asleep. Treading carefully, he moved to the side of the bed to stare down at Alex's sleeping face, tracing each feature with his gaze: the dark lashes resting on pale cheeks, the rosy red lips parted in slumber, and the slim, perfect nose. All of it together made the most alluring sight Gabriel had ever seen in his life. He felt tired, tired of fighting what he wanted, of holding back the hunger and desire inside of him for the beautiful Deviant who forced him to feel things he'd never thought he'd be able to after Rafael died.

Moving to the chair near the window, Gabriel sat down in it to watch over Alex as he slept, keeping his pledge to protect him from the man haunting his dreams. He hoped he could keep his other promise to rescue Jason and that history wouldn't repeat itself. He'd told Alex the truth when he'd said he believed Alex had so much strength, but losing his twin would test that strength beyond anything else he'd ever experienced. Something he'd lived through by immersing himself in the ADA and everything it represented. Until his sexual relationship with Bryan, he'd never allowed himself to think of anything beyond the next mission, just to be able to hold onto his sanity. No matter what happened, he didn't want Alex involved in the ADA. It was too dangerous.

Gabriel found himself drifting off and tried more than once to stay awake, needing to ensure Alex's restful slumber wasn't disturbed by the dreams, but eventually his body forced him to give in. In his sleep, he unconsciously slumped down in the chair, his head lolling to the side slightly. Gabriel's own dreams didn't allow him to rest peacefully. Images of Alex dying, his team destroyed, and finding Bryan's body plagued him. He knew he couldn't allow any of it to happen. If it became necessary, he would trade himself for the others.

What disturbed Gabriel wasn't sounds from Alex or any of the other occupants of the safe house, but the feeling of warm, gentle lips brushing over his. The light pressure registered, and he jerked slightly yet settled immediately when he realized the kiss belonged to Alex. He brought his hand up to cup the side of Alex's neck, his thumb trailing over the slim edge of Alex's jawbone. The wanton sound Alex let out sent heat rushing to his groin, and Alex's hand pressing against his pec caused his chest to tighten with emotion.

Gabriel pulled Alex into his lap when the younger Deviant's tongue teased along his bottom lip. Their bodies molded together easily, as though made for one another, and his heart clenched at the thought of Alex not being in his life. His muscles rippled in pleasure when Alex's slender fingers found their way to his stomach, and he couldn't stop the affection striking through him when he felt Alex smile at the reaction. "Oh, you find that funny, do you?" he said huskily, sliding his lips along Alex's jaw to the sensitive skin of his earlobe, huffing in satisfaction when Alex shivered.

At Alex's whimper of his name and the sudden brush of Alex's palm over his nipple, Gabriel growled and nipped the delicate flesh of Alex's lobe. "Keep that up and you may find yourself in trouble," Gabriel rasped, dipping his tongue into the shell of Alex's ear.

Alex's moan tore through him, enslaving him to the desire raging inside, but the panted "Promise?" broke the last bit of resolve he held and sent him to his feet. He gripped Alex close and covered the short distance to the bed, following Alex down to the mattress. Alex twined his legs around his hips and clutched Gabriel tighter against his body. Gabriel latched onto the side of his throat with his lips, sucking heatedly and lightly abrading the tender flesh with his teeth. Rocking against the obvious bulge pushing into his belly, he captured Alex's mouth in a deep kiss once more.

He slid his tongue between Alex's lips, rubbing his along Alex's. The slick, smooth glide of muscle over muscle stoked his lust even higher. Electricity tingled through his nerve endings straight to his cock at each soft lick, every passionate kiss. He broke the kiss and carefully eased back to look down at Alex. "Are you sure?" he murmured. "I don't want you to regret anything."

Alex reached up to lovingly trace the outline of Gabriel's lips, an emotion sparkling in his green eyes that Gabriel had never seen directed at him. He'd only seen the affectionate, loving look exchanged between Jackal and Theresa. His breath caught, and his heart stumbled, falling and landing once and for all right into Alex's slender hands. "I've never been more sure of anything in my life, and I could never regret being with you," Alex whispered.

If the younger Deviant only knew how those simple words destroyed him. Gabriel groaned and sat up, straddling

Alex's legs to pull at Alex's shirt, yanking it up over his head and carelessly tossing it aside. His own shirt followed a second behind it. His eyes hungrily roamed the pale, firm chest draped with the silver cross and the light rose-colored nipples as Gabriel lowered his body back down onto Alex. Alex's hands gripped at his back with a gasp when he latched onto one of the pink nubs, sucking and pulling it between his lips. He flicked his tongue back and forth over the hard point, relishing Alex's whimpers and moans, the shudders wracking his body.

Gabriel stroked his fingers along the defined contour of Alex's sternum, causing the cross to shift on its chain with a tinkling sound. Drifting lower to the light sprinkling of brown hair leading into his jeans, he stopped to tease the inner flesh of Alex's belly button. He traced the skin just above the fastening on Alex's jeans, dipping under repeatedly. Carefully sliding the button free of its hook, he followed the path of his fingers, using his tongue to bathe the invisible line. Alex trembled when Gabriel slipped his tongue into his navel, his hands gripping Gabriel's head gently. A breathy, "Oh," escaped Alex at Gabriel's fingers outlining his hard cock behind the fabric when his hand slithered lower.

Pinching the zipper of Alex's jeans between thumb and forefinger, Gabriel tugged the fastener down, listening to the harsh sound of metal teeth separating in the darkness. He popped the button free and slowly separated the folds of material, almost groaning when Alex's stiff length sprung upward. At least seven inches of rigid prick jutted out from a small tuft of wiry brown hair. It turned him on even more to know Alex didn't have any underwear on under the jeans he'd worn since the department store.

The moonlight from the window cast just enough brightness for Gabriel to make out the weeping tip and the perfectly shaped mushroom head. He licked his lips and swept the pad of his thumb over the pearl beading at the slit. Alex trembled and let out a small keening noise, so Gabriel did it again. He traced the vein along the underside of Alex's cock, voraciously watching as the column of engorged flesh twitched and bobbed at his touch. "Beautiful," he said in a low voice.

"Gabriel," Alex whined, embarrassment evident in his voice.

Smirking slightly, Gabriel slid his tongue over the rounded tip, gathering the drop of liquid and finally tasting Alex. The younger Deviant's flavor exploded on his taste buds, and he pulled the rounded head into his mouth, sucking gently.

"Oh God," Alex sobbed above him.

Gabriel felt Alex's fingers tighten on his scalp, yanking his hair a little. He began to move his mouth down Alex's cock, drawing more and more of him inside, all the while teasing the sensitive skin with darting licks of his tongue. He swallowed the entire length, burying his nose in the hair at the base, and started back up to the top again. When he reached the head, he reluctantly released the tasty prick to tug Alex's jeans down further, freeing the perfectly rounded orbs beneath it. They drew his attention immediately, and he skimmed the underside of Alex's shaft to the base, nuzzling briefly. He weighed each globe carefully with his tongue before drawing one between his lips, moving back and forth to each until he heard Alex's panting cries echoing off the walls.

He released the one in his mouth and engulfed Alex's shaft once more, sucking heatedly. The tiny jerks of Alex's cock, the ragged breaths wheezing from his lungs, and the quivers wracking his slender body warned him of Alex's impending release. He swallowed around the hard column of flesh, triggering Alex's orgasm. Sweet, salty spice met his taste buds, and he eagerly drank the other man's essence, greedily imbibing the zesty liquid.

Gabriel only released Alex once he'd taken it all, rising up over the dark-haired Deviant. Alex's eyes were closed, his lips parted on shivering breaths. Gabriel smiled affectionately and brushed a lock of sweat-dampened hair away from Alex's cheek. Alex opened his eyes to gaze up at him, wonder and satiation radiating up at him. Unable to stop himself, he leaned down to press a gentle kiss to Alex's lips, nipping lightly at the tantalizing bottom lip. Alex returned the kiss, opening his mouth to accept the slick pink muscle.

Alex's hand slid down Gabriel's side, tracing the defined hardness of his body. When he reached the edge of Gabriel's jeans, he slipped in between their bodies to cup the bulge in Gabriel's pants. Gabriel hissed as Alex squeezed him through his jeans. "Alex," Gabriel warned raggedly, rocking into the palm of Alex's hand.

Alex ignored the warning and squeezed again. Gabriel sat up and quickly divested the remainder of their clothing, removing the condoms from his pocket and setting them on the nightstand. He saw Alex's eyes zero in on them and the auburn-brown eyebrows go up, yet Alex didn't say anything, just slid his gaze along Gabriel's body. Gabriel felt his stare as a tangible touch, his prick bobbing in pleasure when Alex kept his scrutiny there for several long breaths.

Gabriel watched Alex reach out to wrap his fingers around his cock. A groan tore from him at the sensation of Alex's calloused palm against the heated shaft, his knees almost giving out. The tentative, inexperienced strokes Alex gave him caused his stomach to clench, and he extricated himself from Alex's grasp to climb into the bed. "Another time," he said gruffly, leaning down to plant a searing kiss on his lips when Alex tried to protest.

He guided Alex onto his side and then onto his stomach.

Alex looked at him in uncertainty, vulnerability shining out of his bright green eyes. "It's okay, baby," Gabriel reassured huskily, sliding the palm of one hand down Alex's bare back. "I could hurt you if you aren't prepared right."

"I know," Alex murmured, flushing and burying his face in his folded arms.

Tenderness swamped Gabriel, and he swallowed around the sudden lump in his throat. He couldn't deny he was head over heels in love with Alex anymore, definitely not to himself, but would he be able to admit it to Alex? Pushing the thought away for the moment, he started trailing kisses along Alex's shoulder toward his nape and down his spine, stopping at each vertebra. When he reached the swell of Alex's rear end, he cupped the firm muscles in his hands, kneading and slowly spreading them again and again, tantalizing himself with glimpses of the tight rosebud between.

He heard Alex give a choked sound when he slid his tongue into the indent at the top of Alex's crease, and he moved lower, sampling the puckered flesh. His cock hardened further, if that were even possible, when Alex's essence inundated his taste buds. Nothing prepared him for the musky, sinful spice or the delicious cry Alex released. He groaned and tasted Alex again and again, savoring his lover. Needing more, Gabriel pried at the tiny opening, using his tongue to part the folds and delve into Alex's body.

Alex gasped and unconsciously thrust his hips backward, forcing Gabriel deeper inside. Gabriel coaxed Alex to his knees, never once halting his current action. None of the men who'd been in his bed ever brought him to the edge just from the sweetness of their piquancy. He could feel his shaft leaking in lust and tried to hold himself together, thinking of anything which came to mind to keep from plunging balls deep inside Alex before he was ready.

Gabriel reluctantly removed his tongue from Alex's hole

and calculatingly outlined the spit-slick flesh with the tip of one finger, probing lightly. Alex moaned when his finger breached the snug entrance, and Gabriel pushed in, watching his finger stretch the outer muscle protecting the vulnerable orifice.

"Gabriel... oh...." Alex broke off when his finger brushed over the small bump Gabriel knew to be another man's hot point.

He thrust the single digit in and out, allowing Alex the time to adjust, adding a second once the silky chute felt receptive. He wished he'd been more prepared for this, had some sort of lube, but the safe house hadn't been used in a long time. Alex held still when Gabriel's fingers started entering him, a fine tremble shimmering down his thighs. "Relax, baby," Gabriel soothed. "Just push out slightly. It'll help."

Gabriel remembered when he'd taken his first cock, the burn and the uncertainty he'd felt, but how good it made him feel afterward. He knew the moment Alex followed his instructions because his fingers slid in easier, gliding along the hot walls of Alex's hole. He made sure to target the prostate, scraping the pleasure gland on each entrance and exit. Adding more saliva, he wiggled a third digit inside, scissoring his fingers as much as possible, working the grasping muscles carefully.

When Alex began thrusting back into his hand, Gabriel knew that he was adjusted enough to accept him. He slowly slid his fingers free and reached out to the nightstand to snag a condom. Ripping the package, he rolled it down his cock and added more saliva to the lubed latex, biting his lip hard at the pleasure rushing through him when his hand stroked over his straining flesh. Moving until his chest rested on Alex, he murmured into the slender shell of his ear, "I'm coming in."

Guiding his aching prick, Gabriel gently nudged the opening of Alex's body, reassuringly caressing Alex's hip as he pressed forward. "Push out," he quietly instructed once more, gritting his teeth at the taut muscle closing around the head of his cock.

"Gabriel," Alex panted, fingers curling in the sheets.

It took every ounce of strength Gabriel possessed to stop, allowing Alex the time he needed to acclimate to the intrusion. Maybe it only took minutes, but it seemed as if an hour had passed by the time Gabriel felt his hips touch Alex's. "That's it, baby. You've got it all," he said huskily. "Does it feel good?"

Alex moaned. "It… it feels strange. I…."

Flexing his hips, Gabriel burrowed deeper into Alex, relishing the hot sheath wrapped around his shaft. Alex's breath hitched, and Gabriel knew he'd tagged the man's pleasure center. Pulling out about halfway, he watched Alex drop his head and pushed back in, delighting in the way Alex's head snapped up in lustful pleasure.

"Oh my God," Alex cried out, his hands clenching further in the bedsheets.

Gabriel restrained his natural urge to go faster, wanting to ensure Alex's first time would never be regretted. He kept his strokes slow and steady, eagerly studying and delighting in every response, wanton sound, and tremor of Alex's lean frame. Nothing mattered more to him than making Alex feel good, his own passion heightened by the knowledge he was the one bringing Alex such pleasure.

Suddenly a hard shudder wracked Gabriel's body, and he gasped, his eyes widening at the burst of lust electrifying his nerve endings. His orgasm threatened, looming on the horizon as each thrust into Alex came with another thrilling flash. He realized on the third exquisite rush that he was somehow connected to Alex, could feel the pure exultation on every plunge into the telepath beneath him. Alex probably didn't even recognize his power had tangled with Gabriel's, pushing each feeling straight through to Gabriel's senses.

Digging his fingers into Alex's hips, Gabriel threw his head back, closing his eyes. He wasn't sure if he did it to enjoy the sensations flooding him from Alex or to stave off his own impending orgasm. Perhaps a little bit of both. Needing to come and knowing he couldn't until Alex did, Gabriel reached around Alex's body and started stroking the hard length, timing his caresses to each plunge into the snug channel. A matter of breaths later and he felt Alex stiffen, his hole contracting around him, and then a keening cry shattered the silence, more than likely heard by the others in the safe house. At that moment, neither could care, too lost in their desire for one another to wonder or be embarrassed.

Hot jets of liquid spilled over Gabriel's fist, pushing Gabriel's hips faster, sending him careening wildly over the edge into his own ecstasy. Hard, pulsing spurts of come filled the condom deep inside Alex, and Gabriel ground harder into his new lover, bringing his hand up to his mouth to lap at the salty fluid covering it. Finally, unable to hold himself upright any longer, Gabriel managed to roll them to their sides and slowly disengaged his body from Alex's, quickly disposing of the condom and gathering Alex close again.

Both of their bodies glistened with sweat in the moonlight from the window, and Gabriel lazily trailed a finger down Alex's smooth, muscular arm. No words were exchanged, neither of them wanting to shatter the stillness, the perfect moment, wrapped around them. Gabriel's thoughts drifted to how Alex had connected them, made him feel what Alex felt. He'd never been with a telepath before, let alone a level five. Could they all do that, or could Alex do it because he was a level five? Did he even know he'd done it?

Did Alex experience the same thing he did and take on his emotions?

Alex eventually broke the silence by asking softly, "Did you feel it too?"

Gabriel slipped his arm around Alex's waist, twining their hands together. "I did. Wasn't sure if you even knew what happened."

"I don't even know how I did it," Alex replied, turning his head a fraction to look at Gabriel in the darkness.

Leaning in, he nuzzled at Alex's shoulder, dropping a kiss on the smooth skin. "You're a level five, Alex. You haven't even begun to tap into your potential."

"I don't want to learn more," Alex said his voice troubled. "All abilities do is bring misery and pain. If we weren't Deviants, Jason and I would still be on the farm. We wouldn't be running for our lives and constantly looking over our shoulders."

Gabriel frowned. "You can't think that way, Alex. You are who you were meant to be. No one asked to be a Deviant, and I know having abilities isn't easy, but if you train yourself to control them, to blend in, you'll see it's not so bad."

"But why should we have to blend in?" Alex challenged, frustration evident in his tone and face. He sat up and ran a hand through his hair. "I hate hiding. I hate worrying someone is going to find out what I am and I'll have to run again. Why should we have to hide just because someone hates us? It's like the slave days all over again, and the ADA is the underground railroad."

Pushing himself into a sitting position, Gabriel reached up and forced Alex to look at him. "It's a shitty situation. I know it. I've been hiding for eight years. For more than just being a Deviant. My powers manifested because of my anger. You know about Paul and what I did afterward, but I've learned to live with it, to survive, and you will too."

Alex didn't say anything in response, merely picking at the covers in irritation. A few minutes later, a loud growling noise issued from Alex's stomach, and Gabriel laughed, ruffling Alex's hair. "Let's go get something to eat."

They both dressed in the same clothing they'd worn earlier and started downstairs. It was almost three in the morning, so most everyone had already gone to bed. Gabriel noticed a light from the kitchen, and they found Hayley at the refrigerator. "You could have tried to at least be quieter," she grumbled at them, filling a glass with milk. "I think the whole house heard you."

Gabriel merely grinned while Alex spluttered and flushed, burying his bright red face in Gabriel's shoulder. "You're the one who supplied the means, Hayles. So you might want to remember that it's your fault."

"Gabriel!" Alex practically shrieked, smacking Gabriel's shoulder. "Oh God!"

Hayley laughed and winked at Alex. "Relax, hun. Preston and I have the room right next door, so I'm pretty sure we're the only ones who noticed."

Alex groaned and slapped his hand over his eyes, hanging his head. Gabriel tossed his arm around Alex's shoulders, squeezing tightly. "Don't worry, babe. She's just jealous."

The three of them laughed, and then Hayley told them good-night before heading upstairs, holding her glass of milk. Gabriel opened the fridge and pulled out some cold cuts, cheese, and mayo. He set them on the counter and grabbed a butter knife from a drawer. "Turkey, roast beef, or both?"

"Turkey," Alex supplied, sliding onto a stool at the breakfast bar, watching as Gabriel started assembling two huge sandwiches.

"So how old were you when your powers developed?" Gabriel asked, slathering a huge scoop of mayo on the bread.

"We were both five. Jason started first. He levitated his toys, much to our mother's horror. Dad came home just in time to stop her from drowning us, and brought us to Grams out of fear she would try again."

"You haven't had any contact since then?" Gabriel frowned.

"After Grams died, we tried calling them, but Mom hung up on us. They didn't even come to the funeral. It was just me and Jason."

Gabriel made a sound of sympathy in his throat. "I'm sorry."

Alex shrugged. "I barely remember them, to be honest. Grams was more of a mother to us than our own mother was."

Setting a plate in front of Alex, he brushed the back of Alex's hand in comfort. "It still has to sting."

"I guess. I mean, they are our parents, but when you haven't seen or talked to someone for almost fifteen years it makes it kind of easy to deal with." Alex lifted a shoulder carelessly again. "Maybe if we'd been older when it happened it would be different."

"Milk, water, or soda pop?" Gabriel asked after a moment.

"Soda please," Alex requested.

After filling two glasses and settling on another stool across from Alex, Gabriel started asking more questions about Alex's childhood, wanting to know more about the younger Deviant. He hungrily absorbed each detail, knowing it may be all he had left when it was over, because if everything went the way he planned, he'd need the memories of Alex's warm smile and gentle laughter to keep him sane. Neither of them noticed the time passing or the beginning glow of the morning sun peeking over the edge of the horizon.

16

ALEX

ALEX shifted on the stool, wincing slightly as his rear end protested the movement. He could hardly believe Gabriel had made love to him. He'd thought it would take practically tying the stubborn Deviant to the bed and having his way with him to get him to do it. Every single moment was burned into his brain like a movie, bits and pieces replaying as he watched Gabriel preparing sandwiches for them. Every sensation had led to something new and exciting. He'd never imagined it would feel so amazing or that he could connect the two of them together to experience what the other felt. When Gabriel came inside him, he'd felt it as deeply as his own orgasm.

His breath quickened at the remembered awareness. Could he do that again? Would he be able to control it, or would he do it unconsciously next time as well? Would there be a next time, or would Gabriel regret their stolen moments together?

"Gabe?" he started hesitantly, waiting for those amber eyes to focus on him.

Gabriel looked up at him in question, wiping his full lips

with a napkin. Reaching up, Alex touched the silver chain around his neck, and he saw the answer in Gabriel's eyes. "You gave me this," he said, not questioning but stating.

"I did."

Alex picked up the cross resting over his heart and gently fingered it. "Hayley said it means a lot to you. Why did you give it to me?"

Dropping his napkin on the countertop, Gabriel leaned forward to touch the silver charm. "Our father gave each of us a cross when we graduated high school. He said it would protect us in the real world as long as we wore it. I haven't taken it off since the day Rafe died."

"You should keep it, then!" Alex protested, moving to take it off, but Gabriel stopped him, wrapping his hand around Alex's.

"I want you to have it."

"But why? It obviously means a lot to you."

Gabriel's eyes met Alex's, a strange glow in their depths, and Alex's breath caught in his throat. They were still sitting in absolute silence, staring at one another, when Preston walked in. "Good morning, you two."

Alex started, wrenching his gaze from Gabriel's. He wanted to howl in frustration at the other man for interrupting. It took a few seconds for him to dredge up a strained smile for Preston. "Good morning, Preston."

Preston winked at them as he started prepping the coffee pot, seemingly unaware of the moment he'd interrupted. "I heard you two had fun last night."

Gabriel growled and Alex blushed. "Preston, if you want to live to see Hayley again, you better keep the comments to yourself."

Laughter bubbled up in Preston, and he said, "I just wondered if you could teach me some techniques, Gabe. Honest."

Alex choked, coughing. Gabriel stood up, and Preston jumped back, still grinning broadly. "Pres," Gabriel warned, glowering.

"Okay, okay," Preston placated, holding his hands up in surrender.

Gabriel slowly sat back down, eyeing Preston as the other man went back to preparing the morning coffee. Alex stifled a grin, pleasure at the familial teasing rushing through him. It reminded him of being on the farm with Grams and Jason: the laughter as they prepared breakfast together and the way Jason used to pretend he didn't know a spatula from a potato peeler just to get out of cooking. The memories made him feel guilty at being happy while Jason was being held hostage and quite possibly being tortured. His smile dimmed, and he pushed his plate away from him, the second sandwich only half eaten.

"Everything okay?" Gabriel asked, eyeing him.

He tried to force a smile but couldn't quite make it. "Just thinking about Jason."

The dark-haired Deviant gave him a sympathetic look and asked, "Any more dreams?"

Alex shook his head. "No. It's weird, but I didn't dream at all."

Gabriel studied him for a few silent moments before nodding. "Good. We should be able to work on some meditation today. Chris needs another day to finish the research on Vincetti's compound. It's the same one they kept you and Jason in before, except I doubt they're keeping Jason and Bryan in the same area."

"I don't know if I'll be able to concentrate enough for it to matter," Alex muttered.

"This is a good time for you to practice because your mind is not focused. Sometimes we have to push ourselves to forget in order to survive," Gabriel said flatly.

Preston glanced up from the bowl of scrambled eggs he'd started making and interjected, "Why don't you go have Marcus show you the boxes of stuff in the attic, Alex? We found some things left behind from previous Deviants staying here, including some clothing. There may be something which might fit you."

Alex gave Preston a grateful glance and stood, heading off to find Marcus. The Deviant in question was sitting on the living room floor, his back against the couch, and watching some kind of daytime program on an old, grainy television. "Marcus?"

The olive-skinned Deviant looked up at him. "What's up, Alex?"

"Preston said you could show me where I might be able to find something to wear?"

Marcus smiled and nodded, nimbly climbing to his feet. "Sure thing, Alex. One of the others found a few boxes in the attic when they were exploring the house. There were a couple that had clothes in them."

Alex trailed Marcus up to the second floor, barely paying attention to their surroundings. When Marcus stopped to pull down a set of stairs, Alex almost ran into him. "Sorry," he apologized.

"No worries, dude." Marcus shrugged and tugged on the string, the ladder stretching down to the floor.

The attic smelled of pine and mothballs, causing Alex to wrinkle his nose at the unpleasant odor as they went up. "Any idea how long this stuff has been here?" he asked, opening one of the boxes to find some old sweatpants and T-shirts.

"Nah. Preston said they could be from years ago. The house seemed pretty dusty when we got here, so I'd guess at least a year or more." Marcus straddled an old chair and watched Alex digging through the box. "Any word on your brother?"

Alex blanched, and his hand stilled on the T-shirt he'd been about to reach for. "No," he murmured in a pained voice.

"I'm sure he'll be okay," Marcus comforted. "He seems like a strong person."

"He may seem as if he is, but he hides his pain and insecurities behind that façade." Alex sighed and sank down to sit cross-legged. "Ever since I can remember, he's always hidden what he thinks makes him seem weak, using anger and disdain to distract him.

"Grams always said he's like an overgrown rose bush. Prickly with thorns, but once you cut those thorns away, he becomes soft and fragile, easily crushed. Jason has only ever shown his true nature to me. I can only hope whatever they're doing to him isn't going to drive him deeper into his shell."

Marcus tilted his head to the side quizzically. "He's an awful good actor if that's just a front, because I got the distinct impression he's pretty good at taking care of himself."

A flash of Jason covered in bruises passed through his mind, and Alex froze. He didn't know where the memory came from or why. He searched for where he'd seen Jason hurt and alone, but couldn't remember when it was. "Alex?"

He blinked and focused on Marcus. "Are you okay?" Marcus asked in concern, sitting straighter in the chair.

"I'm fine. I… was just thinking." Alex gave Marcus a wan smile and stood up, snatching a pair of black sweatpants and a dark blue T-shirt from the box. "We should probably get back downstairs before they come searching for us."

Skepticism flitted over Marcus's features, but he didn't say anything, merely standing to precede Alex down the attic steps. They parted ways so Alex could shower and change. The others were already sitting at the table when he entered the dining room twenty minutes later. He ignored the sharp amber gaze as he sat in the chair beside Gabriel, but he should have known Gabriel wouldn't let it go.

"Are you okay?" Gabriel murmured into his ear.

"I'm fine." He repeated his earlier sentiment.

Gabriel slid his arm along the back of Alex's chair and stroked his fingers over his right shoulder. "Later," he promised, not letting it rest.

Alex didn't miss the smug grins and curious looks from the others at the table. He knew Gabriel's proprietary embrace confirmed they were together. An hour ago a thrill would have gone through him, and he wouldn't have been able to keep from grinning like an idiot, but the memory of Jason injured haunted him, and he couldn't shake the dreadful feeling in the pit of his stomach that he was missing something. A memory nagged at the back of his mind, but he just couldn't pin it down. The thought kept slithering away whenever he'd get close. What was he forgetting?

He forced himself to eat, mechanically shoving food in his mouth. The eggs tasted dry and bitter, sitting like a rock in his belly. By the time breakfast was finished, his head throbbed and he could feel one of his migraines coming on. He wobbled as he stood, and Gabriel caught his arm, holding him steady. "What's wrong?" Gabriel demanded quietly.

"Headache," Alex croaked out, leaning unconsciously into Gabriel's warm body. He heard Gabriel swear, and then he found himself airborne and being carried upstairs to their bedroom.

Cool sheets met his heated skin, and he barely noticed Gabriel leave the room and come back. A cold, wet cloth pressed against his forehead, and he moaned quietly, squeezing his eyes shut tighter. Gabriel didn't ask him any questions, just soothed his hair back from his face and used another cool face rag over his closed eyelids, cheeks, and neck.

"Shh, baby," Gabriel hushed when he let out a small sob.

"I can't remember," Alex fretted.

"Can't remember what?"

Alex fidgeted, the pain in his head getting worse, and he gripped at his temples, his palms digging hard into the tender flesh. "Jason... I can't remember where...."

He realized his words were fractured, but the more he tried to recall the memory the more his head throbbed, and his throat grew raw from stemming the urge to vomit. "I saw him... hurt... where...."

Gabriel shushed him again. "Baby, relax. Take slow, even breaths. Whatever it is, it will come back in its own time. Trying to remember is obviously hurting you."

Alex felt tears burning beneath his eyelids. Why couldn't he grab hold of the fragmented memory? Every time he reached for it, the images slipped away, just out of his grasp. He tried to do as Gabriel instructed, concentrating on his breathing and letting the image go. He slowly pulled in a deep, even breath and carefully let it out. Eventually the pain began to lessen, fading away on each outward exhalation.

It could have been a half hour or more when Alex was finally able to open his eyes and not feel as if a thousand needles were poking his retinas. He stared up at Gabriel in gratitude. "Thank you."

"After I grab a shower and see about a change of clothes, we are going to meditate," Gabriel dictated in a "don't-argue-with-me" tone. "Why don't you rest here for a bit longer, and I'll come get you when I'm done?"

Alex nodded carefully. "Okay."

"Good. I'll be back in fifteen minutes." Gabriel squeezed

Alex's shoulder and left the room, shutting the door behind him.

Staring up at the ceiling, Alex forced himself to keep his mind away from his twin. Something about the whole situation nagged at him. He could think of Jason and remember him at other times without pain, but just the mere touch of Jason bruised and sitting in the grass somewhere brought pressure racing along his skull.

He carefully sat up and swung his legs over the side of the bed, gingerly testing out his stomach's ability to keep down breakfast. When no nausea hit, he sighed in relief and eased himself to his feet. Gabriel had removed his sneakers at some point, and they lay beside the bed. He picked them up and sat down in the chair next to the window to slip them on.

Alex wasn't sure what made him glance out the window as he bent to tie his shoelaces, but his entire body stilled when he saw Jason standing near the trees lining the property. His breath quickened, and he looked harder to make sure he wasn't imagining his brother being there. "Jace," he breathed, and swiftly tied his shoes, never once removing his gaze from the lean figure at the back of the house.

The second his laces were tied, he shot to his feet and raced out of the room and down the stairs. He heard several of the others call his name, but he ignored them, slamming the back door open. He saw Jason smile and hold his arms out to him, beckoning him forward. "Jace!" Alex cried out.

If he'd have stopped to think, his common sense might have set in, but the hope that his brother really was there stamped the idea of it being a trick deep into his subconscious. He darted down the porch steps and ran toward his twin. "Jace!" Alex keened again.

"Alex, no!" Gabriel's voice roared across the yard, but his warning came too late.

Alex was an arm's length from his brother when the illusion disappeared. A stranger stood in Jason's place, and Alex skidded to a stop. "No," Alex whispered in horror, trying to scramble backward.

The man, tall and lean like Jason but with blond hair and blue eyes, grinned maniacally and grabbed Alex's arm. "Too easy, little mouse."

Alex heard Gabriel running at them, but another man stepped from the shadows and lifted a gun. Horror spread through Alex when he realized they intended to shoot Gabriel. He launched himself at the one with the gun, managing to knock the hand holding it away just as the shot rang out. The man snarled and backhanded Alex, sending him flying into the Deviant who'd lured him from the house. "Keep hold of him, you idiot."

Alex's ears rang from the loud gunshot, and his cheek felt hot from the blow. He saw the other Deviant lift his hand and take aim once more at Gabriel. "No," he slurred and struggled to get away from the hands gripping his arms. "Don't."

A third voice stopped the one about to shoot Gabriel. "Enough. You know he said not to touch him. Let's go."

He couldn't see the owner of the voice, but relief spilled through him that they weren't going to hurt Gabriel. Suddenly, everything shifted and swirled around him. Colors blended, wind whipped past his face, and then it was over. He gagged and dropped to his knees the second the man holding him released him. Bile rose in the back of his throat. What the hell had just happened?

When Alex could finally focus, he looked up and blinked heavily. Minutes ago they'd been standing in a bright, sunlit yard outside, and now they were in some kind of cement room, a mirror dominating one wall. He recognized the place, and fear flooded him, his blood running cold in his veins and the hairs along his nape rising at the goose bumps pimpling his skin.

"I'll inform him we were successful," the gun-wielding Deviant said, sliding the gun into a holster at his waist. "Make sure you don't let him escape."

"Yeah, yeah," the Jason look-alike snapped.

The door snicked shut behind the man, and Alex's stomach finally settled enough for him to struggle to his feet. "What do you want?" he demanded, glaring at them while holding onto the table in the room to steady himself.

The blond snorted. "Ain't us that wants anything, little mouse. Just sit down and relax."

"Stop calling me that," Alex growled, his fingers tightening on the table.

"Sit down and shut up," the third Deviant snarled. "I'm going to get something to eat, Tim. Watch him."

Tim grunted and leaned into the wall, crossing his arms over his chest. "Bring me something back, Joel."

Joel waved him off and left the two of them alone. Alex looked around him, trying to find any possibility of escape, but there wasn't even a window, only the door and the mirrored wall, which he knew had to be a two-way mirror. Was the man called Vincetti watching him from the other side?

"Where is my brother?" Alex demanded.

Shrugging, Tim replied, "I'm sure you'll see him soon enough, little mouse. Why don't you sit down and shut up like Joel said?"

Alex scowled at him. "I want some answers."

"If you don't shut up, kid, I'm going to shut you up," Tim snapped. "You're getting on my nerves."

"I want to see Jason."

Tim pushed away from the wall, taking a step toward

Alex, when a voice came through the speaker in the far right corner. "Enough, Tim. Leave us."

He glared at Alex and strode to the door, slamming it and locking it behind him. Alex turned and stared at the glass, knowing the owner of the voice had to be watching him from there. "What do you want from me? Where's my brother?"

"Your brother is safe. On the other side of the wall from you, in fact. As for what I want from you, I merely need your presence to bring Gabriel to me."

"Why? What do you want from him?" Alex peered at the mirror, trying in vain to see through it.

A deep laugh rolled through the room. "You mean, he hasn't told you how he killed his own brother? Come now, Alex, no need to lie. You know why I want him here."

"No, I don't," Alex protested. "What does Gabriel killing his brother have to do with you?"

The voice didn't respond, and the small room grew quiet. Alex didn't hear anything else until the lock clicked and the door swung open. He gasped and fell backward into the table, the chair shifting, causing the leg to scrape the floor loudly. The scarred Gabriel from his dreams stood in front of him, wearing a contemptuous expression. Scars covered almost his entire face, running down his neck and under the collar of the black long-sleeve T-shirt he wore. Both hands were encased in gloves, and no hair grew along the right side of his scalp, the skin too damaged to allow it. Alex shuddered and shrank back even further. He couldn't see the rest of Rafael's body, but he could only imagine it must look the same or worse.

"Surprised, Alex?" Rafael smirked.

"Why?" Alex whispered, his heart pounding in his chest. "Why are you doing this to your own brother?"

Rafael sneered at him. "I know my sniveling brother told

you what happened five years ago." He gestured to his face. "More than two-thirds of my body was covered in third degree burns. Gabriel will pay for what he did."

"He thinks you're dead! He's barely lived because of the guilt!" Alex protested. "Gabriel never meant to hurt you."

"You're lying," Rafael shouted. "Gabriel knew what he was doing when he threw me into the fire."

Alex looked at the broken mirror image of Gabriel and sadly knew nothing he said would change Rafael's mind. "You've allowed your bitterness to blind you against your own brother, to bury your feelings for him. Gabriel loved you, Rafael, but you turned your back on him first when you sided with Vincetti."

Rafael gave Alex an icy look, and suddenly pain exploded in Alex's head. Alex cried out and dropped to the floor, clutching his head between his hands. "I may need to keep you alive, at least until Gabriel arrives, but I can have some fun in the meantime," Rafael said after the pain ebbed.

A warm fluid trickled from Alex's nose, and he swiped at it with his hand. Red smeared across his fingers. More blood spilled out, and Alex stared in horror at Rafael. Agony erupted along his nerve endings once more, and Alex collapsed to the floor, curling up in a ball and praying for it to be over soon. The look of affection and love in Gabriel's eyes mere hours ago danced through his mind, urging him to find the strength to shut everything else out and remember why he needed to survive. Somehow he knew if he died, Gabriel would blame himself and would withdraw so far into his shell that he'd never allow himself to care about someone again. Alex pushed through the pain, tried to recall his training, and attempted to force Rafael out of his mind. He managed to dull the sensations, but Rafael had years of practice over him, and he couldn't quite stop him entirely.

Cruel laughter came from Rafael as he let up on the

bombardment of Alex's senses. "You think such a pathetic barrier will help you? Your mind is weak. If you join me, become a part of my ranks, I can show you things you'd never even imagined. Ways to use your ability which would astound you."

"Never," Alex replied fiercely, still trying to stem the flow of blood.

"Pity," Rafael said shaking his head. "Gabriel really does need to learn to choose better partners. Paul was weak too. I knew it the moment I met him, and couldn't allow their relationship to go on."

Realization sank in, and Alex stared at Rafael in horror. "You turned him in to those people."

An evil smirk twisted Rafael's lips. "Of course. I had to get rid of Paul somehow, and I knew of Gabriel's ability before he even knew he had one. Mine surfaced a year prior to Gabriel's during a moment of sheer anger. I knew Gabriel's would appear if he were put into a similar situation where he would be forced to use them. Watching his lover die would only serve the purpose."

"How could you do that to him!" Alex exclaimed. "Do you have any idea what he's been through because of it? You've been lying to him even before Vincetti. He believed you when you said your ability came out the same time as his." Rafael's words didn't sink in immediately, but when they did, Alex mentally reeled at the knowledge that Paul had been more than a friend. Why hadn't Gabriel told him they'd been lovers? Did Gabriel still grieve for Paul because he still loved the man? He hid his anguish at the thought, not wanting to give Rafael further ammunition to hurt him.

Disdain flooded Rafael's gaze. "You seem to think I should care."

Alex's heart ached. Gabriel had no idea of the darkness in his brother's soul. All this time he'd tormented himself with thoughts of Paul's murder and the falsehood of his role in his twin's death when none of it had been true. Would Gabriel be able to forgive himself once he knew the truth? "He's your brother."

"A brother who betrayed me, but tonight I will have my revenge on Gabriel, and you'll provide the perfect bait," Rafael sneered.

Dismay flooded Alex. Gabriel's words from yesterday came back to him. He'd insisted on Alex staying at the safe house because he'd be distracted by Alex's presence. Would Gabriel get hurt with him there? "Please don't do this," he begged.

Rafael didn't reply. He pressed a button on the wall near the door, and seconds later Tim entered the room. "Put him in with his brother."

Tim glared at Alex. "Let's go."

Alex struggled to stand, wobbling slightly. He preceded the blond Deviant from the room, blindly following his directions. They stopped in front of one of the glass door cells similar to the one they'd been held in last time. Jason sat on one of the small beds, his face buried in his arms, which were wrapped around his knees. He looked up at the sound of the door opening. "Alex!" he cried jumping to his feet. "What the hell did they do to you? Where are you hurt? Why are you covered in blood?"

He embraced his twin as the door slid shut behind him. "Jace," Alex breathed, happy to see his brother was alive. "I'm fine. Really."

When he pulled back to look at him, he noticed the bruises he'd seen in his memory. "Oh, God."

"It's just bruises. I'm so sorry, Alex. I only wanted to see you. Connor told me I could if I slept. I didn't know they'd be able to follow." Jason paced the small cell.

Alex sank down on the edge of the bed nearby, confused. "I don't understand. What do you mean, see me?"

"You don't remember?" Jason halted and frowned.

"Remember what?" Alex asked.

Jason squatted down in front of Alex and looked up into his mirror image. "The dream, Alex. You really don't remember the dream?"

A dull pain started in Alex's temple, and he rubbed at it, shaking his head. "No. I kept seeing you hurt, bruised, like now. Except it didn't make sense when I hadn't seen you like that. You said you came to me in a dream?"

Swearing, Jason shot to his feet and started pacing once more. "Connor told me he could manipulate people's memories. I bet he erased the dream from your mind."

The ache grew fiercer, and tears stung Alex's eyes. "Who's Connor?"

"He's also being kept prisoner here. They're holding his little brother hostage to make sure he doesn't try to escape." Jason slumped down on the bed next to Alex. "I met him the first night they captured me. He's been bringing me food and is basically my warden.

"They keep injecting me with some kind of serum that strips my power. I can't even lift the toilet seat." Jason scowled, almost pouting.

Alex knew Jason relied heavily on being able to use his abilities to protect himself. "I'm sorry," he whispered.

"For what?" Jason demanded incredulously.

"I never should have left you that night. I should have stayed with you instead of rushing off to find Gabriel."

Jason snorted. "Stop being a martyr, Alex. If you'd have stayed they just would have captured you sooner. I know you love the big bastard, and I would have done the same thing in your shoes."

He nudged Alex and laid his head on Alex's shoulder. "I've missed you, brother."

Alex swallowed hard, pressing closer to his twin. "I've missed you too."

"Do you know if Bryan is okay?" Alex asked after a moment.

Shock colored Jason's features. "They kidnapped Bryan too?"

Alex closed his eyes and nodded. He prayed Bryan was still alive. "They took him the same night they took you."

"Goddamn it. I can't believe that son of a bitch is Gabriel's brother! What else happened that night?"

They sat there as Alex recounted everything that had happened since the night of the attack on the agency. All the parts except the intimate encounters between him and Gabriel. When he reached the part about Lizard, Jason growled and punched the bed, rattling the frame.

He had no idea how long they sat there talking, but it must have been a couple of hours at least when a dark-haired man approached their cell holding a tray. Alex sensed he knew the stranger, but he couldn't quite put his finger on how he knew him. "Connor," Jason greeted warily.

So this was Connor!

Connor gave Jason a sad look. "I had no choice, Jason. You know if I don't do as he asks he'll hurt my brother." Connor had a soft Texas drawl, with his accent putting just enough of a twang on his words to send shivers down any straight woman or gay man's spine.

"Put his memory back," Jason demanded, glaring at him. "That's the least you can do."

Sighing, Connor set the tray down on the bed across from them. Alex looked between them curiously. A strange tension filled the room between the two men, and he noticed an odd look in Connor's eyes. Despite his resolve not to invade someone else's mind without permission, Alex couldn't quite stop himself from reaching out for Connor's thoughts. He picked up the image of a small child no more than eight or nine, stray pieces of conversations Jason and the dark-haired Deviant had engaged in, and the attraction Connor held for Jason. The next bit of information stopped him in his tracks, and he withdrew from Connor's mind immediately. Connor fantasized about Jason in the same way Alex himself had about Gabriel. Those were things he didn't need to see.

Connor gave him a harsh glance. "Invading someone else's private thoughts without asking first is the reason Normals fear us."

"I'm sorry," Alex apologized. "You can't exactly blame me for trying to find out the truth. I will do whatever I can to protect Jason and myself."

Connor gave a stiff nod in understanding and moved to stand in front of Alex. "I have the ability to modify a person's memories. To bury them, erase them, or make them remember things differently or change it all together."

"You did it to me," Alex stated flatly.

"Yes, but I didn't erase them. I buried them in case there ever came a time when I could return them to you." Connor knelt in front of Alex. "I can return them if you'd be willing to trust me."

Alex glanced at Jason, who gave him an encouraging glance. He wanted to know what had been taken from him. He dipped his head in agreement. "First, why does it cause me pain when I try to remember?"

"When I bury the memory instead of erasing it all together, your mind will catch flashes, little things which stand out, but every time you try to pull those images forward, your brain senses the 'wall' they're hidden behind and triggers pain receptors to prevent you from remembering. Just relax. It isn't going to hurt." Connor placed the tips of his fingers on Alex's temples and closed his eyes.

Warmth began to spill out of Connor's fingers through Alex's temples and slowly crept along his skull. It almost gave him the sensation of being tickled. Alex frowned and watched Connor's face, the eyebrows furrowing and his lips tightening at the edges. Suddenly Alex found himself gasping for breath, his head thrown back as images flooded his mind: Gabriel next to the stream, Jason leaning on his palms, the bruises, and Rafael appearing from the shade of the trees. He saw Connor and knew Connor's guilt at removing the memories which would have warned them of the Deviants coming to kidnap him. The realization sank in that he'd betrayed Gabriel to his brother and Rafael knew Gabriel would come for him. He'd done exactly what Gabriel knew he would.

Connor carefully released him and collapsed to the floor. Jason dove to catch him, wrapping his arms around Connor. Alex watched in a daze as Jason lifted Connor and gently set him on the bed across from them. Connor's face was pale, and his hands shook. He gave Jason a grateful smile. "It takes a lot out of me to return the memories. More than to remove them, I'm afraid."

Alex probably would have been surprised at the tenderness Jason displayed in his care of Connor, but all he could think of was his own betrayal. He'd unknowingly revealed Gabriel's plan to Rafael. "How could I?"

Jason looked at him. "Alex?"

"How could I betray Gabriel like that?" Alex whispered, heartsick. "Now Rafael knows Gabriel's plans. He'll be ready for them, and they won't stand a chance."

"You couldn't have known," Jason protested. "You didn't mean to, Alex."

"Whether I meant to or not, I did, and Gabriel knew I

would!" Alex cried, covering his face with his hands. "He didn't want me to know because he knew I'd betray him."

"Alex, stop it!" Jason demanded, shifting to Alex's side. "Gabriel would never believe you'd betray him. Whatever the big bastard may be, he's not stupid. He cares about you."

Misery settled on Alex's shoulders, and he curled into Jason's side. "I wish they'd never rescued us. Lizard would still be alive, and Gabriel wouldn't be on his way here to die."

"Gabriel isn't going to die. He's too stubborn to die," Jason joked lightly. "Give him more credit, Alex."

Alex couldn't speak past the lump in his throat. He prayed Jason was right because he hadn't even had the chance to tell Gabriel he loved him.

17

GABRIEL

G ABRIEL tried to ignore the nagging contentment settling into his gut. He caught himself whistling more than once in the shower and frowned in frustration, only to find his lips curved into a slight smile seconds later. It wasn't right that he was happy when Bryan and Jason were suffering God knows what at the hands of Vincetti, let alone what he'd done to his own brother. He'd accepted that he loved Alex, knew he couldn't and wouldn't change the way he felt for the world, but did he deserve to keep Alex? Did Alex even love him, or know what love is, for that matter? The younger Deviant had barely lived or experienced anything in his twenty years. Would it be selfish of him to hold onto Alex if or when the time came to let him go?

He flipped off the shower and reached out to grab the towel on the rack. He briskly dried and dressed, eager to return to the younger man. Being around Alex brought back feelings he hadn't had in a long time. Not since Paul. Even with Bryan he'd held a part of himself back, and yet now that part he'd locked away for so long sat in Alex's slender fingers.

The shouts of the others calling Alex's name grabbed Gabriel's attention as he stepped from the bathroom. Fear ripped through him, and he raced down the stairs and out the back door to see Alex rushing across the yard toward someone who looked like Jason. "Alex, no!" he shouted, speeding after him.

He could do nothing but watch in horror as Alex came to an abrupt halt and another Deviant came forth from the shadows. The moment the third man touched Alex and the Jason look-alike, they were gone. Gabriel reached the spot too late and dropped to his knees, roaring at the top of his lungs. His fists slammed into the grass where only mere seconds ago Alex had stood. Anger coursed through his veins. Vincetti had taken so much from him already. He wouldn't let the son of a bitch take Alex. Not this time.

"Gabriel?" Jackal queried from behind him, dropping his hand on Gabriel's shoulder.

"They took him, Jackal. They took him, and I couldn't stop them," he murmured.

Jackal squeezed Gabriel's shoulder reassuringly. "We'll get him back, Gabe."

Gabriel nodded and stood up. "We leave tonight."

"Maybe we should wai—"

He cut Jackal off. "No. We leave tonight. Get the team ready to go."

Uncertainty crossed Jackal's features, but he didn't say anything more, just gave a jerk of his head in understanding and turned back to the house. Gabriel followed him slowly, his mind formulating a plan. For whatever reason, Vincetti wanted him after all these years, even with all of the powerful Devs he already had in his grip. Why was he still pursuing Gabriel? Was it because he'd gotten away five years ago? Bruised ego, maybe? He knew what he'd do to get Alex, Jason, and Bryan back. The only thing he could do... trade himself for them. If they were still alive.

They would need weapons and transportation. There was no way they would be able to reach the compound tonight by car. Gabriel pulled out his wallet and slid out a simple white card with a single phone number on it. Bryan had given it to him five years ago and told him if anything should ever happen to him Gabriel should call the number on the card. He'd tried to get Bryan to tell him more about the phone number, but Bryan refused, stating he didn't need to know unless the situation called for it. The person on the other end would be able to provide them with whatever they needed.

Entering the house, Gabriel picked up Preston's cell phone from the kitchen counter and punched in the number. He listened to it ringing and then a male voice. "Hello?"

"Bryan's been kidnapped."

A brief silence met his statement. Then the man spoke: "When?"

"Three nights ago," Gabriel said flatly. "The agency was hit by Vincetti's men. They took him and two others that we know of. We're going after him tonight, but we need weapons and a chopper."

"Where are you?" the stranger barked out.

"A safe house in Kansas."

"Meet me at Griff's out on Route 50 in two hours. Order a glass of milk." The line went dead.

Gabriel carefully lowered the cell back to the counter. Two hours and he'd finally meet the man Bryan held so much trust in. Who was he?

Finding the others, he outlined the details. They'd wait outside while he met with the mysterious man. "Are you sure this is a good idea, boss?" Dear asked. "We don't even know who this is."

"Bryan trusts him. He told me that if anything were to

ever happen to him to call the number. The person on the other end would help us, no matter what we needed." Gabriel leaned against the nearby wall, his arms crossed over his chest. "If Bryan trusts him, then I trust him."

"Good enough for me," Tank replied, casually shrugging.

"Gather whatever we have and meet me at the car in an hour."

Gabriel glanced at Hayley standing in the doorway, her hands twisted together nervously. He walked up to her and set his hand on her forearm in comfort. "We'll get Bry back, Hayley. He's going to be okay."

Hayley smiled tightly. "I know he's going to be okay. I'm worried that you're going to do something stupid."

She knew him too well. Gabriel pulled her into a hug. "Promise me you'll come back too," she murmured, tightening her arms around his waist.

He couldn't promise her that, though. Not if freeing the others meant giving himself up. "I'll try," he whispered.

"No. You are going to," she growled fiercely.

Smiling at her mother bear ferocity, Gabriel pressed a kiss to the crown of her hair. "If I have any choice in the matter, we're all coming back."

Hayley had tears building when she pulled back to look up at him. He could see the knowledge in the depths of her eyes. She knew he wouldn't be coming back, that he intended to trade himself for the others. "Don't do anything stupid," she choked.

"I'll be fine, Hayles. I'm too stubborn to die," he tried to joke, lightly brushing away one of the tears from her cheeks.

She shook her head and turned to rush from the room. Gabriel watched her go, his heart heavy at how much he'd miss her. He'd miss everyone, really. Hayley was like a sister to him.

Chris approached him quietly. "I'm going with you."

"No. You aren't. You need to be our eyes and ears, Chris," Gabriel said flatly. "We need you to watch our backs."

"How, Gabe? There's no equipment here. I'm not staying here while you and the others put your lives in danger to save Bryan. I can watch your backs from there just as easily."

Gabriel studied Chris for a moment and finally gave a brief nod in assent. "Fine, but you're to remain at the rear. I won't lose another squad member."

Chris reached out to touch Gabriel's shoulder. "You can't blame yourself for what happened to Lizard, Gabe. He knew the risks when he joined the agency."

What the hell was with everyone knowing what went on in his brain? Gabriel scowled and shrugged off Chris's hand. "If I had listened to Tank, Lizard would still be alive. Vincetti's men never would have found the farm house."

"We all can lay the blame at our feet," Chris insisted. "How did we miss them breaking through the fence around the property? How did anyone patrolling not see the horde of Deviants entering the escape tunnel? You have to stop condemning yourself for everything that goes wrong. Shit happens every day, Gabe. People die, people mess up, and they aren't always as innocent or moral as we believe them to be. It's not your fault. None of it is."

Gabriel stared at Chris for several breaths, and then he pulled him into a tight yet quick embrace. He let go almost immediately and ignored the heat he felt suffusing his cheeks. "Let's get out of here. Find this place called Griff's."

The five of them piled into the SUV and headed toward Route 50. Griff's turned out to be a honky-tonk bar. Only two vehicles sat in the dirt parking lot when they arrived: a blue run-down truck and a black Ford Explorer with heavily tinted windows. The neon signs in the windows of the bar were lit up and flickered every few seconds. Gabriel's gaze darted back and forth, taking in the details of the squat wooden building. He noted the front door and figured there had to be a back door to the place as well. Only the two escape routes didn't sit well in his belly, but he had to take the chance. If this mysterious person on the other end of the phone could get them to Bryan and Alex, then he'd roll the dice and pray they didn't land on snake eyes.

"Stay here," he instructed his team.

"But, boss," Jackal protested.

"If anything goes wrong, I can't afford you all to be in there. I need you to find a way to rescue Bryan and the twins." Gabriel gave a harsh look at Tank when he went to speak up as well. "Don't. Just do as I tell you."

Tank grunted. "Don't expect me not to come in there after you, boss."

Gabriel waved Tank's words away and climbed out of the SUV. He approached the front of the building, still cautiously looking around, and opened the front door. Despite it being the middle of the day and the sun shining brightly overhead, the interior of the bar was dim, and it took a few precious seconds for his eyes to adjust. There were three others in the bar: the bartender, currently drying a glass, a man slumped over the bar and nursing a beer, and another sitting at a table in the corner farthest from the bar. Gabriel couldn't see the features of the man seated at the table for the cowboy hat the man wore, and his head remained tilted down.

He slowly approached the bar and perched on a stool. "What can I get for you?" the bartender asked in a bored tone.

Gabriel grimaced but asked, "A glass of milk, please."

The bartender's hands stilled, and he looked at Gabriel with a raised eyebrow. The drunk slumped over the bar giggled and said, "He juss order a glash of milk, Harry?"

Harry ignored the drunk and propped a fist on his hip. "We ain't got milk. You know this is a bar, right?"

"Get him a shot of whiskey," a deep voice interjected from behind.

Gabriel turned to see the stranger in the corner staring at him. He frowned and waited for the shot of whiskey before striding over to the man's table. He swung a chair around and straddled it. Setting the drink in front of the man, Gabriel demanded in a low voice, "Who are you?"

"Name's Linc. I can see why Bryan was so infatuated with you," Linc drawled while picking up the shot glass. He tossed the whiskey back in one gulp and slammed the glass down on the table top. Gabriel didn't like the smug look on Linc's face or the sheer arrogance radiating from him. A scar, about an inch long, slashed across Linc's right cheek, and he could just make out the dark brown hair color underneath the edges of the hat. A wide, squat nose, obviously broken at least once, sat above full, firm lips and a squared chin. Gabriel had no idea how tall he was.

Lips thinned in anger at Linc's words and attitude, Gabriel glared at him. "Are you going to help us or not?"

The smug glint in Linc's steel gray eyes died out, smothered by a deadly intent that almost sent a chill down Gabriel's spine. "You know where he's being held?"

"Yes. We need gear, weapons, and a helicopter. We're going in tonight and taking Vincetti and his men out. He won't be expecting us to attack so soon after taking another... of our team." Gabriel stumbled over his words at the mention of Alex.

Linc looked at his watch and then back up at Gabriel. "Let's get out of here."

Pitching some money on the table, Linc tossed a casual wave at the bartender named Harry and stood up. Gabriel's eyes widened when he saw how tall Linc was. He had to be at least six foot six, the top of his hat brushing the motor compartment of an overhead ceiling fan. A dark blue T-shirt covered broad shoulders and a muscled upper torso, while a pair of black jeans hugged thighs almost as wide as Gabriel's head. If he'd met Linc before Alex, he may well have bent over the nearest table and begged him to fuck him. The man nearly took his breath away, but his beauty couldn't compare to the supple length of Alex's body or the sweet mewling cries Alex made as he came.

Gabriel swallowed and stood, offering his hand. "Gabriel."

Linc accepted and shook his hand briefly. "My truck's outside. Your friends will have to follow."

"How—" Gabriel stopped himself abruptly and shrugged.

What surprised Gabriel more than anything, and he supposed it shouldn't, was the beat-up truck belonged to Linc rather than the fancy SUV sitting in the parking lot. He laughed quietly and walked over to the agency vehicle. Tank lowered the window. "Who is he, boss?"

"All that matters is that he's going to help us get Bryan and the twins back. He wants you to follow us."

"How do we know we can trust him, Gabe?" Jackal asked, leaning forward from the back seat. "Why don't you ride with us and we'll all follow him?"

"Like I said back at the safe house, if Bryan trusts him, so do I," Gabriel stated flatly and strode to the run-down truck.

He climbed into the passenger side next to Linc and settled against the seat, one arm on the window, the other at the ready in case Linc tried something. "How do you know Bryan?" he asked after they were on the road.

Linc's expression remained stoic as he spoke. "My little sister was his wife."

Gabriel figured Linc wouldn't appreciate sympathy and merely grunted in acknowledgement. He wondered why Bryan had never mentioned Linc during their time together. "So where are we going?"

"We're almost there."

Linc didn't offer more information, and Gabriel clenched his jaw at how the man claiming to be Bryan's brother-in-law wasn't more forthcoming. "So it was Vincetti?" Linc asked flatly.

"Yes. He attacked the agency a few nights back and managed to capture Bryan as well as several others from the farmhouse."

"I see."

Gabriel could practically hear the accusation hidden in Linc's words, and it set his teeth on edge, but he refused to defend himself to a man he didn't know. No other conversation transpired between them after that. They turned off onto a dirt road minutes later and jostled past dense trees and empty fields. Soon, Gabriel saw the blades of a helicopter in the distance and sat up straighter as they approached it. When he saw the logo on the side of the chopper, he raised an eyebrow. "You're government?"

"Special Forces."

"I thought the government wouldn't interfere in Deviant matters?" Gabriel asked warily.

"It doesn't. I'm not the government. That's all you need to know." Linc brought the truck to a stop near the helicopter. "Get everyone on board. We're leaving in five."

Gabriel didn't even get a chance to ask anything more because Linc clambered out of the vehicle and strode around to the pilot side of the chopper. His team climbed out of the agency SUV and walked to him as he stepped down from the passenger side of the run-down pickup. "Boss?" Jackal queried cautiously, eyeing the well-known insignia for Special Forces.

"Get in. We'll discuss it later." Gabriel understood his squad's reticence about the situation. No one here had ever had a good run-in with the government, military or otherwise. Most of them had been victims of the Deviant camps and the multitude of attacks on them by Normals.

Gabriel took the front passenger seat while the four of them strapped themselves into the back. The noise from the blades prevented any further talking until Linc tossed him a headset. Slipping it on, he heard Linc's voice crackle through the earphones. "How far is the compound?"

"Vermont," Gabriel shouted into the microphone.

"Once we gear up and refuel, we should be able to reach Vincetti's in two hours."

"How long until we get to wherever your place is?"

Linc grinned at Gabriel as the chopper lifted off the ground. "Anxious to get rid of me already?"

Frustration caused Gabriel to scowl, and he flipped Linc off. He only chuckled in a deep baritone. The man was absolutely infuriating. "Anxious to rescue our people."

"Are you and Bryan still…." Linc trailed off.

Gabriel frowned. "No. We're not."

Linc grunted but didn't say anything else. The flight took roughly an hour, and Gabriel spent the time thinking of Alex and fighting off the anxiety tightening his stomach. He didn't pray often, if at all, to be honest, but he couldn't stop himself from sending a message to whatever being existed to protect the younger Deviant. Only a matter of hours had gone by since they'd taken Alex, but it felt like an eternity. His hands balled into fists at the memory of the fear on Alex's face a split second before he'd disappeared.

The helicopter descending shook Gabriel from his thoughts, and he looked out the window to find a large ranch below. Horses raced along the fence of an open pasture, tails flicking high in startled fear of the noise of the engine. Gabriel noticed several men coming out of a barn and another three stepping onto the porch from the house. They piled into a group to await their landing.

Gabriel's team climbed out and immediately flanked him as he approached the men. Linc didn't bother with introductions, barking out orders to several of them to gear up and prepare the other helicopter for a mission. Gabriel watched as four of the seven men scurried to do Linc's bidding. "Curtis, take Gabriel's team to the war room and make sure they have everything they need."

A tall, dark-haired man nodded and beckoned Gabriel's squad to follow him. "War room?" Gabriel queried curiously.

Linc shrugged. "The men call it that, but it's only a storage room where we keep the gear and weapons. Grab whatever you need. We'll leave in an hour."

Curtis led the five of them into the barn and toward the back to a large metal door. He punched a code into a state of the art keypad and turned the handle, pushing the door open wide. Chris let out a small grunt of surprise, and Gabriel couldn't help but be impressed as he gazed at rack upon rack of all types of weaponry: machine guns, hand guns, knives, grenades, and explosives. It was enough to make any weapons expert drool. Bear and Tank each instantly chose a handheld machine gun, while Jackal picked up a couple of 9mm Beretta M9s.

Since Gabriel's team was the last to patrol before Vincetti's men hit the agency, everyone still had their weapons vests, and they started pushing extra clips and grenades into the various pockets. Their own weapons had been left behind at the safe house, as they were useless without bullets. Gabriel still carried his knives in his vest but needed another gun. He gravitated to a Ruger SR9 with a rear sight laser. Picking it up, he flicked on the laser and targeted a nearby wall, looking down the barrel. The 9mm pistol seemed fairly lightweight and easy to handle, with the safety conveniently in place near the thumb.

"Nice choice," Curtis assessed, also picking up a couple of

guns, cartridges, and explosives. "Ruger SR9 is usually Linc's choice too."

Gabriel didn't reply as he popped the magazine free and snapped it back in just as quickly. He slid the gun into its holster and snatched up a few of the clips, sliding them into his weapons vest pockets. He stuck two fragmentation grenades in as well. "Is Linc Special Forces?"

"Used to be. He retired a couple of years ago and now runs the Bar K full time." Curtis lifted a couple of rifles from a nearby rack, setting them on top of a black duffle bag near the door. "Old habits die hard, though. He keeps this stuff for days like today."

"And those men? They all seemed to be well-trained."

Curtis grinned at Gabriel. "Linc only hires on ex-Special Forces or military personnel. Most of those men, including myself, are from his old team."

Grudgingly, Gabriel had to admit to himself his respect for Linc went up several notches. He knew there had to be more to the story than Bryan just being married to Linc's little sister. "What's his relationship with Bryan?" he asked nonchalantly, hoping the other man would reveal what Linc had hidden behind an emotionless mask.

"I think you should ask him that question," Curtis said, his smile dying. "Let's go. The others should be ready by now."

Gabriel and his men trailed after Curtis, through the barn and back out into the daylight. The sun hung low in the sky, casting orange and purple fingers across the normally bright blue. He spied Linc standing with his men near the main house. Linc caught his eye and beckoned him over.

"We'll be using these to communicate," Linc said, dropping a small earpiece in each man's hand. "Marcus pulled up a schematic of the compound in Vermont. We have a fairly good idea where Bryan is being held."

"We have others in there as well," Gabriel replied. "Chris, tell them what you know of the security at the compound."

Chris came forward and began to explain the closed circuit cameras, the security system, and the guards patrolling the grounds. "Last time we went in through a drain pipe on the far side of the compound. I'm sure they've secured it by now. If you have a computer I can use, I may be able to find another way in undetected."

Linc pointed at a stocky, medium-built man with shockingly white-blond hair. "That's Derek. He's the resident tech geek. Derek, take Chris here and see what you can find."

"No problem, Linc," Derek said, motioning for Chris to follow him.

The remainder of the time until they left was spent discussing their plan of attack. Linc and his team would go after Bryan while Gabriel's team went for Alex and Jason. Gabriel didn't let on that he would be breaking off to find Vincetti. He knew if he did, they'd try to stop him, but it was time to end this. No matter what he had to do, even if it meant dying himself, he would kill Vincetti for everything he'd done and everything he would have done in the future.

18

ALEX

ONNOR left them soon after returning Alex's memories, and Alex knew it would only be a matter of time until they came for him again. Rafe intended to use him as ammunition to hurt Gabriel, and in order to do that, he'd need Alex. "Gabriel's coming," Alex said sadly.

Jason hugged him, pulling Alex's head down on his shoulder. *"We shouldn't talk out loud. They're watching and listening."*

"Doesn't matter, Jace. Rafael's like me. A telepath. So speaking out loud or in our minds, it doesn't matter."

Jason stroked his fingers through Alex's hair. "Hadn't thought of that," he said ruefully. "Alex, you love Gabriel, right?"

"Of course," Alex answered emphatically, frowning at the question. "Why?"

"Then you have to have faith that he knows what he's doing and that it's going to be all right." Alex sensed Jason smiling. "And anyone with half a brain can see the big bastard loves you right back. He wouldn't let anything happen to you."

Alex sat up in frustration and ran a tired hand over his face. "That's just it, Jace. I'm scared he's going to sacrifice himself to save me and you and Bryan. He blames himself for so much, things he shouldn't, things he can't and couldn't control. Things he doesn't even know weren't his fault."

Jason leaned forward, bracing his elbows on his knees, hands dangling between them. "He's not coming alone, Alex. The others won't let him do anything stupid. And when this is all over, you can tell him the truth about the things which aren't his fault."

A bitter laugh rose in Alex's throat, but he cut it off, knowing if he let it out it would turn into a sob and then outright crying. "Ironic."

"What is?" Jason asked, eyebrows furrowing.

"Usually I'm the one being the optimist and encouraging you."

"I had to grow up sometime, huh?" Jason teased.

Alex managed a half smile. "Grams always said you just needed something that would force you to mature. She loved you very much, Jace. Loved us both. No matter that we were Deviants and could do things which most of the world thinks makes us freaks. None of it changed the way she felt about us. I really miss her."

"So do I, bro. So do I."

Without a window, neither of them could tell what time of day it was outside. Alex figured the others would come in under the cover of darkness, and he wished he could at least see how late the day had grown in order to prepare himself for what was to come. He hadn't touched the food Connor had brought in, his stomach protesting the idea and his throat tightening in nausea. Jason tried to get him to eat several times, but he'd refused. How could he possibly eat?

The sound of an alarm sent both him and Jason to their feet. Alex wrapped his arms around himself and prayed:

Please, God, please watch over Gabriel. Don't let anything happen to him. Bile stung the back of Alex's throat, and then he heard the sound of the cell door unlocking. Tim, the Deviant from earlier, stood there pointing a gun at them. "You," he said, shaking the barrel at Alex, "come with me."

Alex looked at Jason, horror and resignation covering his features. Jason stepped in front of Alex. "You aren't taking him."

Tim smirked and stepped back to allow two gigantic men to enter the cell. "The one on the left. Bring him."

Jason stood his ground, but Alex couldn't let them hurt his brother. "I'll come with you," Alex said in defeat, moving around Jason.

"Alex, no!" Jason exclaimed, trying to stop him.

He gave Jason a sad smile. "I can't let them hurt you, Jace. You're my brother."

"But—"

Alex cut him off, "Gabriel's here. You said to have faith, remember?"

Jason scowled at having his words of comfort thrown back at him. "That's not fair."

"Shut up," Tim snapped, "and let's go!"

Alex hugged his twin briefly and then walked out of the cell, closely followed by Tim and the two hulking Deviants. Every corridor, every turn, reminded him of his dream, the one where Gabriel's brother had murdered Jason. Except the corridors weren't empty. Dozens of Deviant men and women were preparing for the intruders, guns and abilities at the ready. He heard raucous laughter and bets on who would get the most kills. He shuddered at the sheer violence in their voices.

Tim dug the gun into his ribs when he stopped to stare at one man in particular, Isaac. Alex glared at Isaac, who merely leered at him and waved two fingers in greeting. He grunted at the weapon jammed against his side. "I'm going," he snarled, wishing he could wipe the arrogant look from Isaac's face.

They entered a huge room that looked like a laboratory. Various workstations were set up around the room, some with computers and some with what Alex knew to be chemistry labs. "Take off his shirt and strap him to the table," Tim instructed the two mountain men, who promptly grabbed Alex and dragged him to an upright table in the center of the room.

Alex didn't fight as they cut the shirt from his body and secured his wrists and ankles to the metal slab. What would be the point, anyway; they could overpower him without even trying. He looked around the room, noting the overhead balcony and several doors leading out of the lab. One door opened minutes after their entry, and Rafe stepped in, the scars on his face covered by the metal mask Alex had seen in his dream. Alex managed to keep from flinching as he was once more reminded of the moment in his dream when Rafe murdered his twin.

Rafe instructed the others to leave them, and he came over to Alex's side. Trailing a finger down Alex's cheek, he said, "I wonder how he'd feel if you were scarred like me. Would he still love you without the sheer perfection of such beautiful skin? Or would he abandon you as he did me all those years ago?"

Alex felt sick as he saw Rafe pick up a scalpel from a small rollaway table nearby. "Gabriel isn't like that. He wouldn't care." Alex hoped, anyway.

"Perhaps. Gabriel always was such a bleeding heart. It was delicious to see him tear apart those Normals when they killed Paul. Such power. Pity he was born with it instead of me. Though I am powerful in my own right, his power... I could do so much if I had it."

An explosion sounded not far from their location, and Rafe grinned maliciously. "Sounds as if Gabriel is on his way here. The fun is about to start."

The double doors Alex had been brought through crashed open, slamming into the wall as Gabriel entered the room. Alex's breath caught in his throat when he saw him. "Gabriel!" he cried, his heart beating faster.

Everything afterward became a blur: the pain of the scalpel on his skin, the anguish at Gabriel's offer, the sound of a gunshot, kneeling on the ground next to a slowly dying Gabriel. Tears mixed with the blood from a slice on Alex's cheek, and he fought ferociously when they tried to force him to move away from the man he loved more than life itself. His heart shattered, splintering into a million pieces, as he watched them lift Gabriel's limp body, and he refused to let Gabriel die alone, clinging to Gabriel's bloodied hand and never once letting go. Not even when they tried to tend to his own injuries. Nothing mattered except Gabriel.

19

GABRIEL

GABRIEL directed Linc to land in the same clearing as before and caught a glimpse of the lights from the compound. His heart sped up with how close they were to Alex, but he forced himself to concentrate, knowing any distraction could be dangerous. The other helicopter, carrying Linc's men, landed in the clearing behind them, and all of the men filed out.

Chris laid out the schematics of the compound against the side of one of the helicopters. "Can you point your light here, please?" Chris asked of one of the men, barely aware of anything but his task. It had always amazed Gabriel how intent Chris became while they were running a mission. "I confirmed through CCTV that they have indeed closed off the drain pipe we used last time. I'm afraid you'll have to risk going in at one of the weaker security check points."

He indicated several points around the building. "My suggestion, if you want to take it, that is, is to head for this section here and this one here." Chris ran his finger along one small sector at the very back of the building and another at the far corner of the fencing. "From what I observed on the video feed I hacked into, there doesn't appear to be a guard going past there often, roughly every twenty minutes. Should be more than enough time to get in there without drawing the surrounding guards."

Gabriel could see how impressed Linc's men were and grinned. "Good work, Chris. I think you're right."

"I don't think it's wise for all of us to enter through the same way," Linc said. "Which section is closest to where Bryan is being held?"

Gabriel immediately saw a strange look pass over Chris's features. "What is it, Chris?"

"I... I couldn't locate Bryan in the compound."

"What?" Linc barked, thrusting his face into Chris's. "What do you mean, you couldn't locate him?"

"He's either not in there, or they're holding him somewhere there are no cameras." Chris blanched at the ferocity on Linc's face and backed up slightly.

Stepping in between them, Gabriel glared at Linc. "He's done his job. No need to get in his face."

Linc straightened and moved away, running a hand through his hair in frustration. "Sorry," he bit out. "I promised I'd look out for him."

"We're all worried about Bryan," Gabriel said flatly. "Chris will stay here and keep trying. He didn't exactly have a lot of time."

Chris gave Gabriel a look of gratitude and picked up the bag of equipment he'd brought with him. "I'll keep in touch via radio."

"I'll stay with him, Linc," Derek said. "I can help him."

Linc nodded stiffly. "We'll take the far northwest corner."

"It's best if we maintain radio silence as long as possible," Gabriel instructed. "We don't know the extent of the abilities Vincetti's Devs possess. I've seen a few these last couple of days which even I never expected. He's been cultivating as many level fives as possible."

"Bryan's kept me informed of Vincetti's movements. The bastard made the wrong one this time." A deadly promise stood out in Linc's voice, and Gabriel was glad they were both on the same side.

As the men mobilized and began threading through the trees, Gabriel asked, "You never said, are you a Dev?"

Linc shook his head. "No. Neither was my sister."

"They say the Deviant gene lies in one of the parents," Gabriel replied quietly.

Without answering the silent question Gabriel had posed, Linc slipped into the darkness to follow his team. Gabriel watched him for a moment and then headed after his own squad. He could hear the sound of owls hooting, the wind rustling the tree branches overhead intermittently, and the soft footfalls of the men all around him. They reassured him, made him remember his purpose and why they were there. It had never occurred to him that Bryan wouldn't be in the same compound as Alex and Jason. Why would Vincetti separate them? Because he knew they would come for the twins and for Bryan. If they were successful, he didn't want to lose both.

The lights of the compound started to penetrate the inky darkness, and Linc's voice came through his earpiece. "Cutting off now."

"Be careful," Gabriel murmured.

"Never anything else," Linc responded.

Gabriel snorted lightly. He had a feeling Linc was never careful. If anything, he probably took more chances than anything else. Especially when feelings were involved. Gabriel had picked up on Linc's interest in Bryan as more than a brother-in-law and couldn't stop himself from wondering if Bryan knew of Linc's attraction to him. Linc's questions about Gabriel and Bryan's relationship left no doubt in Gabriel's mind that Linc wanted Bryan.

Shaking his head, Gabriel brought his attention back to the mission at hand and motioned his team toward the back side of the building. As they approached the section of fencing Chris indicated on the schematics, Gabriel realized the compound seemed extremely quiet. Vincetti had to know he'd come for Alex and the others, yet the security seemed lax. He continually scanned the property while Jackal cut through the fence enough for them to slip inside. Gabriel pointed at a rear door leading into the old jail. "We need a way in," he murmured into his earpiece.

"One step ahead of you, boss," Chris came back, and Gabriel heard the lock click open.

They cautiously entered the building, but the corridor in front of them was empty, and Gabriel led the way toward another door. The next corridor connected to the one they'd come through on their previous mission. "Find Alex and Jason," he instructed the others. "Get them out and away from here."

"Gabe," Tank growled. "Don't do anything stupid."

"I have to take him out for good this time," Gabriel said darkly, his jaw clenching stubbornly.

"I'm going with you," Jackal replied, moving to his side.

"No. You'll do as I'm telling you. Get the twins out of here." Gabriel didn't wait for further protest and broke off from the others.

An alarm sounded just as Gabriel set his hand on the door handle. Swearing, he wrenched the door open and entered the next corridor. Two men rounded the other end of the hallway the second he stepped in. He brought up his gun and started firing on them, managing to take out one, but the other kept coming, the bullets bouncing off his skin like pebbles. Gabriel tapped into his power and sent it hurtling at the rushing Deviant. A loud roar echoed along the cement walls, and the man collapsed, his left leg bent at an odd angle.

The Deviant with impenetrable skin continued firing wildly at Gabriel, narrowly missing him several times. Gabriel tossed out another burst of energy and cracked every bone in the man's hand, causing the gun to fall uselessly to the floor. He approached the injured Deviant and kicked the gun away. "Where's Vincetti?"

Cackling, the man spit at his feet. Gabriel grabbed the man's shirt in his fist and shook him. "Where is Vincetti?"

"Fuck you," he snarled.

Gabriel grinned cruelly and concentrated his power on the Deviant's heart, forcing it to expand and the blood vessels to contract tighter. The man wheezed in agony, and blood started pouring out of his nose. "Tell me where he is."

"Gone!"

Ramping up the pain, Gabriel increased the pressure on the bastard's heart. "He's dead!" the man shrieked.

"What the fuck do you mean he's dead?" Gabriel demanded, gripping the shirt twisted in his fist tighter.

"He's been dead," he gasped. "He's not running the operation anymore."

"Then who is?" Gabriel snapped.

"He calls himself the Healer. No one knows his real name."

Gabriel froze, his blood running cold. "You're lying," he said coldly, instantly popping the main artery in the Deviant's heart and watching the life drain from his body.

Tossing the man aside, Gabriel straightened. The names the Healer and the Messenger had always been a joke between him and Rafael. Their parents had named them after the biblical archangels Gabriel and Raphael. When they'd learned the true significance of the archangels during Sunday school, they'd begun calling each other the Healer and the Messenger in secret, knowing their parents would scold them for it. It had been like their own private nicknames for one another. Could this Healer actually be his brother? But he'd watched his twin burn alive that day five years ago. How could he possibly still be alive?

Why would Rafael continue Vincetti's operation? He'd hated the son of a bitch almost as much as Gabriel did. Was that why Alex and Jason had become targets? The countless questions whirled around and around inside his mind. There was only one way to find out. Uncover the truth of who the Healer was. Determination filled every step Gabriel took. "Chris," he barked into his earpiece.

"Boss?" Chris answered.

"I need you to find out where the center of this place is. That's where he'll be." If the Healer was Rafe, he'd want to be in the middle of everything.

"Give me five minutes, boss."

The radio went silent, and Gabriel followed the jail's old, faded signs, figuring they would most likely start him in the right direction. Every turn brought him into combat with another Deviant, barring him from the truth of the Healer's identity. What if it was Rafe? Would he be able to stop his brother again?

Chris's voice came over the radio as he finished off a telekinetic Deviant, easily dispatching the man. "Keep your heading, boss. Turn left at the next corridor and then right. There's a huge area which looks like it may have been the cafeteria, but it's been converted into some kind of laboratory."

Gabriel took the left, and as he came to the right turn, Chris stopped him in his tracks, his chest tightening at his squad member's words. "Boss... Alex is in there."

Anger nipped at the heels of his fear, and his jaw tightened. He rounded the corridor and strode purposefully toward the double doors. No one stood in his way this time. It seemed almost as if whoever was on the other side waited for him.

When he entered the room, his eyes immediately zeroed in on Alex, bare-chested, strapped to an upright table straight across from the door. "Gabriel!" Alex cried out, his eyes wide in fright.

A man stood near Alex with his back to the door. He held a scalpel in his right hand, poised over Alex's cheek. "Hello, brother," Rafe sneered, turning his head enough for Gabriel to see the iron mask covering over half of his face.

Gabriel's stomach twisted, and he swallowed hard, his suspicions confirmed. "Rafe."

"I see you still have a taste for the weak," Rafe drawled lazily, trailing the tip of the scalpel along Alex's cheek. Alex whimpered. "Paul was weak too."

Blood welled along the cut, causing Gabriel's hands to clench at his sides. He ignored the jibe about Paul and demanded, "Let him go. I'm the one you want, not him."

Rafe finally spun around, fully revealing the remainder of his injuries. Gabriel refused to allow himself to feel pity or sympathy for his brother. He knew what he'd done five years ago had been wrong, but his brother had let it twist him, make him into the same monster as Vincetti. "Let him go," Gabriel repeated.

"No." Rafe grinned maliciously and sliced at Alex's chest, laughing as blood spilled out and down the lean lines of Alex's torso. "I'm having too much fun! I knew when I discovered Alex and Jason, their abilities so similar to ours, it would be almost... poetic. Although you didn't even realize when you rescued them what their significance really was. I knew you'd come for them, knew you'd see us in them.

"You've gone soft, Messenger. You never saw the connection, never realized exactly what Alex and Jason were. You still believed up until five minutes ago, when you walked in and saw me, that Vincetti was the one with the brains to orchestrate all of this. Vincetti was weak, just like you. I had to… remove him from the picture."

The red essence of Alex's life soaked into the fabric of his jeans, and rage filled Gabriel. He pushed aside Rafe's words, burying them for consideration and absorption later. Instead, he focused his power on Rafe's hand, attempting to disarm him, but an invisible wall seemed to block his ability, causing him to step backward in shock. No one had ever been able to stop his power so effectively before. Rafe smirked and tipped his head to the side. "Did you really think, after your betrayal five years ago, that I wouldn't have found a way to stop your power, brother?"

Gabriel caught himself and brought his gun up, aiming at Rafe's heart. "Don't make me kill you, Rafe. I will if I have to."

Rafe gave a booming laugh. "I've spent the last five years gathering the most powerful Deviants around me, Gabriel. That gun will have no effect."

He looked toward the balcony overlooking the laboratory. Gabriel glanced up to see a dark-skinned woman standing over them, her hand raised, and suddenly his gun flew from his grip, slamming into one of the cement pillars and falling to the ground in pieces. Looking back at his brother, Gabriel knew the only way he could get Alex out of there safely. "Fine, let him go and take me instead."

"No!" Alex screamed. "No, Gabe. Please no!"

Gabriel gave Alex a look filled with love and sadness all at once. "Let him go, Rafe, and I won't fight you. You can do whatever you want to me."

Rafe lifted an eyebrow. "Why would I ever want to let him go when he's the perfect revenge?"

A cold dread trickled through Gabriel. "What happened

five years ago was an accident, Rafe. I never meant to hurt you."

Snorting, Rafe began carving a letter into Alex's chest. Alex whimpered and squeezed his eyes shut tightly. "Too little, too late, brother. You left me to die. Now I'll make you feel the pain I did, feel the sheer terror of knowing there's nothing you can do to stop it."

Gabriel could see the letter M taking shape, and his lips compressed into a thin line. Rafe intended to scar Alex using his nickname for Gabriel. Taking advantage of Rafe's momentary distraction, Gabriel launched himself at his twin, intent on stopping him from hurting Alex. Rafe flashed him a humorless grin and sidestepped him, sinking the scalpel into Gabriel's side. Alex cried out as Gabriel stumbled and clutched the wound, blood instantly saturating his shirt and vest.

"Healer," a voice called from the balcony above.

Isaac stood a few feet from the girl, his hands gripping the railing. "They've released the other one!"

"Let them take him. I have the ones I want," Rafe replied with deadly calm.

"But they're heading this way, Healer!" Isaac exclaimed. "The others are coming for them!"

Rafe scowled angrily at him. "Then why are you standing here? Stop them."

Isaac rushed off to do as Rafe instructed.

A loud explosion suddenly rattled the walls, and chunks of plaster fell from the ceiling overhead, raining down around them. Gabriel covered Alex's body with his own, protecting the younger Deviant. Alex sobbed against him. "Gabriel...."

Another blast came, sounding even closer this time. Gabriel didn't trust Rafe enough to leave his back turned away and spun around to face his brother, now between his twin and Alex. "You chose to allow what happened all those years ago to twist you, to make you as corrupt as Vincetti. Why? You hated Vincetti for what he did to you, to us!"

Fire burned in Rafe's amber gaze, but a hint of vulnerability shone through the anger. "I hated you more! You were my brother! Look at what you did to me!" He furiously gestured to the mask covering the burned half of his face. "Over 75 percent of my body was burned! Do you know what it's like to smell your own skin roasting? To know you're going to die, and your own brother is responsible for it?"

Rafe glared at Gabriel. "You deserve to suffer like I did, to know the pain I felt for weeks, months, afterward. Nothing can ever take those memories away!"

Pain slammed into Gabriel's mind, and he dropped to his knees, clutching his temples. He'd been so wrapped up in his worry for Alex's safety and the agony in his brother's voice that he'd forgotten to keep his defense against Rafe's power in place. He tried to force Rafe from his mind, but the wound in his side and the high tension running through him kept him unfocused and off balance.

Seconds passed like hours, and then, unexpectedly, Rafe withdrew from his mind. Gabriel gasped and struggled to stand, grasping the edge of the table Alex was still strapped to in order to steady himself. Rafe didn't even notice him, his eyes locked on Alex's. Before Gabriel could truly comprehend the situation, a third explosion rocked the building, the west wall imploding inward at the same time as spidery cracks ran along a huge section of the ceiling overhead.

The dark-skinned female on the balcony above scurried to escape, terror sending her running for cover. Ominous creaks signaled the plaster above getting ready to give way, and Gabriel tore at Alex's bonds, trying to free him before it could come down. He heard Rafe roar behind him and swung around in time to see him lift a gun toward the two of them. Alex sucked in a breath at the deadly looking weapon.

"I will have my revenge!" Rafe screeched, his finger tightening on the trigger.

Gabriel stepped in front of Alex as Rafe squeezed. Everything seemed to happen in slow motion after that. Gabriel knew he could have stopped the bullet, but maybe Rafe was right. Maybe it was his fault that his brother had become so bitter and hateful. Maybe he did deserve to die as restitution. If he died, maybe Rafe could find peace and finally let it go. The bullet slammed into his chest, narrowly missing his heart and sending him thudding into Alex. Fire erupted inside his ribcage, and he bit back a groan.

"Gabriel!" Alex shrieked. "Oh God, no!"

Rafe went to fire again, but the cracking sound of a beam overhead giving way echoed through the large, cavernous room. He looked up in time to see a chunk of cement ceiling the size of a small car break free. He caught Gabriel's eyes for a split second, emotions roiling in their amber depths. Gabriel wrenched his head to the side as the section collapsed on top of his twin brother.

They weren't safe yet, and Gabriel used enough of his power to snap the leather straps holding Alex to the table, pulling Alex free and stumbling out of the path of the still-falling debris. The movements sapped the last of his strength, and he collapsed, gripping his chest. "Alex! Gabriel!" Jackal's voice echoed across the lab.

Gabriel's vision blurred because of the blood loss from both wounds, and he could just barely make out his and Linc's teams swarming into the room before he passed out, slumping to the ground. He figured it was poetic justice that his brother got his revenge anyway. After all, he'd just watched his brother die a second time and hadn't tried to save him.

20

GABRIEL

Wʜᴇɴ he opened his eyes next, he figured it would be in whatever hell he deserved, but when he saw Alex slumped down in a chair next to the bed, his breath caught. The sound must have disturbed Alex, because his eyelids slowly fluttered open, revealing those beautiful green orbs.

"Gabe," Alex said breathlessly and leaned forward to grip his hand. "Thank God!"

"Where... am I?" Gabriel managed to wheeze out. His chest felt as if it were on fire.

"In the hospital. The bullet nicked your lung. It's been touch and go for a few days. I'm just glad you're awake!" Tears welled in Alex's eyes and spilled over, trickling down his pale cheeks, one of which had a gauze pad covering the cut from Rafe's scalpel. Gabriel could see dark circles underneath his eyes, and his hair appeared tousled and unbrushed. He wore a faded blue T-shirt and worn jeans that had seen better days. The sterling silver chain around his throat twinkled in the fluorescent lighting.

Gabriel reached up to lightly run his fingers through Alex's hair. "Don't cry, baby," he shushed quietly.

"Why did you do it, Gabe? You could have died!" Alex demanded while still sobbing.

Gabriel smiled tenderly, and would have laughed if he could have without sending pure agony spiking through him. "Because I love you, Alex. I couldn't let you die."

Alex cried even harder, raining kisses over Gabriel's forehead, cheeks, and finally his lips. "I love you too, Gabriel. So much," he said when he pulled away.

"It's about time!" came from the doorway, and Gabriel looked over to see Jason and Jackal standing there, grinning from ear to ear. Jason moved closer to the bed and gave them a knowing smile. "It's good to see you awake, Gabe."

Jackal stepped forward to give Gabriel a half hug, careful of the tubes running from his body. "Welcome back to the land of the living, boss. Wasn't sure if you were going to come back to us or not."

"Like I said, I'm too stubborn to die," Gabriel joked.

"Gabriel Romero!" a shriek rang out through the hospital corridor, and Gabriel winced, trying to put on a chagrinned look. "You stupid son of a bitch!"

Hayley walked right up to him and punched him lightly in the arm. "You just had to go and make yourself the hero, didn't you? I hope you're proud of yourself, you big dumb ox!"

Gabriel coughed to cover his grin, only to groan in pain. "Serves you right, you jerk," Hayley sniffled, finally breaking down and dropping the affronted act. "You're lucky you kept your promise, or I would have dragged you right back out of the hell you were in to send you back there myself. This baby needs a godfather." She lightly touched her still flat belly.

He gently gripped her hand and pressed a kiss to the back

of it. "I love you too, Hayles, and I would be honored to be your child's godfather."

The doctor came in and cut the celebration short, shooing everyone from the room except Alex, who refused to leave. He moved away to let the doctor examine Gabriel, but he never left, watching intently as the doctor checked Gabriel's wounds and made marks on a chart.

"Everything looks good, Mr. Romero. In fact, your body is healing at an extremely rapid rate. Injuries such as yours usually take at least a week to even begin showing signs of repair. It's hard to believe you were only brought in mere days ago.

"You should be able to go home in a couple of days. We just want to keep you for observation. I do want you to take it easy for a week or so, just until the stitches dissolve and there's no chance of tearing."

"I'll make sure of it, Dr. Sikes," Alex replied, giving Gabriel a stern look.

Dr. Sikes looked at his watch briefly. "I have more rounds to make, but I'll check back in before your release."

Alex instantly resumed his seat next to Gabriel, but was unable to pick up their interrupted conversation because Linc came into the room. "Gabe," Linc said, moving to the bed. "Good to see you awake."

"Thanks. Did you find Bryan?" Gabriel asked.

Anger briefly flitted over Linc's features. "No. They must have had him somewhere else. We located files on other locations where they are performing experiments on Deviants, trying to intensify their powers. We've already started raiding the locations. So far, we haven't found him."

"And Rafe?" Gabriel asked, though he already knew the answer.

Linc shook his head. "He's dead."

Somehow Gabriel couldn't quite bring himself to feel

sorrow for his lost brother. Rafael had died five years ago in the fire. Alex squeezed his forearm lightly in comfort. "The others?"

"You saw Jackal. Bear and Tank were in the cafeteria getting what passes for coffee around here. They're glad to hear you're awake." Linc paused and quirked one corner of his mouth. "I may have to take Chris off your hands. He's the reason we found you and were able to locate the files containing the information on the other compounds. Even Derek wouldn't have been able to hack into those firewalls."

Gabriel scowled at Linc. "Hands off, buddy."

Linc laughed huskily. "We'll see about that."

Alex covered Gabriel's mouth quickly, stemming whatever he would have said. "Gabe needs his rest, Linc. Stop antagonizing him."

"Sure thing, Alex," Linc replied mischievously, winking at the dark-haired telepath. "I'll let you fill him in on everything else. Now that the big bastard is awake, I've got things to do."

Gabriel stuck out his hand to Linc. "Thanks for your help, Linc."

Clasping the proffered hand in one of his own large paws, Linc nodded stiffly. "We're going to find Bryan."

"Once I'm out of here, I'll be joining you in that search," Gabriel said, ignoring the exasperated look from Alex. "It's my fault he was taken."

Linc shook his head, releasing Gabriel's hand. "No. Bryan knew it was inevitable that someday he'd be the focus of an attack, whether by Deviant or Normal. It's not your fault, Gabe. He wouldn't want you to blame yourself."

"Thanks," Gabriel replied gruffly.

"I'll see you around, Gabe," Linc said and left.

Gabriel sighed tiredly and held out his hand to Alex, who promptly took it into his own. Tugging, he urged Alex to stand and immediately yanked him down onto the bed next to him. "Gabe!" Alex squawked, struggling to get back up.

He refused to release Alex and pulled him in to his side, ignoring the tug of the IV and heart monitor. "Settle down," he murmured, threading his leg between Alex's. "I just want to hold you."

Alex ceased protesting and snuggled into Gabriel's side. Gabriel remembered the last moments before the explosion that took Rafe's life. Alex had managed to tap into his power to stop Rafe's assault on his mind. "Thank you," he said tiredly.

"For what?" Alex asked curiously.

"For using your ability to help me."

"Oh." Alex fidgeted with the front of Gabriel's hospital gown. "I don't even know how I did it or what I actually did. Something just came over me when he started hurting you. It was almost as if I couldn't stop myself."

"That's why we need to practice, so you can learn to control it even if you don't want to use it. Your emotions running high can trigger a defense mechanism, and you may end up doing something you regret."

"Like the day Paul was killed?" Alex replied softly.

Gabriel tensed and nodded. "Just like that."

"First you have to rest and heal. Then we can talk about it," Alex promised.

"I'll be fine by tomorrow. I'm a fast healer."

Alex shook his head. "Nope. Dr. Sikes said to rest for a week, and that's just what you're going to do."

Gabriel sighed, and then a grin spread over his lips. "You going to nurse me back to health, baby?"

"I'll be there to get you whatever you need."

"Whatever I need?" Gabriel breathed into Alex's ear, nuzzling at the sensitive lobe.

Alex gasped and shivered, his fingers clenching in the ugly hospital gown. "That's not resting."

"Doc never said I couldn't exercise," Gabriel taunted, sliding his tongue along the delicate shell of Alex's ear. "Seems to me exercising is the best way to regain your strength."

Alex moaned and turned his head, capturing Gabriel's lips with his own. Gabriel deepened the kiss, thrusting his tongue inside Alex's mouth, relearning the taste of his lover. "We should," Alex panted between kisses, "stop."

"It's only kissing," Gabriel growled and stopped whatever protest Alex could form next.

Gabriel allowed himself the right to let go of everything outside of that hospital room. Just for tonight, he thought, combing his fingers through Alex's hair. They could concentrate on everything else tomorrow. All that mattered in this moment was holding Alex and knowing that whatever the morning brought they would face together.

C raving more urban fantasy or paranormal? Spell of the Werewolf is available now!
A werewolf seeks to sever the curse. A hybrid hunter wants him dead. Will the next moonrise be his last?

L ooking for something contemporary? Try Touch Me Gently! Available on Kindle and Kindle Unlimited.
A scarred young man jumping at shadows. A big-hearted, sexy cowboy providing him a safe haven. But is he able to trust his cowboy with his heart?

A NOTE FROM J.R.

Thank you for reading His Salvation. If you enjoyed it, I would truly appreciate if you could let your friends know so they can also enjoy the relationship between Alex and Gabriel. If you leave a review for His Salvation on the site in which you purchased the book, Goodreads or your own blog, I would love to read it. Please email the link to jrloveless@gmail.com

ABOUT THE AUTHOR

J.R. Loveless began her adventure in writing at the young age of twelve. Her foray into creating her own worlds and telling her characters' life stories was triggered by her own love of reading. She currently resides in South Florida with her dog and two cats, and by day works as a manager for a financial lending institute.

Her journey into gay romance began in 2005 when she began posting her original fiction on a forum for feedback and readers' pleasure. In 2010, a good friend urged her to submit to a publishing company, and the day she received the acceptance and contract was the best day of her life. Since then, she has been noted to be one of the most purchased audio books after Fifty Shades of Grey on Audiobook.com and received best gay romantic fiction for Touch Me Gently in the 2011 TLA Gaybies.

J.R. adores her fans and loves hearing from them.

Never miss out on an update or sale by by subscribing to J.R.'s Website. As a thank you, you'll receive a free short novelette called White Rain about two friends who become lovers!

J.R.'s Blog

J.R.'s Facebook Reader Group

facebook.com/authorjrloveless

twitter.com/J.R.%E2%80%99s%20Twitter

instagram.com/jrloveless

amazon.com/author/jrloveless

bookbub.com/profile/j-r-loveless

goodreads.com/jrloveless

Printed in Great Britain
by Amazon